The Christmas Angel

The Cape Light Titles

The Christmas Angel

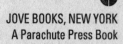

A Cape Light Novel

THOMAS KINKADE

& KATHERINE SPENCER

JOVE BOOKS, NEW YORK
A Parachute Press Book

THE BERKLEY PUBLISHING GROUP
Published by the Penguin Group
Penguin Group (USA) Inc.
375 Hudson Street, New York, New York 10014, USA

Penguin Group (Canada), 90 Eglinton Avenue East, Suite 700, Toronto, Ontario M4P 2Y3, Canada
(a division of Pearson Penguin Canada Inc.)
Penguin Books Ltd., 80 Strand, London WC2R 0RL, England
Penguin Group Ireland, 25 St. Stephen's Green, Dublin 2, Ireland (a division of Penguin Books Ltd.)
Penguin Group (Australia), 250 Camberwell Road, Camberwell, Victoria 3124, Australia
(a division of Pearson Australia Group Pty. Ltd.)
Penguin Books India Pvt. Ltd., 11 Community Centre, Panchsheel Park, New Delhi—110 017, India
Penguin Group (NZ), 67 Apollo Drive, Rosedale, North Shore 0745, Auckland, New Zealand
(a division of Pearson New Zealand Ltd.)
Penguin Books (South Africa) (Pty.) Ltd., 24 Sturdee Avenue, Rosebank, Johannesburg 2196,
South Africa

Penguin Books Ltd., Registered Offices: 80 Strand, London WC2R 0RL, England

This is a work of fiction. Names, characters, places, and incidents either are the product of the authors' imagination or are used fictitiously, and any resemblance to actual persons, living or dead, business establishments, events, or locales is entirely coincidental. The publisher does not have any control over and does not assume any responsibility for author or third-party websites or their content.

THE CHRISTMAS ANGEL

A Jove Book / published by arrangement with Parachute Publishing, L.L.C.

PRINTING HISTORY
Berkley hardcover edition / October 2005
Berkley trade paperback edition / October 2006
Jove mass-market edition / October 2007

Copyright © 2005 by The Thomas Kinkade Company and Parachute Publishing, L.L.C.
Cover image: *St. Nicholas Circle* copyright © 1993 by Thomas Kinkade.
Cover design by Lesley Worrell.

ISBN: 978-0-515-14357-7

JOVE®
Jove Books are published by The Berkley Publishing Group,
a division of Penguin Group (USA) Inc.,
375 Hudson Street, New York, New York 10014.
JOVE is a registered trademark of Penguin Group (USA) Inc.
The "J" design is a trademark belonging to Penguin Group (USA) Inc.

PRINTED IN THE UNITED STATES OF AMERICA

22 21 20 19 18 17 16 15 14

DEAR FRIENDS

❦

WHEN I WAS A YOUNG BOY, ONE OF MY FAVORITE Christmas traditions was trimming the tree. We had many ornaments, but the ones I liked best were those that had been handed down from generation to generation, and I hung them with great care, selecting very special places on the tree for their display.

But there was one ornament that everyone in my family agreed was the most beautiful. It was the angel ornament that topped the tree. I can still picture her. She wore a red velvet gown. Her long blond hair sparkled under a golden halo, and her gossamer wings shimmered with a silver glow. She was unquestionably our most treasured ornament, the one that made the tree complete.

That Christmas ornament was my first vision of an angel, and since then, I've seen many like her, and I've met many too, but the ones I've actually known didn't have golden halos and shimmering wings.

An angel may be a stranger who lends a helping hand or a friend who knows when you're in need. Or it may be someone who reminds you of your own capacity for goodness and love.

In Cape Light, as in my life, angels take many forms. Emily Warwick realizes she's been blessed by an angel when she finds an abandoned baby in the church crèche, a baby who changes her life, challenging her to reexamine and deepen her bonds of love.

Reverend Ben, struggling with self-doubt, will find angels at work in his own congregation.

As you enter Cape Light, I hope you enjoy your time with the good people there and the angels they meet, and my Christmas wish for you is that God's angels will bring the gift of hope and faith and love into your life too.

—Thomas Kinkade

CHAPTER ONE

ℰMILY FOUND THE BABY PURELY BY ACCIDENT. LATER,
looking back, she decided it hadn't been an accident at all.
It was one of those things that was simply meant to be.

She'd nearly skipped her morning run that day, and realized later that a few minutes on the clock either way
would have made all the difference. She could have turned
onto a different path. Or she could have been so caught up
in her rambling thoughts, she would have missed that tiny
flicker of movement in a place where it definitely shouldn't
have been.

It was the day after Thanksgiving, an unofficial holiday
with schools and many offices closed and most people
sleeping off the bounty of the day before. Emily had rolled
over when the alarm sounded, snuggling deep under the
down quilt. But finally she forced herself to get up out of
bed, pull on running clothes, and creep downstairs, shoes
in hand.

She sipped a quick cup of coffee and pictured her husband, Dan, still sound asleep. She sighed and double knotted her laces. Better run now than regret it later when her clothes felt too tight. She did some quick stretches, grabbed her gloves, and headed out the door.

The cold morning air was like a slap in the face. She stretched and started at a slow pace, drawing in deep breaths, exhaling frosty clouds. There had only been a dusting of snow so far, but the legendary New England winter was quickly setting in.

Emerson Street was empty; the only sound was her own breath and the beat of her steps on the pavement. She pushed herself around the corner and headed down the long hill on Beacon Road to the village. She liked to run to the village green and along the harbor before looping back. As the mayor of Cape Light, she sometimes felt her early morning treks were a way of checking up on things, a quiet surveillance of her domain. It was silly to think that, she knew. You couldn't tell much by merely glancing at the outside of houses or stores. But still she felt as if this tour kept her in touch with the beating heart of the place.

She rounded the turn onto Main Street. The wide thoroughfare stood silent, the Victorian buildings and old-time storefronts like a painting on a Christmas card that captured an elegant, bygone era. The shops and restaurants were decorated for the holidays, the window displays filled with gentle slopes of fake snow, sparkling stars, and gilded-winged angels. Bright pine wreaths with red bows brightened the wrought-iron lampposts. Holiday garlands swooped across the avenue, and each of the parking meters had been covered with red and white stripes, creating a row of free-parking-for-shoppers candy canes. The village maintenance crew hadn't reached the end of the street yet, but she knew they'd complete the job today. Tonight was the annual Christmas tree lighting on the green. Everything had to be ready by then.

It was hard to believe the holidays were here again. It felt as if she and Dan had held their highly original and very public New Year's wedding ceremony on the green just weeks ago. Now here they were, almost a year later. The months had passed in such a happy blur, it was impossible to describe.

It was one thing to find love when you were young: that was expected. But when you've all but given up and it comes at you out of the clear blue, you appreciate it in a different—and deeper—way.

How many tree lightings had she presided over now? Into her second term as mayor, she was losing track. But she loved her job, the demands and challenges of it, too. She loved feeling she made the lives of people in this town better in some small way. That was a privilege, she knew, and a blessing.

Where Main Street met the harbor, Emily turned right and ran along the far side of the green. Out at the end of the dock that ran to her left, she spotted a lone but familiar figure—a black knit cap pulled over his head, his body huddled against the cold in a thick coat, a yellow Labrador sitting patiently at his feet.

Digger Hegman and Daisy were a common sight at the waterfront in the early morning. But Emily didn't call out a greeting. She knew Digger was deep in his contemplations, appraising the harbor and even the birds for his daily forecast, or maybe lost in recollections of his own days at sea.

She headed instead toward the stone facade of Bible Community Church, which faced the green. As usual, the church's decorations this year were beautiful in their simplicity, a thick pine wreath on the wooden doors out front and a large crèche, with almost life-size figures, sheltered by tall trees.

Emily ran past, giving the display a quick glance. Her thoughts raced ahead to the workday. Village Hall would be empty today; it would be a good time to catch up on the paperwork that seemed to flow up from some inexhaustible stream below her in-box.

A few steps past the church doors, she slowed and looked back over her shoulder. Had she seen something moving in the crèche? Something in the cradle?

It couldn't have been the plaster figure of the infant Jesus, she reasoned. The figure of the baby wasn't added until Christmas Eve night. Except for some straw, the wooden cradle should have been empty.

But she was almost positive she'd seen something in there. A squirrel or maybe a cat? No, whatever it was it had looked too big, even for a cat.

Emily glanced back again at the display, sure now that there was something odd about it.

She turned and retraced her path, then slowed to a walk as she reached the crèche. She stood stone still, mesmerized by the sight of a tiny hand rising out of a bundle of rags and straw in the carved wooden cradle.

It couldn't be. Yet there it was again, as clear as the sun above. A tiny hand. Popping up out of a mound of cloth.

Emily ran forward and pushed the corner of a tattered blanket aside. A rosy cheeked baby wearing a pink wool cap stared up at her.

The baby blinked huge blue-grey eyes. Then suddenly its tiny face crumpled and it began to cry.

Emily scooped up the child and the wad of blankets that cocooned it. Bits of straw clung to the precious bundle.

"There, there. It's okay. It's all right now," she soothed the baby.

She lifted the child to her shoulder and gently patted its back. *Who in the world would do such a thing? How long had the child been out here? The poor little thing must be freezing.*

A hundred questions raced through her head as Emily jogged to the church, the baby clutched to her chest. She yanked open one heavy door and slipped into the dark, sheltering warmth. She walked into the sanctuary and sat down in the last pew, resting the baby across her lap.

The baby had stopped crying but still fussed in her arms. Though Emily loved children, she knew next to nothing about taking care of them, especially tiny babies.

"Are you hungry? Is that it?" Emily said aloud. "I wish I had something for you."

As if on cue, the baby started wailing again, louder this time, putting all the force of its tiny body into the effort. The cries echoed around the empty sanctuary, and Emily jumped to her feet and started pacing up and down the middle aisle.

She bounced, patted, and cooed to no avail. Suddenly she noticed a pacifier hanging from a long string that was attached someplace inside the blankets. She took out her water bottle, cleaned off the pacifier, and stuck it in the baby's mouth.

The baby sucked eagerly, eyelids drooping in contentment. The church was instantly silent again.

Emily sat down with the baby in her lap once more and examined the wrapping, wondering what else she might discover. The outer blanket looked like a piece cut off a larger comforter. White acrylic stuffing trailed out of one end. Beneath that layer, she found smaller blankets, none very thick. The baby was dressed in one-piece, terry cloth pajamas, which at least covered its feet. The pajamas were worn and stained, with a hole in one elbow and a faded yellow duck embroidered on the chest. The baby's nails were dirty and jagged. The child wasn't well cared for at all. A wave of sadness filled Emily's heart.

"God bless this poor child," she whispered.

Fumbling with the blankets again, she felt something else stuck in the folds: a piece of paper. She pulled it out and unfolded a small note written in blue ink. The handwriting was childish looking, she thought, round with loop-ing script letters. The message was just a few lines long.

> *Please help my baby, Jane. She's a good girl.*
> *I can't keep her no more. I am so sorry. Please*
> *find her a good home. God bless you.*

Staring down at the little girl, Emily couldn't imagine how anyone could have abandoned her. The pink hat had slipped off entirely and Emily set it aside. Tufts of reddish gold hair covered the baby's head. With her huge eyes and cherubic face, the child was positively beautiful.

What would it take to give up such a sweet, innocent lit-tle girl? The simple note suggested the baby's mother was not a monster. She must have been desperate, though, with some serious reasons for avoiding the usual process of giv-ing up a child for adoption.

Emily didn't condemn her; she didn't even judge her. She understood the situation too well. Over twenty years ago, Emily had made the momentous decision to give up her own newborn daughter, and now the mother's scribbled note stirred up long-buried feelings.

As if sensing Emily's distraction, the baby reached out and clutched at the air. Emily stuck out her finger. The baby latched on, surprisingly strong, and Emily felt the force of their connection deep in her heart, like an electric circuit closing its loop.

"Don't worry, Jane. I'll help you," Emily whispered. "I promise."

She stared down at the child another moment and sighed. But how? What to do now? A call to the police seemed in order, though for some strange reason, she felt reluctant about the idea.

She shifted the baby to one side and felt around her jacket pocket for her cell phone, then fumbled with it in one hand.

"Emily? Are you okay?"

Emily jumped at the sound of Reverend Ben's voice. She turned to see the minister standing at the end of the pew, staring curiously.

"Reverend Ben, you won't believe it. I was jogging through the green this morning and I found this baby. Right in front of the church, tucked into the cradle of the crèche."

Reverend Ben stepped closer, squinting at her through his gold-rimmed glasses. "Found a baby? In the crèche?"

Emily nodded.

"That's . . . unbelievable."

"Isn't it?" Emily turned back to the baby. "Her name is Jane. See, there was a note." Emily handed him the note and watched as he quickly read it.

"How sad. Sad for the child and for the mother." He came closer, eager to get a better look at the baby. "Is she all right? It's awfully cold out there."

"She seems to be okay. She was wrapped in a few layers of blankets. I think she's just hungry right now and probably needs her diaper changed."

"My, she's a beauty."

"Yes, she is."

"Have you called anyone yet?"

"I was just about to dial the police." Emily stood up. "Here, could you hold her a moment?"

"Yes, of course." Ben took the baby easily into his arms. "Hello, little girl. You poor little thing," he crooned.

Emily dialed the local police department, a number she knew by heart. She quickly reported the situation to the officer at the front desk, who was more than surprised to hear the story, especially coming from the town's mayor.

"We'll send a car and an ambulance right away, Mayor."

Emily hadn't realized an ambulance would come, too. But it made sense. The baby would need to be examined by a doctor.

"Thanks. I'll be waiting." Emily ended the call and turned back to Ben, who now struggled a bit with his tiny charge.

"Here, I'll take her," Emily offered. Ben handed the baby back, and Emily cradled her in one arm, using her free hand to find the pacifier again. The baby calmed and Emily felt like a genius.

"I think she's hungry," she said quietly.

"Yes, she must be." Ben was quiet, watching Emily with the baby. "You've made friends quickly. I think she likes you."

Emily didn't know what to say. She looked down at Jane, who seemed to be smiling.

Emily heard the big wooden doors open and saw Officer Tucker Tulley walk in. "What have we here? I heard the call but I didn't believe it. Thought someone on the radio was pulling my leg."

"It's a baby, all right, Tucker," Reverend Ben said. "A little girl."

Tucker shook his head and stared down at the child. "I don't think we've ever had a baby abandoned in this town. Not since I've been on the force, anyway."

Emily couldn't recall such a thing either, though her mother, who was a great authority on town history— especially the transgressions of local citizenry—might be able to cite a precedent.

"There was a note. But I don't think you can tell much from it." Emily handed the note to Tucker. He looked at it briefly, then stuck it in his pocket.

"Not much. I'll keep it for the report, I guess."

They all turned at the sound of the ambulance siren outside. Emily felt the baby's body grow tense in her arms.

Tucker turned back to Emily. "Would you like me to take her from you now?"

She didn't know what to say. She knew she had to give the baby up, yet her arms couldn't seem to let go of the child, who now rested so comfortably against her shoulder.

"I . . . I can carry her out. It's all right."

She felt Tucker and Ben watching as she stood up and

stepped out of the pew. The two men moved aside and let her walk out first. She felt self-conscious, as if she were playing a part in a strange play. Even the warm weight of the baby in her arms seemed somehow unreal.

Tucker reached forward and pushed open the church door. Emily paused and glanced back toward the pew. "Her blankets. She'll get cold."

"I'd better take those. They might be needed as evidence," Tucker said. "They'll have plenty of clean blankets in the ambulance."

"Yes, of course." Emily nodded and finally stepped outside. She walked quickly toward the ambulance, which was parked on the green. A stretcher stood on the sidewalk in front of the church.

One of the paramedics met her and, without a word, took the baby. Emily stepped back, feeling surprised and suddenly left empty, as if something had been stolen from her.

"Where will you take her?" she asked.

"To the hospital at Southport. She'll be checked in and examined. A social worker will meet us there to take care of all the paperwork."

"Yes . . . of course." Everything was happening so fast now. *Too fast*, Emily thought. Reverend Ben stood beside her, watching.

The EMS attendant placed the baby on the stretcher, in a baby-size foam form. He pulled belts across her body, securing her. The baby started to cry and Emily grew concerned.

"Can I ride with you to the hospital?"

She could tell from Ben's look that he was surprised.

The paramedic looked at her and then at Officer Tulley.

"She can go along if she wants. No rule against that." Officer Tulley rested his hand for a moment on Emily's shoulder.

The paramedic nodded. "Hop up in back. It will probably be easier anyway for the social worker to get the story firsthand."

Emily climbed into the back of the ambulance and positioned herself close to the baby. She wasn't sure why she felt so relieved to go along. She just did.

BEN WATCHED THE AMBULANCE PULL AWAY, THEN RE-turned to his office, where he saw the light on his answering machine blinking. He leaned over the desk and pressed the button to play back the message.

"Reverend Ben? I'm sorry to cancel on such short notice," the thin voice of Vera Plante began, "but I'm not able to come tomorrow morning to that coat-drive meeting. I just had my whole family here for Thanksgiving and I'm beat. I am sorry. I do want to help. I'll be working on the Christmas Fair this year, though. On the bake sale. I'm just thinking now that volunteering for both is a bit too much for me. Hope you understand."

He did understand. Vera wasn't young—of course she was tired after a houseful of company. Still he had to resist the temptation to call her back and tell her that baking cookies for the Christmas Fair was well and good, but it wasn't going to put decent coats on the poor kids in Wood's Hollow this winter.

When he asked for volunteers to run a coat drive for the community center at Wood's Hollow, a run-down area on the edge of Cape Light, only Vera and Grace Hegman had come forward. Ben had a meeting penciled in for this morning, at nine thirty. The two women were to meet him at the church and they'd drive together to the Wood's Hollow community center to figure out the details and how to get the word out around town.

He realized now that he hadn't heard from Grace all week either. Not a good sign. But it was barely eight o'clock. Too early to call, he thought. He would wait a few minutes, at least until a quarter after.

His office seemed so quiet. The church secretary had the day off and so did the sexton, Joe Tulley. Finding Emily and the baby in the sanctuary had been a rousing start to the day. But now the silence closed in on him, feeling oppressive.

He picked up a letter that sat open on his desk. The postmark was from a Native American reservation in Wyoming. The handwriting was tight and neat, determined and efficient, much like Reverend James Cameron, the man who had penned it.

> *Dear Ben,*
>   *Sorry I haven't been in touch. We've been so busy, it's hard to know where to begin. Life here is interesting and the work full of challenges. I try not to push it but there are so many in need, so much to be done. Day by day, we make progress in small steps. Leigh is a terrific help—the best wife in the world, far better than I deserve. And our little Julia is the joy of my heart. She'll be a year old in just a month or so, as I'm sure you remember. I am truly blessed.*

Ben stopped reading for a moment, picturing Leigh, the woman who had arrived in Cape Light last year, on the run from an abusive ex-husband, and Julia, the beautiful baby she had given birth to on Christmas Day. James had wanted to help Leigh and wound up falling in love and marrying her.

The letter continued for several pages, with James describing his mission work on the reservation. As usual, he sounded focused and productive. Ben envied him that. It was hard to admit, but he did.

He missed having James around, a colleague and a confidante and a good friend. More than that, he missed the younger man's energy. Even in poor health, James's spirit never failed him.

Ben sighed and leaned back in his chair. He'd always been perfectly content in Cape Light, preaching at this church. But the letter from James had gotten under his skin. James's work seemed so meaningful, while lately life at this church seemed routine and, frankly, uninspiring.

How had that happened? He wasn't sure. Certainly, serving a small congregation like this was a world away from the hands-on missionary work James was called to. And yet each calling had value in its own way. The people of Cape Light needed spiritual nourishment as much as those in any far-off corner of the globe.

But maybe he'd lost his zeal, Ben reflected. Maybe this wonderful, comfortable place was just too comfortable for him after all these years. He'd gone soft, lost his inner fire. Lately, it seemed he couldn't even rouse his congregation to help their own neighbors in Wood's Hollow. They seemed far more interested in debating whether red or gold bows should be used to decorate the garlands at the annual Christmas Fair.

This Sunday was the first in the season of Advent, the beginning of preparation for Christmas. It was a phase of the holy calendar that always energized him. This year, however, Ben felt strangely distant, unmoved. What had come over him? He was never prone to such dark thoughts.

And what did he have to complain about? Two winters ago, his wife, Carolyn, had been at death's door and their son, Mark, had been almost a stranger to them. Now Carolyn was completely recovered from her stroke and Mark was happily living at home, working at a bookstore, and preparing to start college again. *I should be counting my blessings this Christmas season,* Ben thought, *not indulging in self-pity.*

He knew he could never run out to some desolate place

and do what James was doing. He could never leave this church. No, that would be impossible.

I'll stay here until I retire or die . . . or for as long as they'll have me. I'm just caught in preholiday blues . . .

He bent his head and closed his eyes. *Dear God, I'm not sure what this strange mood is about. Please help me be mindful of my blessings and help me shake off this self-indulgent malaise. I know there's always meaningful work for me here. Please help me regain my focus and feel productive again.*

Ben checked his watch, then picked up the telephone and dialed the Hegmans'. The phone rang several times. He was just about give up when Grace answered.

"Good morning, Grace. I'm glad I caught you. I just wanted to confirm our meeting at nine thirty."

"A meeting?" Grace sounded confused, and his heart sank.

"About the coat drive for Wood's Hollow?"

"Oh . . . oh yes. I remember now. I'm so sorry, Reverend. I can't make it down there today. My dad's come down with a chest cold. I told him not to go out walking this morning, but you know, there's no stopping him. He doesn't sound good at all. He can't watch the store for me today, and I hate to leave him alone feeling so poorly."

Ben took a breath, struggling to mask his disappointment. Grace was devoted to her father, Digger, who was not in good health these days. She also ran a business single-handedly. Perhaps it had been asking too much to have her head this outreach, but everyone was so busy all the time. At least she'd volunteered. At least her spirit was willing.

"I understand, Grace. I hope Digger is feeling better soon. Keep me posted, okay?"

"Yes, I will."

"I suppose tomorrow isn't any good for you either?"

"Gee . . . no, I'm sorry. It's a big weekend at the store. The Christmas shoppers will be out in force, you know."

"So I've heard. Why don't you check your calendar and see if there's some time next week that will work for you. The cold weather is setting in fast. The kids down there do need coats," he reminded her.

"Oh, yes. I know," she said solemnly. "I will get back to you," she promised.

Grace hung up and Ben sat at his desk a moment, feeling deflated and ineffectual. Was there anyone in the congregation he could call on such short notice to help out? Many faces came to mind—Lucy Bates, Sophie Potter, Jessica Morgan, Fran Tulley—but he eliminated each in turn, knowing they were either too busy with their lives and responsibilities, already taking part in some church activity, like the Christmas Fair, or simply not interested in donating their time to this type of effort.

He couldn't help but think the lack of spirit in the congregation somehow reflected back on him, on his own failure to inspire them and to open their eyes to the needs of their neighbors, families who lived in the shadow of their relative affluence. It was not a good feeling.

There were a few families from Wood's Hollow who had recently joined the church, making Ben more aware of the pressing needs there. It was a forlorn and mostly forgotten corner, one many residents of Cape Light didn't even acknowledge. The last few months Ben had been trying to arouse some awareness in his congregation for the people living there. So far, he had to admit, without great results.

Vera and then Grace both bailing at the last minute on the coat-drive meeting was just the most recent in a string of frustrations. He would go down to the community center on his own, he decided. Maybe once he got the ball rolling, Grace and Vera would help, or someone else would step forward. It wasn't ideal, but it was the best he could do this morning.

Determined to see the thing through, even if nobody else in the congregation was interested, Ben slipped on his coat and scarf and set out.

EMILY SAT IN THE EMERGENCY ROOM WAITING AREA IN A hard plastic chair, a tattered copy of *National Geographic* in her lap. Her sight was fixed on a pair of swinging doors that opened to the examining rooms, where the paramedics had taken the baby.

The ride to Southport had taken about an hour. After the baby had been brought in, medical personnel had taken over. She'd been more or less brushed aside and told to wait for the social worker, a Mrs. Preston.

Emily shifted on her chair. She wished she could see what was happening. She wondered if the social worker would let her see Jane again, take one last look.

The baby's face filled her mind's eye, and she could almost feel her warm weight in her arms. She thought again of the brief note, the mother's sadness and desperation.

She might speculate, but she would probably never know what had driven the baby's mother to such a desperate act. In her heart, though, she knew the feelings that woman had experienced. She knew them far too well.

When she was eighteen, right after high school graduation, Emily had eloped with Tim Sutton, a local fisherman. The pair had run away to live on the Maryland shore. She had had no contact with her family for over a year when she and her young husband were in the car accident that took Tim's life. Widowed and eight months pregnant, with no place to turn for help, Emily finally called home. Her mother came down and stayed by her bedside while Emily lay in the hospital, trying to heal from both the injuries that complicated her pregnancy and the shock and grief of losing Tim.

Her mother had been no great comfort, though: all the while she insisted Emily was too young to take care of a baby. How would she support it or raise it properly on her own? She hadn't gone to college, choosing to run off and get married instead. She couldn't even support herself, her mother pointed out. Emily was not only naive but also selfish to think only of what she wanted, Lillian Warwick had claimed. Making sacrifices is the first lesson of motherhood, she'd told Emily.

And Lillian made it very clear that Emily couldn't expect to bring the child back home to Cape Light and have her family take both of them in as if nothing had happened. Not after the way she had defied her parents and run off to get married.

It was her mother's way of getting even, of punishing Emily for defying her wishes—all presented in the best interests of the child, of course.

Finally, sick, weak, and confused, Emily had given in to her mother's arguments. Memories of that dark time now brought familiar pain. It was a choice she had made and then regretted for the rest of her life.

Two years ago, in answer to her prayers, Emily's daughter, Sara, had found her. Having Sara in her life again seemed like a gift from heaven above for which Emily was forever thankful. But the reconnection with Sara, now in her mid-twenties, had never fully made up for the loss of giving her up as an infant.

How could it? The wound was still there, barely healed over. Now this baby and her plight drew all those painful, submerged feelings to the surface again.

The doors swung open and two women walked toward her, the admitting doctor, whom Emily had spoken to briefly, and a tall woman in a long blue overcoat. Her short brown hair was mixed with silvery grey, worn in a short, no-fuss hairstyle. She walked quickly and carried an overstuffed briefcase. Emily guessed it was Mrs. Preston.

The doctor quickly made introductions and left Emily and Nadine Preston alone together.

The social worker sat down next to Emily and took out a notebook and pen. "Thank you for waiting, Ms. Warwick. I won't take much of your time."

She proceeded to ask Emily questions about when and how she'd found the baby. There wasn't much to tell.

"Did you see anyone else nearby? Did you pass anyone while you were running?"

"Hardly a soul. Only Digger Hegman, out on the dock. He lives in town over the Bramble Antique Shop with his daughter, Grace. He's out on the dock every morning with his dog."

Nadine Preston noted the information on her pad. "I'll have to speak with him, too, I suppose."

It was possible that Digger saw the person who left the baby, Emily realized. Though Digger was so confused lately, she wasn't sure if any information he offered would be reliable.

"What will happen now?" Emily asked.

"The baby will be given a complete examination, blood tests, X-rays, and all that. She may need to stay in the hospital for treatment if some problem is uncovered."

"Such as?"

"Well . . . any number of things. She might be dehydrated or anemic. Or she might have more serious problems, like hepatitis or being HIV positive. It's likely that the child's mother had a problem with drug use."

"Oh . . . I see." Emily thought she should have realized that.

"She'll be treated, of course. There are some great drugs now for pediatric HIV. Very effective," the social worker went on.

Such sobering possibilities for the baby made Emily feel sad. "I hope there's nothing that seriously wrong with her, though."

"Yes, let's hope so."

"What happens if she's healthy? Where will she go?"

"She'll be placed in foster care while we look for her mother or a close relative. The investigation takes about a month. If we don't find anyone after that time, the baby will be put up for adoption."

Emily considered the child's fate. Neither possibility seemed that positive to her.

Nadine Preston smiled briefly and gave Emily a curious look. "I haven't covered many cases of abandoned children, thank goodness, but I have seen enough. I can imagine it's been a trying experience for you."

"For me? Well, certainly an unusual start to the day." Emily was caught off guard by the question, but Nadine Preston's quick smile put her at ease again.

"I guess what I'm trying to say is, it's only natural to feel concerned. To feel involved with the child. But you have nothing to worry about. We're going to take good care of her."

"Yes, I'm sure you will." Emily watched Nadine Preston closing her notebook and stowing it in her briefcase. The interview appeared to be over.

"Would it be okay if I called you in a few days, to see how she's doing?" Emily asked.

"There are privacy issues. We're really not supposed to give information to anyone outside of the case . . ."

"I just want to know how the tests come out, if she's healthy and all that," Emily said quickly. She wasn't used to being in this subordinate position. Civil servants like Nadine Preston were usually eager to accommodate her.

The other woman hesitated a moment before answering. "I suppose you could call for an update if you really want to, Ms. Warwick." She took out a card from her briefcase and handed it to Emily.

Emily quickly slipped it into her pocket. "Thanks."

"It's all right. I understand." Nadine Preston smiled

kindly. Then she stood up and slung her heavy bag over her shoulder. "Thanks for your help."

"You're very welcome."

The two women said good-bye, and Emily watched Nadine Preston push through the swinging doors and disappear. She'd really hoped to see the baby one more time before she left, but it seemed best not to push her luck. The social worker had already granted her one favor and also hinted she didn't think Emily should get too involved.

I can't help the way I feel, Emily reasoned. The situation was . . . unusual. Extreme. It's only natural to feel interest in the child's fate. The social worker even said so herself.

"Emily? Are you all right?"

Emily looked up to find her husband, Dan, striding toward her across the waiting area. Tall and lean, he was easy to spot even in this crowd. He looked as if he'd dressed in a hurry, wearing his down jacket over a grey sweatshirt and jeans, a baseball cap covering his thick, silvery blond hair. His pale blue eyes searched for her in the crowd. He looked concerned, as if she'd been in an accident.

She'd called him earlier for a ride back to town, but the phone connection had been full of static and she'd barely explained about the baby.

"Hi, honey. Thanks for picking me up. I'm fine," she assured him. He hugged her hello, holding on a little longer than usual.

"I don't like getting calls from a hospital emergency room first thing in the morning. And what's all this about a lost baby?"

She could tell that her ex-reporter husband, "just-the-facts Dan," wanted the whole story.

"I was jogging through the village green, past the church, and I saw something move in the big crèche, in the cradle. I went back and it turned out to be a baby. A little girl," she added. "Her name is Jane."

Dan frowned. "How did you figure out her name?"

"There was a note. Not much else though. It's so sad. She's really a beautiful baby, about three months old. I wish you could see her." Emily glanced wistfully at the swinging doors that now separated her from the baby.

Dan stared at her a moment. "That's quite a story. Quite an experience."

"It was . . . odd. I took her into the church. Reverend Ben helped me call the police."

He touched her shoulder. "You've had some morning. Are you all done here?"

Emily nodded. "I guess so."

Dan slipped his arm around her shoulders and they walked out into the parking lot. Although there was nothing more she could do, Emily felt strangely reluctant to go. But it was hard to put her feelings into words.

Once they were in Dan's car and driving away, she said, "I wish I could have seen her one more time, just to say good-bye. But I didn't want to ask the social worker. I had a feeling she would have put me off, so I didn't ask."

"It's probably just as well. I'm sure the baby will get good care now. You don't have to worry."

"That's what the social worker told me. Her exact words." Emily stared out the passenger side window.

Dan reached over and touched her hand. "You've been through a strange experience, honey, like helping out at the scene of an accident. I think you're a little in shock."

Emily didn't know what to say. She certainly felt . . . not quite herself.

"Are you still going in to the office?" he asked.

"Yes, I need to catch up. I can get a lot done this afternoon."

"Let's stop in town for lunch first. I bet you haven't eaten all day."

She was hungry, she realized. Maybe some real food in her stomach would relieve the floaty, unreal sensation she'd been feeling ever since she'd found the baby. Emily felt as if she were in a trance. Maybe Dan was right; maybe she was in shock from finding the baby.

But it had been a wonderful kind of shock, she reflected. And one of the most amazing moments of her life.

She already knew she wouldn't have missed the experience for the world.

CHAPTER TWO

━◟

ALTHOUGH DAN DIDN'T ASK ANY MORE QUESTIONS about the baby on the way back to Cape Light, the child's image was never far from Emily's mind. How, Emily wondered, could this little being whom she'd known so briefly have made such a deep impression?

Dan drove into the village and parked in front of the Clam Box. Emily was sure that by now everyone in town knew about the baby and she'd be barraged with questions at the diner, the town's unofficial news hub. Then again, she would be answering questions wherever she went today.

It was already past twelve and the Clam Box was nearly full. Emily spotted Charlie Bates, the diner's owner and cook, second generation. He was at his usual post, working hard at the grill behind the counter. He deftly slipped a burger onto a waiting roll, added a side of fries, and then spun around and dropped the dish under the heat lamp at the service station.

"Order up." He slammed the little bell on the countertop.

His wife and head waitress, Lucy Bates, ignored him, greeting Emily and Dan with a warm smile. "I have your favorite table by the window set up."

"Thanks, Lucy." Emily took a seat as Lucy handed down the menus. "I'll just have a bowl of chowder today and a salad."

"Me, too," Dan said. "I'll have the same."

Lucy laughed. "Soup and salad seems to be everyone's choice today. I guess we all ate too much turkey and pumpkin pie yesterday." She jotted down the order on her pad. "Hey, Emily, Tucker said you found a baby on the village green this morning. Is that really true?"

Emily took a sip of water. "It's true, all right."

"I can't believe it. I thought Tucker was joking." Lucy's blue eyes widened, and then her expression grew more serious. "What an awful thing, to abandon a child like that. What did they say at the hospital? Is the baby okay?"

"They're running some tests. They won't know for a few days. But she seemed pretty healthy to me," Emily added.

"Lucy? Baconburger? Table five? The dish can't walk across the restaurant on its own, you know."

Charlie stood at the end of the counter, scowling at his wife. Emily wasn't sure how Lucy put up with him. She had left him about two years ago but had come back, for the sake of their children, Emily suspected. Someday when the two boys were grown, Charlie might not be so lucky.

Charlie was Emily's only real political rival. He'd made a run for mayor in the election two years ago when Emily ran for her second term. His defeat had only sharpened his ambitions. He'd remained active in town politics, never letting an opportunity pass by to stir up trouble for her.

Emily tried to imagine how Charlie would interpret her finding the baby. Undoubtedly, he would figure out some way to put a negative spin on it.

Emily came to the diner anyway. The food was reliable if not gourmet, and she needed to show Charlie she wasn't afraid of him. Besides, she liked and admired Lucy, who managed to put up with her onerous husband, work full time at the diner, raise two boys, and go back to school for a nursing degree. Though she was only able to take a few courses each semester, and was still years away from finishing her degree, Lucy plugged doggedly away.

"Catch you later. Charlie's on the warpath." The pretty redhead rolled her eyes. "But I want to hear more about that baby," she said over her shoulder as she walked away.

Emily felt Dan watching her. "Are you okay?"

She looked up at him. "Me? Sure. I'm fine. I guess everyone's heard by now. Better to answer all the questions and get it over with."

He smiled mildly at her. "It might be more efficient to hold a town meeting and invite the press. But I guess that would be a little extreme."

He glanced out the window and his smile widened. "Speaking of the press, look who's coming this way. Now you'll really be interrogated. I've heard this girl is tough."

Emily turned to see her daughter, Sara Franklin, rush toward the restaurant and pull open the door. Sara glanced around, spotted Emily and Dan, then quickly walked over. She looked very professional and smart, Emily thought, in a knee-length tweed coat and high black boots. Sara slipped off her coat and swung her long, dark hair over her shoulder. Her blue turtleneck matched her eyes perfectly. Emily realized that Sara—who always seemed to have her mind on more idealistic matters—didn't really know how pretty she was.

"Hi, guys." Sara leaned over and kissed Emily's cheek, then slipped into the booth beside her. "I lucked out and saw your car parked outside."

"Luck had nothing to do with it. She's like a little bloodhound, tracking down a story," Dan teased.

Though he claimed to be perfectly happy retired now for almost two years, Dan still missed running the newspaper and running after stories. He had given Sara her first chance writing professionally and liked to take credit for teaching her the ropes. She had done well on her own merit, though, with a talent for writing and an intuition for ferreting out news.

"You want to know all about the baby, I guess," Emily said.

"Everything." Sara pulled a notebook out of the leather knapsack that also served as her purse and sometimes seemed to contain everything but the kitchen sink. "What time did you leave your house this morning?"

Emily sat back. She could tell this was going to take awhile. She had been interviewed by Sara before: her daughter was relentless in her quest for detail.

Emily answered Sara's questions right through her soup and salad and into coffee. Finally, Sara seemed satisfied.

"Now please don't make a big deal out of it, Sara. I didn't do anything heroic, just what anyone would have done in the situation."

"Okay, but how many people find a real live baby in a manger scene? It's practically . . . a miracle," Sara pointed out.

Emily didn't reply, because Sara's casual use of the word struck a chord in her.

"I wouldn't go that far. This isn't a piece for the grocery-store tabloids," Dan cut in. "It seems pretty logical to me that someone chose a cradle as a place to park a baby."

"Logical, perhaps," Sara agreed, "but it still makes great copy. Maybe some relatives will see the story and come forward. Maybe I can help find the mother or whoever abandoned her."

Emily hadn't thought of that. The idea of finding the mother disturbed her. If the mother was found, would she be allowed to have the baby back after abandoning her? And what about relatives? Emily hoped that if any came forward, they would be more responsible than the child's mother.

Sara took a last sip of coffee and excused herself to go write up the article.

"She'll get good copy out of this," Dan predicted as Sara disappeared out the door. "Everybody wants to read about an abandoned baby. Front page, above the fold."

"You sound as if you wish you were writing this one yourself."

"Been there, done that." Dan grinned at her; then his expression turned serious again. "Are you sure you're all right? You just don't seem like yourself."

Emily was about to claim again that she felt perfectly fine, but instead she shrugged, touched that he'd noticed. "I feel a little . . . unsettled, I guess."

"You want to talk about it?" he asked gently.

Emily sensed that he knew old feelings about Sara had been stirred up—how hard it had been to give her up so many years ago, and the shame, guilt, and regret that were with her still.

"No. I mean . . . I'm not ready to talk about it right now," she admitted. "But thanks for asking."

"All right, I'm here when you're ready." He reached across the table and touched her hand. "Do you still want to go in to the office? Why don't you just come home with me and relax?"

"That's a tempting offer, but I really need to take care of a few things on my desk today," Emily insisted.

The truth was, her office was the best place to hide away. There she could bury herself in work, her foolproof method for avoiding her painful memories.

"IT WASN'T MY FIRST FRONT-PAGE STORY, OF COURSE. But I think it came out pretty good. I got a great quote from

Officer Tulley," Sara added. "He said something like, 'I thought the dispatcher was playing a joke, but I knew it wasn't April Fool's Day.' "

"Yes, I read it. I read it twice," her boyfriend Luke Mc-Callister teased her. "I've saved it in a scrapbook for you."

Sara shrugged and smiled slyly. "You ought to get together with Lillian. You could have a scrapbooking party. I hear it's the latest thing."

Sara's grandmother, Lillian Warwick, actually did collect Sara's articles and paste them into books. But Lillian openly disdained Luke and told anyone who would listen that he wasn't good enough for her granddaughter. The very thought of sitting in Lillian's parlor and working on scrapbooks together was so bizarre, it made Luke laugh out loud.

"Now you're scaring me," he joked, slinging his arm around her shoulder as they walked steadily up a steep hill in the village of Newburyport. Filled with shops and restaurants, bookstores, galleries, and even a movie theater that showed foreign films, Newburyport was a popular destination on Saturday nights, and the sidewalks were crowded with couples. "But even the idea of scrapbooking with Lillian won't dim my appetite. I'm starving," he said. "Where do you want to eat?"

Sara shrugged, feeling comfortable and warm cuddled up against him. Luke was tall, though not quite six feet. He wore his brown hair short, almost in a crew cut. With their faces so close, she could just about discern the thin, faded scar that ran from the corner of his eye down his lean cheek. His changeable, hazel eyes matched his temperament, introverted and often moody. Luke had a rough-around-the-edges quality she found incredibly attractive.

"I'm not sure what I'd like to eat," she said honestly. "Let's walk a bit." She slowed her steps to look at a shop-window and Luke stopped alongside her.

"Do you want to go inside?"

She shook her head. "Not really. I'm not ready to start Christmas shopping yet. I can't believe it's the holidays already."

"Neither can I. Doesn't it seem time goes faster when you get older than when you were a little kid?"

"Yeah, it really does." Sara nodded, wondering if it went even faster for Luke, who was ten years older than she was. "Listen, I've been meaning to tell you, my folks want me to come down to Maryland this year for the holidays."

"Are you going?"

"I think so. Would you like to come with me? They said to ask you," she added quickly.

Luke glanced down at her for a moment. "How about you; do you want me to come?"

She nudged him in the ribs with her elbow. "Of course I do, silly. But it's pretty boring. Family stuff. My town makes this place look like New York City."

Luke laughed. "I'm sure it's not that bad. Besides, I like your parents," he added. "They're cool."

Sara rolled her eyes. "I don't think *cool* is a word I'd use to describe Barbara and Mike. But it's sweet of you to say."

Her adoptive parents, she meant, Barbara and Mike Franklin, who had raised her in the small town of Winston, Maryland. All through college Sara had been obsessed with finding her birth mother. Right after graduation, she came to Cape Light on her own and located Emily. Their relationship had been rocky at first and Sara had nearly gone back home. She had felt so angry, as if she could never forgive Emily for giving her up. But Emily's sincere love and understanding had eventually won her heart.

As much as Sara loved her adoptive parents and knew that no one could replace them, she now couldn't imagine her life without Emily. Sara had carved out a place for herself in Cape Light these past years and rarely thought of returning to Maryland anymore, though she did sometimes dream of someday moving to other, more exciting places.

Sara paused to gaze into another window where colorful ski sweaters with matching scarves were cleverly displayed on a row of fake snowpeople.

"I just dread all the holiday shopping," she confessed. "I'm not a shopping kind of person. I start off pretty good. Then about an hour or two into it, I panic and end up buying everyone sweaters or calendars."

Luke laughed. "You need a good list. That's the whole secret. Plan your attack and don't deviate."

She glanced at him curiously. "You sound as if you're already done."

"Not exactly. But I have started my list," he admitted. "It's shaping up nicely."

The glint in his hazel eyes made her even more curious, but she didn't pursue it. They'd come to a jewelry store and Luke made them stop.

"How about jewelry?" he asked casually.

"How about it?"

"Would you like some for Christmas?"

"It's not necessary," she said. Luke always got her lovely gifts, but this suggestion seemed extravagant. "Come on." She tried to tug him away. "You don't have to buy me jewelry. It's a sweet thought, but this store is way too expensive."

Luke wouldn't budge and, as he was much bigger and stronger, it was hard to get him moving again.

"Let's go inside," he said, tugging Sara along in his wake. "I want to see something."

"I thought we were going to have dinner," she protested. "I don't really feel like shopping right now."

"We're not shopping; we're browsing. I just want to get some ideas of what you like. For my list," he reminded her.

They were inside the store now. A tall saleswoman with bright red lipstick and glossy dark hair seemed to swoop down on them. "Can I help you with something, sir?" Her bright smile was fixed on Luke, Sara noticed.

"We're just browsing," Sara said.

"We'd like to see some rings," Luke said, almost at the same time.

The saleswoman ignored Sara. "Anything in particular?"

"Not really. That case would be a good place to start, I guess." Luke pointed at a nearby glass case and Sara's mouth dropped open. It was filled with diamond engagement rings.

The woman's smile widened. "Just a moment. I'll get the keys." She walked away quickly as Sara grabbed Luke's arm.

"What are you doing?"

He patted her hand. "Calm down. This is going to be fun."

"Luke, I'm serious. We can't waste this woman's time. She's trying to make a living. This isn't a joke."

"I'm not joking. Didn't you ever want to try one of those on? Hey, that one looks like your taste, and it's a good size, about two carats, wouldn't you say?"

"I have no idea," Sara sighed. Almost against her will, her gaze was drawn to the case, zeroing in on the ring he was talking about.

It was a beautiful ring, a sparkling round stone in a simple setting that blended platinum and gold. Classic, but with a slightly unexpected, artful touch, just the kind she would like, if she ever wanted a diamond. Luke did know her taste by now; she had to grant him that much.

The saleswoman appeared again with a big key ring. "Have you found something you like?" she asked cheerfully.

Sara smiled through gritted teeth. "I don't think so. Sorry we—"

"That round solitaire in the second row caught my eye," Luke told the saleswoman. "May we see it?"

"Yes, of course." Before Sara could protest again, the saleswoman had the ring out on a dark blue velvet cushion and was describing the stone and setting in great detail.

Luke picked it up and held the diamond to the light. Then he looked at it under a magnifying lens, all the while asking the saleswoman questions.

Sara realized there was no way to get him out of the store before he was good and ready. She just had to play along.

And where had Luke learned so much about diamonds? He was asking some very informed questions about weight and flaws and countries of origin.

The saleswoman stepped away for a moment and Sara nudged him. "When did you turn into a diamond expert?"

Luke shrugged. "I was at the dentist last week. There was an article about diamonds in *Smithsonian*. Fascinating stuff."

Right. *Smithsonian* magazine. More like *A Guy's Guide to Buying Chicks Expensive Stuff*. That would be more Luke's speed, Sara thought.

The saleswoman suddenly appeared again, smiling coaxingly at Sara. "Would you like to try on the ring now?"

Sara stared at her, feeling like a deer caught in the head-lights. Luke picked up the ring, then picked up Sara's hand. "Don't be shy. I want to see how it looks, Sara."

He slipped the ring on her finger and met her glance. There was a sexy teasing glint in his eyes that touched her heart. She wasn't sure what it was about Luke that drew her, but it worked every time.

She glanced down at her hand. The ring did look lovely. It was just the right size, too.

"What do you think?" he asked, smiling at her.

"I . . . it's . . . so . . ." Sara found herself atypically at a loss for words.

She looked down at the ring again. This wasn't a piece of costume jewelry. It was a real diamond, the kind people wear when they plan to get married.

What was happening here?

She suddenly felt smothered, as if she couldn't get a

breath of air. She yanked the ring off her finger and tossed it on the velvet mat.

"I can't do this." She felt the saleswoman staring at her, as though she'd gone mad, but there was nothing she could do. She turned and bolted out of the shop.

With her hands jammed in her pockets and her head ducked down, Sara walked at a quick pace down the crowded street toward Newburyport's waterfront. She couldn't think straight; she could hardly even see straight. She wasn't sure if she felt shocked or just plain angry at Luke. Had that all been a huge joke? Or was it his not-so-subtle way of hinting he wanted to get engaged?

She hadn't even reached the corner before she felt a hand tug her shoulder and turn her around. Luke stared down at her, breathing quickly from his chase.

"Sara, wait up. Where are you rushing to?"

She didn't answer him. She turned and started walking again, and he fell into step beside her. They walked along in tense silence for a while.

Finally Luke asked, "Mad at me?"

She glanced at him but didn't answer. She wasn't sure. It was hard to be mad at a guy for wanting to buy you a two-carat diamond. Still, there was something that had happened back there that just didn't sit right.

"You took me by surprise," she said finally. "More than surprise, you tricked me into going in there. We've never even talked about getting engaged or any of that stuff. Now, all of a sudden, you want me to pick out a diamond ring?"

Luke stood back and crossed his arms over his chest. He was wearing his favorite leather jacket with a dark grey turtleneck sweater underneath. He looked very attractive, which was an annoying thing to notice at a moment like this.

"How else could I do it? You never want to talk about 'that stuff.' Every time I bring it up, you change the subject. You start talking about your job, your landlady, your cat—"

"Okay, okay. I get the idea."

Sara sighed. She couldn't deny it; the accusation was true. Luke did try to talk about their relationship and where it was going, about making a real commitment. She was the one who always avoided the conversation.

"Just tell me one thing; would you have gone into the store with me if I had been up front with you?"

Sara didn't answer for a long moment. "No," she said at last. "I wouldn't have."

Luke winced, then said quietly, "See, that's what I mean."

"No, I don't see," she insisted. "It seems to me if I wouldn't have gone in willingly, that's all the more reason not to . . . bamboozle me."

He rubbed the corner of his eye with his fingertip. It was a nervous gesture he had when he didn't want to lose his temper.

"The thing is, once you went in and tried on the ring, you seemed to enjoy it, Sara. I was there. I saw you. It wasn't exactly torture."

He had a point. What was she complaining about? Most of her single girlfriends were stuck in just the opposite situation, trying to figure out a way to trick their boyfriends into the jewelry store. And she *had* enjoyed trying on the ring. She'd never worn a diamond before. She understood now why they were so special and symbolized so much.

All the more reason to be upset at Luke for tricking her.

"That just isn't the way I want to choose a ring or get engaged to someone. I want to do it in a thoughtful way. I'm not an impulsive person. If you don't know that about me by now—"

Luke raised his hands in surrender. "Okay, I get the point. That was too spur of the moment for you, too off the cuff."

"That's right. You know I'm not like that."

"Yeah, I know," he said. "It's just that sometimes you

can miss out by trying to plan everything so carefully. Sometimes you just jump in feet first and it feels right. Didn't you ever feel that way, Sara?"

Yes, getting involved with you, she wanted to say. But she didn't tell him that. Instead, she twined her arm through his. "I know what you mean, but this is too important."

They continued down the street to the harbor. She could tell he wasn't happy and probably not done talking about the situation, but at least they weren't arguing anymore.

The night was clear and calm. Sara found the chilly air refreshing, clearing her head after the stuffy little shop.

Built on a large hill during the colonial era, the village of Newburyport rose up behind them like a folk art painting, the famous gilded steeple a focal point, the winding streets paved with stone, and millions of glittering white lights rimming rooftops and trees, setting the town aglow for the holidays.

They walked along the harbor for a while, then sat close together on a bench facing the bay. Settled under Luke's arm, Sara nestled against his warm, strong body. She didn't need to talk. She didn't want to.

If only they could stay just like this, without any conflicts or changes, without taking any huge, life-altering steps. What was wrong with just being together? Why did their relationship have to change?

"I'm sorry, Sara. I guess I should have brought this all up even if it's difficult to talk about. I want us to get engaged for Christmas. That's what I've been thinking of. That's what this is all about."

Sara sat without answering. She was surprised and not surprised. Certainly their trip into the jewelry store had given her some hint. Still, the idea of taking such a momentous step made her stomach clench. She knew in an instant that she wasn't ready, and wouldn't be in time for Christmas.

Finally, she looked up at him, her eyes wide. "Luke . . . I just don't know . . ."

"No, wait. Let me talk first. When I came here two years ago and we first met, I was a mess. My life was a big blank. I wasn't a cop anymore. I'd lost my identity, my reason for getting up in the morning. I had no idea what was going to happen to me. But I came to this place and I found myself here. My real self, not just the cookie-cutter identity my father had stamped on me." He turned to her and smiled into her eyes. "I couldn't have done that without you, Sara. I would never have stayed if you weren't here. You know that, don't you?"

She nodded slowly, feeling almost moved to tears by his heartfelt admission. When she thought back to the days when they first met, she saw it much differently, casting herself as the wounded one who had come to Cape Light in search of her birth mother, Emily Warwick. She had felt too frightened and conflicted to confront Emily and confess her real identity.

Luke was the only one who knew her secret, who encouraged but never judged her. He wasn't the only reason she had stayed in Cape Light, but she couldn't imagine her life without him, without his loyalty and love.

"I could never say this to you before," Luke went on. "But I finally realized I'm in a good place now. I'm happy with my life and proud of what I've accomplished with New Horizons."

Luke had set up a center in Cape Light to help at-risk inner-city kids before they wound up in trouble. After some initial local resistance, the program was now thriving.

"I'm ready to take a new step in my life with you," he went on. "I want to get married and have some kids of our own. I love you, Sara. I want us to start a real life together."

Sara swallowed hard. She didn't know what to say. It wasn't that she didn't love Luke. Since meeting him, she had never seriously considered dating anyone else. She had had a brief flirtation with Dan's son, Wyatt Forbes, during the short time he ran the newspaper, but Wyatt had never really mattered to her. It was always Luke.

But marriage? Children? Those were words for someday, a place far off in her life agenda.

Before she could put her feelings into words, Luke leaned forward and gripped her shoulders. "I know why you got so mad at me. I forgot to propose. That was it, right?"

He slipped down on one knee and took both her hands in his own. "Sara—" he began.

"No, don't." Sara took his face in her hands and kissed him hard on the mouth. "I love you, Luke," she said, drawing him to his feet. "I love you so much . . ."

They kissed again, holding each other close. But as Luke pulled back, she could see that he thought she had been saying yes to his still unspoken proposal.

Sara bit her lip and looked down, unable to meet his gaze.

"You don't want to. Is that it?" His voice was soft, but she heard the sharp edge of hurt and sadness.

She looked up at him again. "I'm the one who wouldn't have made it all this way without you."

He shook his head slowly. "That's not what I'm asking you."

She took a breath. "I'm just not ready yet. I know it's hard for you to understand, but you're in a different place than I am right now."

Luke was ten years older, a difference that usually didn't matter between them. She knew that he didn't like to be reminded of it, but maybe it was more important than they had realized.

Sara chose her words carefully. "Please try to understand. This is all coming at me so quickly. So out of the blue."

"We've been together for two years now, Sara. We've talked about the future, spending it together. It can't be that much out of the blue."

"Luke, please. You know what I mean. I need some time. Christmas is just too soon for me."

He stepped back and stuck his hands in the pockets of his leather jacket. His brooding look reminded her of the past, of the expression he wore when they first met. She had been drawn to him despite it. Or maybe because of it.

"I thought that's what I've been doing, giving you time. How much time do you need? Do you even know?"

She shook her head mutely. What a question. Unanswerable.

He let out a long breath and turned away, walking farther down the dock. She didn't follow. She didn't know what more she could say. She knew that despite her professions of love, she had hurt him. And now she didn't know how to make it better.

She caught up with him, took his hand. "There's no one else in the world I'd rather be with, Luke. I don't know what I'd do without you. Please, just be patient with me?"

He stared down at her, his expression unreadable. She couldn't tell what his reaction was going to be and felt her heart beating hard against her ribs.

Finally, he sighed and touched her cheek with his hand.

"All right. Since we aren't going to buy any diamond rings tonight, I guess we ought to have dinner. Any ideas?"

"You choose. I'm hungry for anything," she said quickly.

He took her hand in his warm, reassuring grip, and they started back up the hill toward the town and lights. "How about that little Indian place on Choate Road?"

"I was just thinking of that place. I'm really in the mood for tandoori chicken and those yummy breads."

"I knew that," he said smugly. "See how well I know you?"

Sara smiled despite herself. Why even answer when it seemed he could read her thoughts?

"THERE'S DESSERT AND COFFEE IF EVERYONE'S READY," Emily announced, resisting her own urge to get up from the table.

Sunday lunch at her mother's house was often a challenge to her nerves, but today the gathering seemed particularly trying, maybe because they'd all been together just three days ago, on Thanksgiving. Or maybe because she dreaded more talk about the abandoned baby and was hoping today to outrun it.

Emily tried to keep the momentum going—salad course, entree, dessert, coffee, and then home.

"Coffee and dessert already? I've hardly touched my food," Lillian complained, waving her silver fork in the air. Emily was not surprised. Her mother was the world's slowest eater and much preferred airing her views to finishing her lunch. "It's hard to eat with those children raising such a ruckus. Always fussing and jitterbugging around. They can't seem to sit still for a minute," Lillian added, glowering down the long table at her two grandsons, Jessica and Sam's boys. Born in mid-September, Tyler was a little over two months and their adopted son, Darrell, was now eleven.

"They're just little boys," Dan said. "I think they've been very good sitting at the table all this time."

"Maybe so, but it unsettles the digestion. I hardly feel as if the food is going all the way down."

Lillian glanced to her right at her old friend, Dr. Elliot, for confirmation. He chortled into his napkin. "Nonsense. Having children around keeps you young, keeps the blood flowing, Lillian. Didn't you ever hear that?"

"Mere common consensus hardly makes a statement true," she replied.

"You ought to talk less while you're dining then," Ezra

told her bluntly. "Too much talking. That's what makes you dyspeptic."

Lillian's eyes widened. "Is that your diagnosis?"

Dr. Elliot pushed up his gold-rimmed glasses with the tip of one finger. "Yes, ma'am, it is. But I won't bother to offer you my remedy for your troubles, at the risk of being asked to leave the table before dessert is served."

Dan laughed out loud, then deftly turned the sound into a cough. Emily saw her sister, Jessica, and her husband, Sam, both smother their reactions with their napkins over their mouths. No one but Dr. Elliot seemed able to speak to Lillian so boldly and get away with it, and even he didn't always escape unscathed by her rapier tongue.

A clattering from the far end of the table drew everyone's attention. Sam jumped up. "Don't worry. It's just water."

He grabbed some linen napkins and quickly started to wipe up a wet spot on the table. It seemed that Darrell had tipped over his water glass.

"I'm sorry." Darrell stood up and stared around, looking embarrassed.

"That's all right, Darrell," Emily said kindly. She grabbed a hand towel from the sideboard and quickly covered the wet spot. She placed a reassuring hand on her nephew's shoulder. He did try so hard to behave well in his grandmother's house. He had caused havoc the first time he had been here, though, and her mother had never forgotten it.

"Is it broken? Is the glass broken?" Lillian stood up and glared at the boy. "That's antique Waterford crystal, you know. That pattern is discontinued. It's irreplaceable.

"Nothing is broken, Mother, thank goodness." Jessica stood up and righted the glass, showing her mother it was in one piece. "I don't know why you won't just give them plastic, or at least some ordinary glasses that aren't irreplaceable."

Lillian sniffed and sat down again in her armchair. "Why don't we all just eat in the kitchen, off paper plates?"

Good idea, why don't we? Emily nearly retorted. But she held her tongue. Sam picked up the baby from Jessica's arms and then took Darrell by the hand. "I'll take the kids into the living room. They can play for a while."

Lillian's eyebrows shot up. "Play? In my living room?"

"We brought a few plastic baby toys, Lillian," Sam said. "Tyler is a little young yet for touch football."

Her mother replied with a heavy throat-clearing sound as her son-in-law and the boys left the room.

Emily cleared some plates and carried them into the kitchen. Jessica soon followed with another stack. "Is the coffee ready?" Her tone was desperate and Emily felt sorry for her.

"It's all done," she said, pouring the coffee from the electric coffeemaker into the silver coffeepot her mother preferred. "Can you take the sugar and cream? I brought a pie and ice cream from the bakery." She touched her sister's arm as she brushed by. "I'm sorry Mother's such a pill about the boys. I love having them here."

Jessica smiled quickly at her. "Thanks. I guess I have to stop expecting her to be any different. Sam's family makes such a fuss over Tyler. You would think he was the first baby ever born in the world."

Emily laughed. "As it should be."

"Any news about the baby you found on the green?"

Emily picked up the tray that held the coffee, pie, and ice cream and started toward the dining room. "Nothing more to report. She's undergoing tests. I guess they'll know more tomorrow." Emily set the tray on the table and started to pour the coffee. "The social worker said I could call her and get an update."

"What social worker? Who are you talking about? That baby you found on the village green?" Her mother peered up at her.

"Yes, we were just talking about the baby, Mother," Emily explained calmly. She had hoped to avoid her mother's views on the topic, but there didn't seem much chance of that now.

"Such a horrid story, abandoning a child that way. I don't know what society is coming to."

"Now, now, Lillian. Foundlings are hardly a modern invention," Dr. Elliot reminded her.

"It's unheard of in this town, Ezra. I assure you that there's never been such a disgraceful incident in Cape Light. And I can tell you exactly where that child came from. I don't see what all the mystery is about."

"Where do you think the baby came from, Lillian?" Dan asked evenly.

"Why, from that trashy little pocket down near the lake, Wood's Hollow. Where else?" Lillian said definitively. "It's not really even part of our village. Just over the borderline toward Rawly, I believe."

"It's definitely within our town limits," Emily corrected her.

Lillian's head popped up again. "It wasn't always. The town line must have been moved recently."

Of course the town line hadn't been moved. Neither had the equator. But Emily didn't argue with her. Few in the village wanted to acknowledge the neighborhood—or trashy little pocket, as her mother called it—of Wood's Hollow.

Set off from the main road, the area consisted mainly of two or three ancient hulking structures standing beside a small lake. They had been hotels and boardinghouses in a bygone era and not even the best accommoations the town had to offer back then. In the 1960s, the buildings had been turned into small apartments and furnished rooms. Since then the residents had all been low income, many of them transients. There were also two or three stores there, a laundromat, and grocery, Emily recalled, and a small storefront community center that mostly stood empty and inactive for lack of funds and volunteers willing to work there.

Investors would periodically come to Cape Light and stir up talk of developing Wood's Hollow, inspiring debates at town-council meetings about knocking down the buildings considered a blight on the community, perhaps by changing the zoning laws. But no one was ever sure how it would be done.

As if on cue, her mother now expressed the popular sentiment. "The place should be cleaned out. Those old buildings should be knocked down before they fall down. You'll get rid of that unsavory element living there. You won't have any abandoned babies around here then. I guarantee it."

"Most of those families are just poor people who work hard but can't afford anything better. Where would they go, Lillian?" Dan asked.

"Who cares where they go? They would leave our town; that's all I'm concerned about. They would go away, back where they came from; that's where they'd go. And they would take their babies with them, one would hope."

Emily stopped pouring the coffee and stared down at her mother. "It's not a crime to be poor, Mother. At least, not yet, thank goodness. I have to think that the child's mother, wherever she came from, had to be absolutely desperate. Even respectable people fall on hard times."

Her mother looked as if she was about to deliver some scathing reply, and then her mouth puckered. She drew in a long breath and sat back in her chair.

Bull's-eye, Emily thought. *I finally hit her "off" button.*

Her reply had been a not-so-subtle reminder of the time during Emily's adolescence when their own family faced financial hardship due to her father's imprudence and misjudgment. Her mother had bravely faced the situation and taken control, selling off just about everything at a humiliating public auction, including the mansion and estate that had been in the Warwick family for generations. Though Lillian's present home on Providence Street was one of the finest Victorians in town, it was more than a step down from the family's former glory.

Emily hadn't meant to hurt her mother's feelings, but she could only tolerate so much of Lillian's closed-minded braying.

Her mother glared at her with narrowed eyes. "Just don't get so involved all the time, Emily. You can't save the world."

"Involved with the baby, you mean? I'm just going to follow up with a phone call. I don't consider that overly involved."

Emily sensed Dan watching her. She knew he shared her mother's opinion and concerns about the baby—one of the few times they had ever agreed. She was grateful that he didn't chime in.

"You know very well what I mean," her mother insisted. "I know that look in your eye better than anyone," she added in a cutting tone. "It's best to let the social workers take care of it now. That's their job. That's what they get paid for."

Before Emily could reply, a loud crash sounded from the living room. Everyone turned and stared at the doorway as Tyler's piercing wail broke the silence.

Jessica jumped up and ran toward the noise. "Sam, is everything all right in there?"

Lillian got to her feet and grabbed for her cane. "Let's survey the damage. I feel like the Red Cross walking through a disaster area," she said dramatically.

In a strange way, she sounded almost pleased, Emily thought. Pleased to be proven right about the children being destructive?

Ezra rose and slowly followed. "Don't worry, Lillian. You can cover your losses on eBay, even the discontinued china patterns."

Emily watched as the others left the room. She stood at the table, her mother's pronouncements echoing in her mind. Did the baby come from Wood's Hollow? She had thought of that herself, then dismissed it. Now she couldn't seem to get the thought out of her mind. Was the baby's mother that close—only a few miles away? If she were to go down there, could she possibly find her? Did she even want the child's mother to be found?

Don't get so involved, she heard her mother's words again. *You can't save the world. Leave it to the social worker.*

Emily sat down slowly, feeling suddenly tired. The trouble was, every time she thought of the baby now, she didn't know what she wanted, or what she should do. Or even if she should do anything at all.

CHAPTER THREE

~

$\mathcal{E}$MILY WAS IN MEETINGS ALL MONDAY MORNING, BUT that didn't prevent her from calling Nadine Preston. Eager to hear about Jane's test results, she called twice before noon, reaching the voice mail both times and leaving a message.

She was wrapping up a weekly briefing with the town's attorney, Warren Oakes, when her intercom buzzed. "It's someone named Nadine Preston, returning your call," her secretary said.

"I'm sorry, I need to take this, Warren," Emily apologized.

Warren picked up his folders and waved a quick good-bye. Even before he'd left the room, Emily grabbed the phone and quickly said hello.

"Sorry it took so long to get back to you, Mayor Warwick. I was making some home visits this morning."

"That's quite all right. Please call me Emily. I didn't

mean to bother you. I just wanted to check on Jane. How did her medical tests turn out?"

"No serious conditions like HIV or hepatitis."

"That's good news," Emily said, feeling relieved.

"Yes, of course," the social worker agreed. "But she will need to stay in the hospital a bit longer."

Emily sat up sharply. "Oh? Why is that?"

"She seems to have a respiratory infection. Her doctor is treating it with some strong antibiotics. She should show improvement in a day or two, but she can't be released until it's completely cleared up."

"That's too bad. Is she in any discomfort? Any fever?"

"She has trouble getting a full breath at times, and they're giving her oxygen. The fever is very mild though, so that's not a grave problem."

Taking oxygen? The poor little thing. Emily's heart went out to her. She felt suddenly sad and helpless, wanting to do something for the baby but having no idea of what that something might be.

"How do you think she got the infection?" Emily asked, unwilling to let the conversation end.

"It's hard to say. Most likely she had a cold that wasn't treated properly, so it developed into something more serious. We did catch it before it turned into pneumonia, though."

"Yes, that's one good thing," Emily said. "Can I come and see her?"

The question just popped out. Emily surprised herself, and she could tell by the stunned silence on the other end of the line that Mrs. Preston was surprised as well.

"Visit her at the hospital, you mean? I'm not sure we can do that . . ."

"I read somewhere that it's good for babies that age to be held a lot, especially if they're in a hospital environment. I read that there are even people who come into hospitals to do that—volunteer baby holders. It helps the babies' brain development or something like that."

Though she'd never raised a child, Emily knew a lot about child development. Long after she had given Sara up, Emily had read countless books on the subject in a subtle form of self-torture, while she wondered what stage her daughter had reached. Could she roll over yet? Sit up? Grab a block? Call out for her mommy in the middle of the night? Was she getting enough care, enough nurturing and stimulation?

Of course, once she met Sara, she realized those worries had been needless. Sara's adoptive mother and father had been the most caring of parents.

"It helps in any number of ways," the social worker finally answered.

"It might be good for her, don't you agree? I mean, all things considered, I suspect that her mother's care was lacking, and now, being in the hospital all alone . . . I'm sure the nurses are attentive, but nurses are so overworked these days . . ."

"I understand what you're saying, Ms. Warwick," Nadine Preston interrupted her. "I suppose if you really want to visit, you may. I'll let the hospital know you have my permission."

"Thank you. Thank you very much," Emily said quickly.

"But you really ought to . . . to be careful."

"About the baby? Is she contagious?"

"I don't mean that way." Nadine Preston paused. "Never mind. Perhaps I'll see you at the hospital. I have to run. I'm late for a meeting."

"Of course. Thanks again." Emily said good-bye and quickly hung up the phone.

As she anticipated seeing the baby that night, she felt a wave of happiness well up inside. Then she thought about calling Dan to let him know she would be home late. She knew she could call his cell and speak to him directly, but instead she decided to call the house and leave a message there. She suspected he wouldn't be happy to hear she was driving to Southport tonight to visit Jane. He would probably try to talk her out of it, so better to avoid the confrontation.

Her mind was made up. She was going.

WHEN BEN PULLED INTO THE DRIVEWAY ON MONDAY night, the house was ablaze with lights. The seasons had once again brought the shortest days of the year, and at six o'clock inky blue night had fallen. The rectory, a cozy retreat flanked by evergreens, looked warm and welcoming. Hanging from the front door was a large pine wreath decorated with dried flowers and a satin bow. That hadn't been there this morning, he mused. It was getting to look more like Christmas around here by the hour.

"Hello? Anybody home?" he called from the foyer.

"Back here," Carolyn called from the kitchen. Ben hung up his coat and scarf and followed the enticing smells to the heart of the house. There he saw pots and pans covering the stove and his wife peering at something in the oven. It looked like a holiday dinner was in the making.

Then he remembered: the children were coming. Rachel and her husband, Jack, and little William. Between his job at the bookstore and his social life, Mark was rarely around, but was making a point of coming home tonight to visit with his sister and her family.

Normally, Ben loved seeing his children and grandson. He loved having the house full of activity and watching the way Carolyn became so animated and joyful. But for some reason he wasn't in the mood tonight. He was more inclined toward a quiet dinner followed by a good book. But there was no help for it.

"Hi, dear. You're late. I thought you'd be home in time to set the table," Carolyn called out to him.

"Oh, sorry. I can help now if you need me," he offered as he walked into the kitchen. "Let me wash the pots," he said.

He slipped off his sports jacket and rolled up his sleeves, then stepped up to the sink. "What time will they be here?"

"Any minute." She glanced up at the kitchen clock, her chin-length blond hair flopping across her eyes. She checked another pot, then finally sat down in a kitchen chair. "I was out all day, shopping for Mark."

"Christmas shopping?"

"Not really. For school. He needs so much. It's hard to know where to start."

Ben laughed. "Mark needs just about what he can fit in that backpack of his, dear. He's a grown man who lived on his own for years before coming back home to us. I don't think you have to exhaust yourself shopping for him."

"Well, I suppose you're right. I'm just anxious for him. I hope he enjoys school this time. I hope he sticks with it."

Ben paused in his scrubbing and glanced at her. "I think he will. In fact, I'm sure of it."

Carolyn sighed. "I wish he didn't need to go so far away. Portland, Oregon, for goodness sakes. It will be like before. We'll hardly see him anymore."

"Not exactly. It won't be like that," Ben said gruffly.

For several years after Mark quit Brown University in Rhode Island, he wandered around the country taking odd jobs and remaining completely out of touch with his family. All attempts to make contact with him, by Ben or Carolyn or even his sister, Rachel, were rebuffed. But when Carolyn fell critically ill with a stroke two years ago, Mark was summoned home and finally made amends with his family.

"No, of course not," Carolyn agreed. "I liked having him home though," she admitted.

Ben felt wistful. He knew Mark couldn't stay with them forever, even if he wasn't starting school again. Though he was thankful to have finally made peace with his prodigal son, thankful to see him back on track, he still felt an edge of envy for his son's youth and flexibility. So many choices ahead, so many possibilities. Mark could pick up and go wherever he pleased, without any responsibilities or commitments tying him down. Ben wondered if he had ever felt that footloose and free. Yes, of course he had. He just couldn't remember quite when, though.

Ben rinsed off a large pot cover and set it on the drain board, then picked up a fry pan and scrubbed away.

Mark had already lived and worked in more places in his short life than Ben had in his sixty-odd years. With the exception of going to school in the South, where he'd met Carolyn, Ben had barely made it from his hometown of Gloucester up the coast to Cape Light.

But it's the depth of experience that counts most, isn't it? He didn't need a big city to dazzle him. He believed in microcosms: all levels of life and complex society could be found in a tide pool. Even the tide-pool community of Cape Light bore infinite variety if you looked long and closely enough.

Why was he feeling this twinge of envy over his son's departure? Why did he feel lately as if his ministry in this congregation was draining him? *Dear Lord, please help me understand and overcome this . . . negativity.*

"Ben, are you all right, dear?" Carolyn's voice broke through his silent prayer.

"Yes, of course. I'm fine." He scrubbed down the sink with a sponge and sprayed off the soap.

"Is there anything going on at church?" she persisted.

"The usual." Which was the trouble. "I'm just tired."

"Maybe I shouldn't have asked the kids on a Monday night. Mondays are hard for you. You're still tired from Sunday."

"No, it's all right. I'm looking forward to seeing them."

He was, too. Once they all arrived and filled the house with their talk and laughter, he'd be distracted from his murky thoughts.

"I had a frustrating morning" he admitted. He told Carolyn how both Grace and Vera had canceled at the last minute on the meeting to start the coat drive and how he had then gone to Wood's Hollow on his own. "There was a volunteer from the neighborhood association at the community center, and we talked a bit. They really need so much help—more than just a coat drive. I wish the congregation would take a stronger interest. I can't do it all myself. That's not what it's about."

Carolyn nodded. "I'm sure it's just timing, Ben. Everyone's distracted now with Christmas and getting ready for the fair."

"That's just the problem. It's easy to work on the fair. That's fun. This is harder work but more important. Why can't they see that? Why can't I make them see?"

Carolyn's gaze was sympathetic. "Don't blame yourself, Ben. You've been trying. It might take more time than you think to get the message across. As you would say, let God into it. Ask Him for tolerance and patience."

It was hard to hear his own tried-and-true spiritual counsel coming back at him. Ben nodded, placing the last pot on the drain board. "Yes, I have prayed about it. I'll continue to, of course."

He sat in a chair across from Carolyn at the kitchen table. "Maybe these *are* challenges I'm meant to face for some reason I don't understand right now. But I'm starting to wonder if God is trying to tell me something through all this, trying to send me a message. I mean, I wonder sometimes if the congregation can even hear me anymore. Maybe I'm just too familiar. Maybe God is trying to tell me that it's time to move on."

"Oh . . . well, I didn't mean that," Carolyn said.

"Have you ever thought about moving away from here, to someplace new?" he asked.

Now his wife looked positively shocked. "Move away? What are you talking about, Ben? Why would we want to move?"

He shrugged. "I was just thinking out loud. That's all."

"I guess I'd like to see more of the world on vacations . . . but you said, move away."

"Yes, well, I didn't mean a vacation. I meant a real move. But maybe not forever. Just temporarily, see how it is to live someplace new and give service in some different way."

Carolyn stared at him curiously. She didn't say anything at first. "What would we do?"

"Oh, I don't know. Maybe some sort of mission work. Something more hands on, like James is doing right now. I just got a letter from him last week."

"How is James?" Carolyn asked with interest. "And how are Leigh and the baby?"

"They're all doing well. James sounds very happy, very productive. I think he thrives on hard work."

"Bring the letter home. I'd like to read it."

"Yes, I will," Ben promised. "You know, James said he could use some help there. Well, he hinted at it anyway."

"I can see how that type of work might draw you, Ben. But I think I'd miss the kids too much, especially William. And Rachel is talking about having another baby. She'll need me more than ever then."

"Of course she would." Ben nodded. He could sense that though she had tried to keep her tone calm, his vague talk had scared Carolyn. She had been so happy when he'd come in. Now she looked sad and confused.

He reached across the table and patted her hand. "I was just talking off the top of my head, dear. Don't look so worried.

She sighed. He could see she wanted to believe him, but she wasn't quite convinced. "We are getting close to retirement age, Ben. I suppose we have to figure all this out sooner or later."

"Sooner or later, but not tonight," he assured her. "We have time. I don't feel old, not when I look at you."

He smiled at her and had finally coaxed a smile in return when the doorbell rang.

"I'll get it," she said, rising from her chair.

"Let's go together," Ben said, following her.

The children came in all in a rush, Rachel and her husband, Jack, leading a waddling little William wrapped in so much winter wear all Ben could see at first were his big brown eyes and the tip of his nose.

"Look, Grandpa." As his mother peeled off his coat, William held up a ragged stuffed tiger.

"My, my. He looks fierce. Does he bite?"

"Only if he's hungry." William shook the tiger at Ben, making everyone laugh. "His name is Willie, too."

Ben picked up his grandson, who held the tiger up to face him. "Are you hungry, Willie?" Ben asked the tiger in a scared voice.

"Cookies, please," William answered in his tiger voice.

"We can find some of those for you. Not a problem," Ben promised respectfully.

The door opened and Mark came in. "Am I late? Hope not."

"Right on time," Carolyn called out. "Everything's ready. Why don't we go right into the dining room?"

Following the appetizing smells that filled the warm house, they traipsed into the dining room. Ben came last, leading his grandson by the hand. He felt a wave of love and happiness. His family's laughter and energy seemed to suddenly fill the house, burning away his dour mood like sunshine burns away the fog on a summer day.

Perhaps the truth was that deep down inside he felt just the way Carolyn did about moving away. He really couldn't do it. He couldn't leave his family or his congregation; he would miss them all too much. Surely his calling and work here were as important and worthwhile as in any far-off place.

This strange, restless mood will pass, Ben told himself. *I need to focus here, where I belong.*

IT'S HARD NOT TO LOVE THE GUY, SARA THOUGHT WITH A secret smile.

She stood watching Luke from a distance as he played volleyball with a group of kids in the gym at New Horizons. He was so involved in the game, he didn't even notice her.

He'll be a great father, Sara thought. Kids loved Luke because he had a special way of talking to them, of figuring out what they needed and encouraging the best in them.

Would she be a great mother? She worried about that sometimes. She liked children. She had been tutoring at the center since it opened and always grew very attached to her students. She missed them when they returned to the city. But those were big kids, usually at least ten years old.

Sara had to admit, she didn't feel quite the same about babies. They seemed so fragile, their needs so hard to figure out. She could hardly imagine being responsible for a baby or being pregnant. Sometimes she wondered if being adopted and searching so long for her birth mother had left her with mixed emotions about becoming a mother herself. Some women her age already seemed quite sure about wanting children. But she definitely was not.

Luke's pressing for a commitment had made her think about it lately. But even before that, she had been secretly quite interested in her aunt Jessica's pregnancy. As eager as Jessica had been to have a baby, when her body began changing, Sara could see it had come as a shock. Now, though her figure was trim and sleek once more, Jessica seemed different. Motherhood changed a woman, Sara knew, though she couldn't exactly say how.

Was she ready for those changes? She knew in her heart that she wasn't. Would she ever be?

"That's it. You got it, Valdez. Point for blue team!" Luke cheered on the kids.

Luke said he was ready for fatherhood, ready to start a new stage of his life. Sara knew that was true. He had come such a long way since moving to Cape Light.

It was still amazing to her that Luke had managed to build this place: the gym and classrooms, the cottages turned into dorms. He had truly made something out of nothing. She remembered the night he told her about his plan, when it was just an idea he had, an inspiration to do some good in the world.

They were both living on these grounds, each renting a cottage when the land was still owned by Dr. Elliot. She had been working at the Clam Box as a waitress while she figured out how to approach her birth mother, Emily Warwick.

Luke had come to town drawn by childhood memories. His family had spent summers at the cottages in Cape Light, and he remembered it as a place where he would find peace at times when his life was totally at loose ends.

He had quit the Boston police force under a cloud of suspicion and humiliation after a shoot-out that left his partner dead and Luke with permanent scars and a metal rod in one leg. But the physical damage was the least of his injuries; stripped of his identity as one of Boston's finest, Luke was adrift, feeling his life was meaningless.

Then he got the idea to buy the Cranberry Cottages and property when Dr. Elliot put them up for sale. Soon after, Luke heard of an organization devoted to helping at-risk inner-city kids—kids who got in trouble at school or had minor scrapes with the law, kids who still could be guided from moving in the wrong direction. The idea intrigued him: preventing crime by preventing kids from choosing those wrong turns in life.

Suddenly, it all made sense to him. He found what he wanted to do with his life. But even after he made the connection with the New Horizons foundation and found the funding, many town residents fought long and hard to keep the center from opening.

Luke persisted and, with Emily's help, won that battle, too. Cape Light was now proud to be the home of a New Horizons center and many, including Sara, volunteered there.

Maybe he had never been a supercop on the streets of Boston, but in Sara's eyes, Luke was a real hero where it really counted. She knew she was lucky to have him in her life.

"Hey, Sara. What's up?" Luke waved to her and started to walk over. The game was still going strong, but another coach took his place.

"I just finished tutoring. Thought I'd say hello."

"Hello." He smiled and kissed her on the cheek. "Want to stay for dinner? I'm having mystery meal—whatever doesn't walk out of the fridge when I open the door."

She laughed. "Sounds good to me. I was having the same at my place."

They left the gym and started down the path to Luke's cottage. He still lived in the same one he rented when Dr. Elliot had owned the place, but he had substantially renovated it.

Luke had saved the wood-burning stove in the living room. As Sara entered, he picked up a few logs from the pile near the front door and quickly built a fire.

The cottage had an open floor plan: one large room with a sitting area on one end and a small kitchen on the other. A kitchen counter broke up the space. The vaulted ceiling and new, large windows gave the rooms an airy feel. The wooden floors had been refinished and covered with area rugs.

"Okay, let's take a look in here if we dare," Sara joked as she pulled open his refrigerator door.

"My, aren't you the brave one." He walked up beside her and rested his hand on her shoulder.

It wasn't too bad, she thought. Though the pickings were spare, they did manage to find the makings of a cheese omelet, a salad, and a bag of frozen French fries.

They cooked together in the small kitchen, with Luke teasing Sara about her lack of culinary skills. "You modern women," he said. "How will you ever hook a guy if you don't know how to cook?"

"I thought I'd already hooked a guy. He didn't seem to notice."

Luke grinned and kissed her quickly as she beat the eggs. "He noticed. He just didn't mind that much."

Sara turned back to the eggs, her mind troubled. Luke was so sweet; he always made her feel so well loved. Why did she have to be so contrary, so stubborn? She should just tell him, yes, let's get engaged. What in the world was her problem?

But she couldn't do that. It might feel good for a moment to make him happy, but she knew in her heart she just wasn't ready. She had to tell him tonight. She had to try to make him understand why.

They ate at the small table, sitting across from each other. "This isn't bad," Luke said, tasting a bite of the omelet.

"At least I didn't burn it this time. Well, not your half," she added.

"You'll have to make this for us at least once a week when we're married." She could tell from the glint in his eyes he was teasing, but not entirely. More like testing the water. The thought made her uneasy.

She moved a bite of food around her plate without picking it up. "Luke, there's something I'd like to talk about," she began.

He didn't answer at first, just kept looking down at his food. Finally, he picked his head up, his expression unreadable. "I hate when people say that," he quipped without smiling.

"Yeah, so do I," she admitted. "It's just that I've been thinking a lot about Saturday night, what happened at the jewelry store. I need to talk about it more with you."

His expression softened and he sat back. "What's on your mind? I have a feeling you're not going to ask me to run over to Newburyport tomorrow and buy you that ring."

That was Luke. Making it easy for her, even when it probably hurt him to say such a thing. She reached across the table and touched his hand.

"I've been thinking about our talk, about your proposal—"

"You never actually let me propose," he pointed out, "but go ahead."

"Honestly, I love you so much and I love the way we are together. I feel so good with you. I can't see myself with anyone but you. But I'm not ready to get engaged, not for Christmas. My life is just still too unsettled to make that commitment."

"Unsettled?" He sat back with a puzzled expression. "How is it unsettled? You have a good job on the paper; you're doing well there. And you have a great relationship with Emily now."

She shrugged. "I can't see myself writing for the *Messenger* my whole life."

"Of course not, but you haven't been there all that long."

"I know. But a small paper in a small town—it gets tiring quickly." She paused. "I've been thinking of applying for a job on a bigger paper, in Boston maybe or some larger market. I sent some of my clips around just to see if anyone's interested."

"Why didn't you tell me?" She could see the admission had stung him. They usually told each other everything.

"I don't know," she said honestly. "I just did it on the

spur. I was going to tell you if anyone answered. So far, I haven't gotten any replies."

"So you want to be a reporter in Boston. What about me?" Now he was angry; she heard it in his voice. "We'd see each other on weekends? Maybe? Even less than we see each other now?"

Sara took a breath and looked down at the table. "Well . . . actually, I thought maybe you might move back to Boston with me. I mean, if anything ever came of it— and so far, nothing has—you could take that job at New Horizons, the one they offered you awhile back?"

Earlier, when they went through other problems as a couple, Luke had considered an offer from the main office of the New Horizons foundation as a liaison who would find new sites and start up centers around the country. Finally, they had made up and he had turned down the job, preferring to stay close to Sara.

"That was two years ago, Sara. Besides, even if they still wanted me, I'm not interested in working at the main office. There's a lot more I want to do right here. I can't just drop everything and run into Boston because you feel restless and want to work for a bigger paper." He shook his head, looking distressed. "I don't know, Sara. Where would that leave us? You haven't said a word about getting engaged or married. Does that fit into your agenda at any point?"

Sara didn't know what to say. She hadn't thought this conversation would be easy, but she hadn't expected him to be so hurt and angry. She was trying to be honest with him. Didn't that count for anything?

"I've never thought of moving on without you in my life, Luke. That's the truth. I do want to marry you . . . someday. But I just can't get there in my head right now. I don't know exactly why. Maybe I need to feel I've accomplished more in my career before I make that commitment. Maybe I have to do more with my life. You're older than me," she said finally. "You're at a different place."

"Oh, the age thing now." Luke rolled his eyes. "I should have seen that one coming."

"Luke, please. Don't make it sound ridiculous. It's just a fact. Ten years is a big difference. You know you were different when you were in your early twenties."

He let out a long breath. Although he was trying to hear her out, it was hard for him to come up against this particular stumbling block. Luke had always been protective of her, a handsome guardian angel who seemed to swoop in when needed most. He had never acted condescending or treated her like a child. If anything, she often felt like the more mature one. They just seemed to suit each other from the start. Their age difference never seemed to matter, though Emily had once warned her that someday it might.

Well, it looked like her mother was right. *Someday is here*, Sara thought.

"Yes, I am in my thirties and you're still in your twenties," he acknowledged. "But honestly, Sara, if we weren't more or less at the same place emotionally, if this didn't work for us, do you think we would have stayed together this long? Let's not measure our relationship against whatever the *typical* thing to do is, okay? I don't think we're the typical couple. But maybe that's a good thing. Maybe it just works for us."

"I'm not trying to turn us into the typical anything," Sara protested. "You know that's not what I want. But you're at a different place in life than I am."

Luke stood and left the table. He walked over to the stove, tossed another log inside, then poked the embers around until they glowed.

"I hear what you're saying. I just don't think that's true. I think you're just scared of making a commitment, or marrying me, or something. As far as accomplishing more with your career, I would never hold you back, Sara. You know that. But plenty of women manage to work and have a marriage. It's the latest thing, haven't you noticed?"

"Is it really? Wow. Maybe we'll even get the vote," she said, matching his facetious tone.

"Okay, that was a little out of line, but give me a break. You make it sound as if the two are just impossible to reconcile. Besides, I don't understand all these newspaper ambitions. You used to tell me how all you wanted to do was write a good novel or a book of short stories. If you're bored at the paper, maybe you should go back to your real writing."

Sara felt stung by his remark. Who was he to say what was real writing and what wasn't? Who was he to decide how she would spend her time or her talent? "Writing for a newspaper *is* real writing," she corrected him sharply. "Some might say fiction isn't."

He rubbed his cheek with his hand. "So you're not interested in writing a novel anymore? Is that it?"

"It's just not what I want right now. I'll get back to it someday, when I've lived longer and have more to write about. I'm a reporter. I like it. Besides, what difference does it make what kind of writing I do? That doesn't solve anything between us."

"If you were focused on your own writing, you wouldn't be talking about moving to Boston," Luke pointed out. "It would solve that problem at least."

When Sara didn't answer, he added, "So you don't want to get engaged for Christmas. I got it. We won't talk about this anymore until you're ready, okay?"

She nodded, feeling let off the hook but still upset and unsettled. She hated fighting with him.

"Okay, fine," she said quietly.

"If you want to talk about it, if you want this discussion to go any further, you'll have to be the one to bring it up. I'm done," he said simply, but his words had an ominous ring.

"I will bring it up," she promised. "You'll see."

"I guess we will have to wait and see." His look gave her a chill. Had she gone too far and damaged their relationship beyond repair? She suddenly felt so scared of losing him, she nearly ran across the room and threw herself into his arms. At that moment, she was willing to agree to get engaged, get married, even have a dozen kids if that's what he wanted.

But she didn't. She stood up slowly and cleared their dirty plates from the table. The phone rang, but Luke made no move to pick it up. Sara brought the plates to the sink and started washing them. The answering machine picked up on the third ring, and Sara heard a woman's voice come on the line.

"Hi, Luke, it's Christina." Her tone was somehow breathy and energetic at the same time. Though Sara didn't mean to eavesdrop, she found herself listening. "Sorry I didn't catch you in. I'm just working out my schedule for this week and wanted to make a date for our interview. Give me a call when you get a chance. You can call late. I'm a night owl, remember?"

The caller laughed and Sara paused in her task, caught by the intimate note in the woman's tone. Who in the world was Christina? She turned to look at Luke, but he was sitting on the sofa, reading the newspaper.

"I'm really looking forward to seeing you," Christina added in her warm, velvety voice. "It will be great to catch up."

Finally, the mysterious siren hung up.

Sara rinsed the last dish and shut off the water. "Who was that?" she asked.

Luke kept his eyes on the paper. "Just an old friend, an old girlfriend, actually—Christina Cross. I mentioned her to you."

"No, I don't believe you ever did. The name doesn't ring a bell." Sara winced inwardly at the jealous note in her voice.

"Sure I did. Christina and I went out years ago. We totally lost touch, but she found me on the Internet or something. She's writing a book and wants an interview."

"Oh, she's a writer?"

"She used to be a reporter, covered the courthouse. That's how we met. She gave it up a few years ago. She's doing a book now on cops who have left the force and what they've done with their lives since. She thinks the way I started a New Horizons center out here will make a good chapter."

"Yes, it definitely would," Sara said evenly. She walked over to the armchair and sat down, facing him.

This woman was going to devote an entire chapter to Luke in her book? That was going to take more than one get-together, Sara thought.

Luke peeked at her over his newspaper. He patted the seat beside him. "Why don't you come over here and sit next to me?"

She met his gaze but didn't budge. "It's nice and warm by the stove," he coaxed her.

She stood up, walked the short distance to the couch, and sat down next to him. He put his arm around her shoulder and pulled her close. "See, I told you it was warmer."

She turned and grinned up at him despite herself. She rested her head against his shoulder and felt his fingers twine in her long hair, stroking it back from her cheek.

"I'm sorry we had a fight," she said quietly.

"I'm sorry, too." He leaned down and kissed her on the forehead. "You don't think I'm too old for you, do you?"

She looked up at him, surprised by the question. "No, of course not. That's just . . . ridiculous."

He sighed and smiled again a little. "Okay. If you say so."

She settled her head on his shoulder again. She felt his strong heartbeat against her cheek, his warmth and strength enfolding her.

"I love you, Luke. Please don't be angry. I don't want to lose you."

He didn't answer for a long time, and she wondered if he had even heard her.

"Don't worry. I'm not going anywhere," he said finally. "You know me."

He leaned his head down and kissed her, a long lingering kiss that made everything feel right between them again.

I do know you, Sara thought. She could depend on his love, his patience, his loyalty. He would wait for her to make up her mind, however long it took.

He would wait.

"SHE'S OFF THE OXYGEN NOW. SHE ONLY NEEDS TO WEAR the tube when she's sleeping," the nurse explained. "It's all right to pick her up. It's good for a baby to be held."

"Yes, I know. That's why I came." Emily's gaze was fixed on Jane lying in her plastic hospital crib. She'd been cleaned up, was dressed in a pale yellow gown with a drawstring bottom, and wore a tiny plastic bracelet on her wrist.

She was in a small room with four other such cribs. The glass wall that looked out onto the corridor had a few paper Christmas decorations taped on it, lending some cheer to the sterile environment.

Some of the other babies were attached to monitors and machinery, probably with much worse medical conditions, Emily realized. The sight of so many sick children saddened her. It didn't seem fair for illness to touch the young.

Jane was lucky. It was only an infection, Emily reminded herself. She would be better soon and able to leave this place.

"We try to cuddle them when we can. But we rarely have time," the nurse admitted quietly. She picked up the baby in a knowing manner and handed her over to Emily.

Emily took her in both arms and cradled her across her chest. She looked down at the baby's small face. Jane stared back with big blue-grey eyes, a quizzical expression on her face. For a moment Emily thought the infant might cry, but she just lifted her fist and stuck it in her mouth.

"It's me. Emily. Do you remember me?" Emily asked in a small voice.

The baby blinked and puckered up her mouth a bit.

"Is she hungry?" Emily asked.

The nurse checked the chart. "She could use a feeding. Here, sit in that chair. I'll get a bottle."

Emily walked over to a comfortable-looking rocker. She sat down slowly, mindful of the baby as she sank into the cushions and eased into the rocker's rhythmic motion. Soon she felt Jane relax in her arms.

"Here you go. You know the correct way to feed her, don't you?"

Emily looked up at the nurse, embarrassed to admit that she didn't really know there was a right way and a wrong way. Didn't you just stick the nipple into the child's mouth?

The nurse leaned forward and demonstrated. "Try to keep the bottle at an angle like this, so she won't be sucking in too much air. When she's finished about a third or so, take a break and burp her."

Burp her? Well, I'll worry about that when I get to it, Emily thought. She nodded and took the bottle.

The baby never missed a beat in her sucking, she noticed. Soon her big eyes drifted closed, her thick brown lashes curling softly against her cheek. She was so beautiful, Emily thought, such a darling.

"You're a gorgeous girl," Emily whispered. "A real showstopper. I wish Dan could have seen you the other day."

Dan. She had left a message but hadn't spoken to him directly. He hadn't called on her way to the hospital, and she had shut her phone off as soon as she entered the nursery. Well, she would call him on her way back to town, or explain when she got home if he wasn't already asleep.

She looked down to see that the bottle was more than a third empty. Emily scolded herself for not watching more closely, though she guessed this baby-care business wasn't an exact science.

"My, you're a speedy one, aren't you?" she asked the infant.

She set the bottle aside and lifted the baby to a sitting position. Jane looked a bit confused and put out to have lost her bottle, Emily thought.

"Time for a little burp. Nurse's orders, sweetie," she added kindly.

She sat there a moment, wondering how to get the baby to burp, when the nurse breezed by again. "That's it, sit her on your knee and just pat her back a bit. Toward the bottom is good."

The nurse gave Jane a gentle pat or two, producing instant results.

"Wow, that was fast." Emily stared down at the baby. "You get right down to business, don't you? I'm like that myself. A job begun is a job half done, I always say."

The nurse breezed by again. She smiled at Emily. "Having a nice conversation?"

Emily nodded, moving the baby back into feeding position again. "Yes, we are. A very nice little visit."

Jane quickly consumed the rest of her bottle, had her appropriate burps, and promptly fell asleep in Emily's arms.

Emily sat with the baby resting against her chest for a long time. Jane seemed so peaceful, Emily was afraid to shift her arm or even breathe too deeply for fear of disturbing her. Yet she liked being the baby's soft resting place.

Visiting hours had ended, and the lights on the floor were dimmed. Emily hummed and rocked and found that she, too, was nearly falling asleep in the darkened nursery.

Finally, the nurse returned. "She probably needs to be changed and then I'll put her back in her crib," she said in a soft voice.

Emily looked up and forced a smile. She really didn't want to give the baby up quite yet. But it was probably best for Jane to return to the crib and take her oxygen again, she reasoned.

She followed the nurse back to the crib, where she changed the baby's diaper with quick efficiency, wrapped her in a blanket, and had her back in the crib in no time flat.

"How long will she stay here, do you think?" Emily asked the nurse.

"Hard to say exactly. She's doing well. A few days more. Until the end of the week, I'd guess." She looked up at Emily. "Will you come back to see her again?"

"May I?"

The nurse shrugged. "You can check with Mrs. Preston, but I don't see why not. Volunteers come through here all the time. You're good with her, nice and calm. Do you have any children of your own?"

Emily hesitated before answering. "One daughter. She's grown up now though. She's twenty-four."

The nurse looked surprised. "You must have been a young mother."

"Yes . . . I was," Emily admitted.

"You ought to come visit again," the nurse said. "We can always use the help."

"I'll call Mrs. Preston to make sure it's okay. I'm the one who found her."

The nurse smiled knowingly. "I know. I read about it in the newspaper, and I recognized your name when you signed in. You can stay with her until she falls asleep if you like."

"Thanks. I will stay." Emily smiled at the nurse as she walked away.

Then she stood by the crib alone, looking down at the baby, watching her breathe. The nurse had inserted plastic oxygen tubes in her nose, but the sound of her breathing was still a little raspy, a bit labored, she thought. The poor little thing. Hadn't she had enough struggle?

Emily reached out and touched Jane's soft, wispy hair with her fingertips. It felt like feathers, like an angel's wing.

The closest I'll ever get to one in this lifetime, Emily thought with a small smile.

CHAPTER FOUR

~~

$\mathcal{E}$MILY RETURNED FROM HER RUN ON WEDNESDAY
morning to find Dan sitting at the kitchen table in his usual
pose, sipping coffee from a big mug and paging through
the morning papers. He subscribed to three and read them
all quite thoroughly.

She'd married a newshound . . . and a handsome man,
she noticed, though not for the first time. Even unshaven
with his hair rumpled and still in his blue plaid bathrobe,
he was awfully cute. Long and lean, a few inches over six
feet, his height and build suited Emily fine. At five-ten herself, she often felt self-conscious, towering over many of
the men she knew. Dan's hair had remained full, a straw
blond color that had gone mostly silver grey complemented by a complexion colored by the sun and wind during hours spent aboard his beloved sailboat.

She leaned over as she passed his chair, put her arm

around his shoulder, then kissed his cheek. "So what are you up to today?"

"The library in Salem. Research for the book."

Dan was writing a book about local history, the ship-building industry mostly, but it included the histories of famous families and folklore of the region. It was the second book he had worked on since his retirement. He finished the first last year, just before their wedding. That book was going to be published soon.

"I'll probably stay in Salem and meet up with a buddy of mine for dinner," Dan explained. "We worked together on our first newspaper jobs. I won't be home until about ten or eleven."

"Oh? That's fine."

Emily poured herself a cup of coffee while her two cats, Lucy and Ethel, twined around her legs, begging for their breakfast.

With Dan out until late she was free to visit the baby again. Yesterday she had called Nadine Preston to ask about Jane's condition, and the conversation soon evolved to more than a simple update.

She knew she had to fill Dan in on the news. During her run, she had thought about just the right way to begin, but though she drummed up her courage and adrenaline outdoors, now that she was back in the house she seemed to have lost her nerve.

But Dan wouldn't be home tonight, and this conversation really couldn't wait.

She turned and sat down at the table across from him. "Can you put down the paper a minute, Dan? I want to ask you something."

"Oh?" Dan folded the paper and stared at her curiously. "This sounds serious. What have I done now?" he teased her.

"It's just something I've been meaning to talk to you about. Something important." She folded her hands on the tabletop. "You remember that I went to visit the baby at the hospital on Monday night, right?"

"Yes, I remember."

"Well, I spoke to the social worker yesterday, Nadine Preston. I called to see if I could go see Jane again—"

"Again?" Dan stopped himself. "Go on, I'm listening. I didn't mean to interrupt you."

"We got to talking about what's going to happen next to Jane. After she's released from the hospital, I mean. Mrs. Preston told me that she'll be released in a few days and the court will appoint a temporary guardian."

"A foster parent, you mean?"

"More or less. Of course, they want to find the mother. That's their primary focus. But they're also looking for any relatives now, any family who can take the baby. That should take about a month. In the meantime, she'll be placed with a temporary guardian until they either find her family or someone to adopt her."

Dan folded his glasses and slipped them into the case. "What does this have to do with us, Emily? Or dare I ask that question?"

He was still almost smiling, but she sensed he was terrified of her answer.

"Nadine Preston asked me if we would be interested in applying. To be the baby's temporary guardians, I mean."

"And what did you say?" he asked in a guarded tone.

"Well . . . I said yes." Dan's eyes widened in shock and his jaw dropped. Emily swallowed and plunged ahead. "But I told her that I had to discuss it with you first, of course."

"Well, thanks. I'm glad you remembered that I exist." The words came out with a sharp edge.

"Dan, please? Can't we just discuss this calmly without getting into an argument?"

Dan rose from his chair and tossed the newspaper on the table. "What is there to discuss? You know how I feel about this. We agreed when we got married: no children. You have Sara and I have Wyatt and Lindsay. We're past that stage of our lives."

"We're too old, you mean," she finished for him.

"I wasn't going to put it that way but since you did, yes."

"I'm not too old. And neither are you. I'm only forty-four. And a half," she added, since she would be forty-five at the end of May. "Women my age are having children every day."

Dan pressed his hand to his forehead. "You're serious, aren't you?"

"Of course I am. We have to sign the papers and send them back today. Most of it's done, just routine information. But there are still a few things to fill in—"

"You've already started the paperwork? Without even asking me?" Dan's voice rose on every word. "How could you do such a thing, Emily?"

She took a breath. He didn't understand. He didn't want to. He was thinking only of himself, not about the baby at all.

"I had to. The social worker said we had to apply right away. I was afraid she would find another couple."

"There, don't you see? That means that there are lots of highly qualified couples willing to take this child."

"I'm not sure that's the case," Emily corrected him.

"Whether or not it is, is beside the point. I can't understand how you could rush ahead like this without me. That isn't at all fair, Emily."

"I agree. It was impulsive and not fair to you," she admitted. "But I was afraid if we waited to talk about it, we would argue. Like we're doing now. And then we would miss out."

"This isn't like you," Dan said, "this jumping-in business. Is this what I can expect for the rest of our marriage? You'll feel free to make these major decisions without consulting me whenever you think I will disagree?"

He had a point. She would feel the same way if the situation were reversed. She was too used to political life, perhaps. She had cleverly circumvented her husband and, in doing so, had undermined her cause.

Emily sighed. "Dan, please try to understand. I admit I got a bit carried away, asking her to send the forms before talking it over with you. But this is something I want very much. So much . . . I can hardly express it. I didn't even realize how I really felt until she asked me."

She looked up at her husband, everything she was feeling welling up in her eyes. She didn't want to cry. Dan might even suspect she was using tears to persuade him. But she could barely hold them back.

He stared at her and then looked away. "I know this is hard for you, Emily. It's only natural to feel involved, to feel responsible for the baby, especially being the kind of person you are. Your empathy, your compassion—those are some of the things I love about you most," he added quietly. "But I just can't see it. How would we ever manage to take this on?"

"We could do it. And it wouldn't be forever. We'll just be taking care of her until the investigation is completed. Mrs. Preston said that would take about a month. If a close relative isn't found, the baby will be placed with adoptive parents."

"That could take a very long time," Dan pointed out. He sighed and jammed his hands into his pockets. "Try to think logically about this, Emily. Why would we ever take on this commitment? It's just insane. You're in an office all day and at meetings most nights. Who's going to take care of this baby—me?"

"Of course not. I've thought this out. It's not impossible. I'll rearrange my hours. You're always saying I work too much. I'm sure I can cut back if I try. And I'll get a nanny. Jessica will help us, too. I'm sure of it. I can even take the baby to work sometimes. In a pinch, I mean," she added, noticing his doubtful expression.

Dan paced across the room and stared out the window. She could see he was trying to gather his composure so that he wouldn't lose his temper again. She knew it was probably best to wait and say nothing, but she couldn't help herself.

"Dan, please try to keep an open mind about this. Most women who have children work. Besides, I just can't stand the idea of some questionable stranger taking Jane. You hear horror stories about children in foster care all the time," she pointed out. "I just couldn't sleep, worrying where she might end up next."

Dan turned to her and sighed. "Emily, I think you're getting a bit dramatic now. You're letting your imagination run away with you. The social worker will do her job. The baby will be placed in a safe environment. Why turn our lives upside down? I don't think you understand what you would be getting us into. There's a reason why they say, 'It takes a village,' " he reminded her. "I know what it means to have a baby around. Normal life, as we know it, will be over."

What's so great about normal life? Emily wanted to rail at him. She felt thoroughly upset and frustrated. Dan was so logical, so practical. Most of the time she admired those traits, even identified with them. But sometimes they caused a big blind spot. The important things in life weren't always logical.

She forced a measure of calm into her voice. "Listen, I can't argue with you. Everything you've just said is true. But my feelings about this aren't logical or practical in any way," she admitted. "They're just very real and very important to me. I want to take care of this baby, even if it's only for a short time. I feel . . . it's meant to be. Can't you just see this as a compromise?"

"A compromise? A compromise to what?" He frowned at her, looking more confused than angry.

"Do you remember that time you took me out for New

Year's Eve? We were dating but we hadn't made any commitment. You were still planning to sail off into the sunset without me," she reminded him with a small smile.

He groaned and made a face. "Oh, yes. The blockhead phase. How could I forget?"

Emily tried not to laugh. "I told you flat out that night that I wanted to get married again and have another baby. Do you remember?"

He nodded. "You were very up front with me. You put your cards right on the table, and I admired your honesty. I also remember that I ran the other way. We didn't speak to each after that for several weeks."

"But you couldn't live without me. You definitely couldn't leave on your long-awaited sailing trip."

"No, not without you I couldn't." He sighed. "But you have Sara now. You have a wonderful relationship with her. Doesn't that change things?"

"I thought it would, honestly. But it's not that simple."

"I guess not," he said with more tenderness in his tone. He walked over and sat at the table again, facing her. "Emily, I don't want to seem like an ogre. I don't want to disappoint you. But we talked all this out before we got married. We agreed that we weren't going to start a family. I thought this was all settled between us."

"I remember. And I'm sorry to go back on my word. But things change. Feelings change. Finding a baby— practically falling over one—changes things for me, Dan."

She tried hard to keep the impatience and frustration she felt from seeping into her voice. From the flicker in Dan's eyes, she could see that she hadn't been entirely successful.

"I know I should be grateful just to have Sara back and have such a wonderful connection with her. You know how much I love her. She's a miracle to me, honestly. But for so many years, I felt a hole inside after giving her up. And now, even though I have my daughter back, I still feel . . . violated. Like something was stolen from me. Especially when I see Jessica with Tyler," she added. "It makes me realize how much I've missed. Twenty-two years of being a mother, to be exact."

Dan moved closer and put his arm around her. He pressed his cheek to her hair and kissed her. "I'm so sorry, dear. But you can never make up for that."

"Maybe not." Emily put her hand over his where he held her shoulder. "But it doesn't mean it doesn't still hurt."

Dan had no answer. He tugged her to her feet, put his arms around her, and hugged her close.

"You've caught me between a rock and a hard place, my love," he said finally. "I feel for you, Emily, for all the years and all you went through. I wish I could make it right for you, believe me. But I just can't see taking on the responsibility of a baby. And taking her temporarily seems like an even worse idea. Once we had the baby here, do you honestly think you could give her up when she's adopted? Wouldn't we be setting ourselves up for the same painful situation you went through with Sara?"

Emily pulled back from his embrace. Secretly she had been hoping that once they had the baby, Dan's feelings would soften and he would agree to applying to adopt. But she could see now that was just a wild fantasy.

Emily did not cry easily. There were countless times when she had felt as if her heart were splitting open yet she had remained dry eyed, holding her grief inside. But now she felt the tears start to flow, and there was nothing she could do to stop them. She covered her eyes and then turned to grab some tissues from the counter.

Dan stood behind her and put his hands on her shoulders. "Honey, please. Don't cry. I'm just trying to do the right thing, to do what's best for everyone—you especially. And the baby."

She knew he was sincere and did have her best interests at heart, or what he thought were her best interests. Dan wanted the safest course for them, though not necessarily the path that would yield the richest rewards a life fully lived had to offer.

She sniffed loudly and wiped her eyes. "I know you don't want to see me get hurt again. I agree, that's a risk. But this isn't about being safe or logical or even practical. I know this baby wasn't in our plans, but life can't always be planned down to the last detail."

With her back still turned, she couldn't see his reaction to her words, but she sensed it in his touch.

This was an issue that came up often between them. Dan could be too faithful to his plans at times, like a lemming diving over a cliff just because he was too stubborn to change direction. She had nearly lost him entirely because of that trait. He had grown more flexible since their marriage, she thought, but obviously not flexible enough.

"I know what you mean, Emily," he answered quietly. He gently rubbed her shoulders. "But this isn't just a question of me being more laid back and carefree, you know. It's much more complicated than that—"

"Not at all," she cut in quickly and turned to face him. "It's a matter of the heart, plain and simple." She touched the center of her chest. "After you ran away from me that time, and I thought our relationship was over, my heart was broken. But I wouldn't have changed a thing. It *is* better to have loved and lost than never to have loved at all. That's really true.

"This is about loving—experiencing love and giving it, Dan. Even for a short time. Can't we see our way clear of all the practicalities and reasons why this won't work, and just take this risk? Can't you do that for me?"

She stood staring up at him for what seemed like a very long time, not knowing what he would say and dreading the worst.

He let out a long breath and looked down at the floor. For a minute she thought he wasn't going to answer her at all. Finally he looked up again.

"Oh, Emily. . . ." He sighed. "How soon would we need to decide?"

She could hardly believe his answer and felt a jolt of shock and joy through her entire body. She wanted to jump into his arms.

"Right away. We have to sign the forms and send them back today. You can come down to my office later and we'll take care of it. Then we need some references from people who know us, and we also get interviewed. We might not even qualify," Emily added.

"Of course we'll qualify. You're a shoo-in." He smiled slightly. "I should have known something like this was going to happen. But honestly, I've been completely blindsided. This is a lot to lay on a guy. You're not asking to bring home a puppy. This is a real live baby we're talking about, a miniature person."

"Yes, I know. She's a precious little thing," Emily said. "Wait until you see her. You can come with me tonight to Southport. You won't believe how beautiful she is."

"I believe you." He put his arms around her and pulled her close. "I'm doing this for you, Emily. Because I love you and I can see how much it means to you. I just hope we're doing the right thing."

Emily hugged him back with all her might, pressing her cheek against his strong shoulder. "We are, Dan. Trust me . . . and thank you. You'll never know how much this means to me."

JESSICA AND SAM'S HOUSE WAS A FEW MILES FROM THE village center. Located down the winding Beach Road, it was challenging to reach in bad weather, but whatever the old Victorian house lacked in convenience, it more than made up for in beauty. Trimmed with pine garlands and tapers glowing in each window, it looked even more inviting than usual.

Set on a span of property that included a pond and a flowering meadow, the house had been abandoned for many years when Sam bought it at a bank auction. He had rescued and renovated the place, not realizing that before he was done, he would live there with a wife, and now a family.

Emily normally didn't pass their house on her way home from Village Hall, but on Thursday afternoon she had been at a meeting in Essex, and she wanted to return one of Jessica's special cake pans that she borrowed for Thanksgiving. Her cake hadn't turned out that well, she reflected, though the expensive pan could hardly be blamed.

Once I have the baby around, maybe I'll learn to be a better cook. The thought made her smile as she turned and steered her Jeep up the long, narrow drive. She parked in front, then noticed the van from Willoughby's Fine Foods parked farther up the gravel drive. Molly Willoughby, Sam's sister, was often here at this time of day. Jessica often watched Molly's two girls after school, and now that Darrell and Tyler had come along, the older kids were helping Jessica with the baby.

Emily liked Molly, a straight-talking, hardworking single mother who had been a Jill-of-all-trades for many years before starting her own gourmet shop and catering business, which was now quite successful. Jessica and her sister-in-law were like night and day in many ways, but over time they had learned to appreciate each other and had become fast friends. It was nearly dinnertime, and Emily guessed the two women were bound to be in the kitchen, chatting and cooking together.

The back door was open. Emily knocked and then poked her head inside. "Hi, everyone. May I come in?"

"Emily, what a nice surprise!" Jessica came to greet her quickly. She wore a long apron over her work clothes, a slim grey skirt and pale pink silk blouse. After the baby was born, Jessica had managed to keep her job at the bank by cutting back to part time. Those were the two sides of Jessica's personality, Emily thought: her sharp business side and her homemaker side. She seemed to find the time and room for both.

"You look great in that color," Emily said, kissing her sister hello. She did, too, with her long, dark curly hair and pearly complexion. "You should wear it more often."

"Didn't you hear? It's a law now," Molly called out from the kitchen. "Everyone has to wear pink at least twice a week."

Emily laughed as she followed Jessica into the kitchen. "I heard the bill passed the House but is still in the Senate." She handed Jessica her pan, which was wrapped in a paper bag. "I just wanted to return your pan."

"Oh, thanks. Why don't you sit and have some coffee or something?" Jessica coaxed her.

Emily glanced at her watch. "I can stay a few minutes, I guess." She sat at the big kitchen table, an antique oak pedestal with matching chairs.

Molly was sitting there, too, chopping vegetables on a cutting board.

"What are you two cooking?" Emily asked. "It smells great."

"Molly's teaching me how to make a braised pork roast. With sage and leeks," Jessica added.

Molly kept her focus on the cutting board. "It simmers on top of the stove so it doesn't dry out."

"That would be a huge improvement at our house," Emily said. "Everything I cook tastes like sawdust."

"Why don't you call Dan and have him meet you here?" Jessica suggested. "We have plenty."

"Oh, we can't. But thanks. Another time," she added, smiling at her sister. She paused. "I really shouldn't stay long. I have to get home. We're having some company tonight, too. Well . . . not company exactly . . ."

The two women glanced at her, their curiosity aroused. "Sara and Luke?" Jessica guessed.

Emily shook her head. "No, it isn't anything. Well, it is something but . . ."

Molly stopped her chopping and gave Emily a long, mock serious look. "Give it up, Emily. You're not leaving until you spill the beans."

Emily took a breath. "Dan and I have applied to be temporary guardians of the baby I found. A social worker is coming tonight to interview us and do a home visit." She stopped and waited, watching their expressions.

Molly smiled and nodded, then started chopping again. "I had a feeling it was something good. That's terrific, Emily. I hope it all works out for you."

Jessica leaned over and hugged her. "That's great news. Wow, what a surprise." She sat down near Emily and glanced at her. "Why didn't you tell me sooner?"

Emily could see her sister felt hurt that she hadn't been let in on the process. They usually told each other everything.

"It just happened so fast, that's all." Emily reached out and touched Jessica's hand. "Dan and I only decided yesterday. I guess I'm a little worried about how it will all turn out."

"I think it will be fine," Molly said with great certainty. "Who wouldn't like you and Dan?"

"Thanks, but I think they look at more than social skills. Dan thinks we might be too old."

Jessica didn't respond for a moment. "Well, it is hard work taking care of a baby, harder than I ever expected. I'm just exhausted at the end of the day. I'd much rather go in to the bank and work on loan applications," she added with a laugh.

Emily knew that wasn't completely true. Since Jessica had returned to work part time, she felt torn about every minute she spent away from Tyler and Darrell.

Still, her reply hadn't been the vote of confidence Emily had expected. In fact, her sister sounded surprisingly like Dan. And Jessica was ten years younger. *Maybe she thinks I'm too old, but doesn't want to come right out and say it*, Emily realized.

"What about your job? Are you going to take a leave of absence?" Jessica asked

"I didn't even think of that. I'm not sure if I'm eligible. I would probably have to step down altogether if I wanted that much time off."

Jessica shook her head sympathetically. "It's going to be hard for you. You work such long hours."

"I'll cut back, that's all. I'm in the office too much as it is. I'll have to learn to delegate more."

"What about Dan?" Molly asked curiously. "How does he feel about it?"

"He wasn't in favor at first," Emily admitted. "In fact, I think he said it was totally insane. But he's come around. He's willing to be a temporary guardian at least."

"Don't worry. That baby will have him wrapped around her little finger in no time." Molly had finished cutting the pile of leeks and whisked them from the board into a large bowl.

"That's what I'm hoping," Emily said wistfully.

Lauren, Molly's older daughter, came to the doorway. "Tyler needs his diaper changed. And it isn't pretty, gang." She made a face that made the women laugh.

Jessica started to get up from the table but Molly was faster. "I'll go. You sit and visit with Emily. This is big news. She needs some pointers from a pro."

Jessica hesitated a moment, but then sat down again. "Thanks, Molly. That's sweet of you."

Emily sat with Jessica for a moment without either of them talking.

"You don't seem that happy for me, Jessica," she said at

last. "Do you really think I'm too old? Lots of women have babies in their mid-forties these days."

Jessica shook her head. "No, that's not it. I'm sorry, Em. I am happy for you. It's a surprise, though, I must say. I thought that with Dan retired, you two were going to have a different sort of life—more traveling and being carefree."

"Dan just got tired of running the newspaper. Calling him retired makes him sound like a senior, for goodness sake. He's only fifty-one," Emily pointed out. "We did have a different plan about what our lives would be like, and it didn't include an infant," she added truthfully. "Dan and I argued about this, too. But I couldn't turn my back on this baby."

"I can see that," Jessica said quietly. "Do you think it has something to do with me having Tyler? I often thought that must be hard for you, considering what happened with Sara."

Emily nodded, moved by her sister's honesty. "Yes, that was part of it. I won't deny it . . . but it was more than that. Something seems to be pushing me in this direction. Did you ever feel that way?" she asked her sister. "As if something was really meant to be? As if God was trying to tell you something? Even when you resist, you find yourself back in the same place again."

Jessica nodded. "I guess I've felt that way once or twice. But you need to be careful, too, Emily. You said this was only a temporary arrangement. What happens after that? Will Dan agree to adopt the baby if that's what you really want?"

Emily shrugged. "I don't know. I'm just hoping I'll know the right thing to do when the time comes to decide."

"I hope so, too. I hope you don't end up getting hurt and disappointed if this doesn't work out. It's not just Dan you need to worry about. Someone could come forward any day and claim the child."

"Yes, I've thought about that a lot." Emily sighed. "You

know me, Jessica. I'm not exactly Miss Impulsive. But sometimes you just have to take a chance."

Jessica nodded and smiled warily. "Yes . . . I guess you do." She stood up and quickly hugged Emily. "I hope this works out. I really do. I'm going to say a prayer for you."

"Thanks, Jess. It is a little overwhelming. And I feel like such a novice about all the baby stuff. Will you help me?"

"Of course I will. I thought that went without saying," her sister assured her. "I'm new at this game myself, but I probably have every baby book ever written," she added with a grin.

Emily laughed. "Great, you'll be hearing from me."

When Emily arrived home a short time later, she called to Dan from the front door.

"I'm back here, in the kitchen," he replied.

She quickly walked through the house, pleased and even surprised to see that Dan had straightened things up, picked up his trail of newspapers and coffee mugs, and tidied up the living room. The kitchen was in surprisingly good shape, too. He had the table set for dinner and was warming something on the stove.

"We'd better eat. That woman will be here in about half an hour, right?" he greeted her.

"Yes, just about." Emily walked over and kissed him on the cheek. He smelled good, fresh from a shower and smoothly shaven. He was dressed in khaki pants, a dark blue sweater, and a good shirt.

"Thanks," she said, smiling at him.

"It's just some spaghetti sauce you had stashed in the freezer. Don't get too excited."

"No, I mean for going through with this interview. I know it's all happened very suddenly."

He glanced at her. "I still have my reservations, Emily, you know that. But I'm willing to do this for your sake. Don't worry. I'll put my best foot forward for this social worker."

Emily smiled at him. "I'm not worried. She'll adore you . . . but I saw you first."

The corner of Dan's mouth turned up in a reluctant smile. "You're a very charming, persuasive woman. You'd be great in politics. Did anyone ever tell you that?"

Emily laughed but didn't answer. Hopefully her charms would work as well on Mrs. Preston.

They ate hurriedly, and Dan cleaned the kitchen while Emily ran around the house and cleaned up a bit more. The doorbell rang promptly at seven, and she felt her stomach flutter nervously.

Dan squeezed her hand as they headed to answer the door together. "Don't worry. It will be fine," he whispered to her. She glanced at him and forced a smile, grateful for his encouragement, all things considered.

"Mrs. Preston, please come in," Emily welcomed her. She quickly introduced Dan, who took their visitor's coat. Then they all walked into the living room.

"Please, call me Nadine." The social worker took a seat on the couch and removed a large leather binder from her briefcase. "This won't take all that long. I have another appointment tonight at nine. Perhaps you could show me around the house first, before we talk?"

"Oh, sure. Just follow me." Emily fixed her face in what she hoped was a pleasant smile and gave a quick tour of their house, upstairs and down, all the while wondering if this other appointment meant some other couple was applying to be Jane's guardians. She wanted to ask but sensed it wasn't appropriate.

When they came to the master bedroom, Emily said, "We thought we could put the crib in here with us at first. We also have an extra bedroom we can turn into a nursery . . . eventually."

She glanced at Dan, wondering if he would show some negative reaction to the suggestion of having the baby for a prolonged period of time, but he had a calm, composed expression on his face. He didn't look wildly eager to take in a baby, Emily thought, but he didn't seem totally averse to the idea. But suddenly his hair looked so grey to her, the blond, flaxen color faded out in the low light. Did Nadine Preston think they were too old for this assignment?

She hoped not. She truly hoped not.

Back in the living room, Nadine sat on the couch with Emily while Dan took an armchair. Nadine made some notes in her binder, then started to review their application. "So, Dan, you have two children?"

"Yes, a daughter, Lindsay, who's married and lives in Hamilton. She runs the newspaper here in town now. And a son, Wyatt, he's a photojournalist on the West Coast for the *Los Angeles Times*," Dan added proudly.

Nadine smiled. She turned to Emily. "And your daughter, Sara, she's also a reporter?"

"Dan gave her a job on the paper before he left. It's worked out well for her. And it's been wonderful having Sara in town these past two years so that we could get to know each other."

"Emily has a terrific relationship with Sara. They're very close," Dan cut in quickly. "Sara adores her. Really . . ."

Emily cringed under the weight of his exuberant compliments. "We do have a good relationship. I'm very grateful for that. Sara is a special person, though," Emily added.

"Yes, I understand." Nadine smiled at Emily, then looked down at her book again.

Emily had already told the social worker the story of how she had given Sara up for adoption and then how they had been reunited two years ago. Nadine had seemed sympathetic and understanding, yet Emily still wondered again if that act—that horrible mistake she had made when she was so young—was going to count against her.

"And how will you manage the child care?" Nadine

asked. "I see you work at home, Dan. Would you be watching the baby?"

"Why, no. That wasn't our plan. I didn't think it was anyway." Dan coughed into his hand and glanced nervously at Emily. She felt her heart sink. She had never even suggested that on the application, though it was certainly a fair question.

"I'm going to take a week off from work at first," Emily rushed in. "At least a week. Just to get Jane comfortable in her new surroundings. And then we're going to hire a babysitter. Dan will be home some days, too, to help out. But he does a lot of research for his writing, and his deadlines are very demanding, so it wasn't our plan to have him responsible for child care, too."

Oh, dear. Here we are, sounding like a dual-career couple with no time in our lives for a baby. What must this woman be thinking?

"And you would be willing to take child-care classes at the hospital, Emily?" Nadine asked.

Emily had already indicated on the application that she would. "Oh, yes, absolutely."

"And you, Dan? Would you be going also?"

Once again, poor Dan looked totally taken by surprise. Emily realized she had probably checked that box off for him and hadn't mentioned it.

"Uh . . . sure. Sure I would," he said, working up a hearty sounding voice. He sat up straight in his chair and cleared his throat again. "I did raise two kids awhile back," he added in a lighter tone. "But I know ideas about child rearing change. I wouldn't mind brushing up on a few things."

Emily stifled a sigh. He made it sound as if his fatherhood days dated back to the Victorian era.

"Theories about raising children do change," Nadine agreed. "But the fundamental principle never changes. Children thrive on love and encouragement."

"Yes, they do." Dan nodded solemnly. "I know that Emily and I would make that our priority, especially considering the poor little girl's circumstances. We know that taking in this baby will change our lives, and she will be the most important person around here."

Nadine smiled at him, looking impressed.

Emily was impressed, too. She beamed at her husband with a wide, warm smile. Maybe they wouldn't be chosen to be Jane's guardians, but it warmed her heart to see Dan making his best case for them. She knew he was doing it for her.

The social worker concluded her interview and packed up her briefcase. Emily felt half relieved and half anxious to see her go. Had they made the right impression? Had they given the right answers to her questions?

Nadine paused by the door, and Dan helped her put on her coat. "I should have a decision for you tomorrow or the next day."

Emily tried to read her expression but couldn't get a hint one way or the other what that decision would be.

Nadine smiled and shook her hand. "I'll certainly call by Saturday. That's when Jane should be released from the hospital."

"Oh, of course." Emily felt a little jolt in her heart.

Dan stood behind her, and she felt him rest his hand on her shoulder. "We'll be waiting to hear from you," he replied. "Thanks again for stopping by."

Nadine Preston said good-bye, then stepped out into the cold night. They watched as she got into her car, and then Dan closed the door.

Emily turned to him. "Well, what do you think?" she asked.

"I think it went all right. I think we were honest."

Emily swallowed hard, suddenly feeling a lump in her throat. "Thank you, Dan. I appreciate everything you said and how you sounded so positive—and committed."

"You don't have to thank me. We're in this together. I know you'll be disappointed if we're not chosen, but at least we tried our best, right?"

She nodded, unable to hold his gaze any longer. "Now we just have to wait to hear what the social service agency decides."

"Yes, it's probably not up to her entirely," Dan added. He slipped his arms around Emily and pulled her close. The hug was some comfort, though she knew nothing would really take the edge off her nerves until she heard back from Nadine Preston.

It's basically up to God now, she thought. She closed her eyes and said a silent prayer, hoping she and Dan would be allowed to take Jane home and care for her, even for a little while.

By Friday night, Ben felt he had pushed himself through a long week, but the Christmas Fair committee was holding an important meeting that he didn't want to miss. He took a seat near the back of the group, which was gathered in the Fellowship Hall on folding chairs set in rows. Sophie Potter sat up front, calling the group to order.

He knew tonight would mostly feature talk about the nitty-gritty details of running the event, but he hoped that at some point he might steer the group around to discussing Wood's Hollow, at least to propose that some of the money raised by the fair be donated there, maybe to the community center.

The Christmas Fair raised a considerable amount of money each year, but most of it was earmarked for the church budget. From time to time, however, the congregation decided to donate some, or even all, of the proceeds to a worthy cause. Last year, they had sent several thousand dollars to a mission project in Central America where

James had been the director. Perhaps this year their hearts would be awakened to a cause much closer to home.

"I think we're covered on the pageant costumes," Sophie Potter said, checking her list. "We still have all the wonderful costumes Vera and Leigh Baxter made last year. So that saves us a lot of work."

Sophie paused and checked her clipboard again. As usual, she was the Christmas Fair coordinator, organizing every detail from the golden halos on each pageant angel to the red and green sprinkles on the bake sale cupcakes. She had done it so splendidly for so many years now, no one else even thought to volunteer for the post.

Ben sat listening to this year's plans. He couldn't help feel that this fair would be no different from the last, or the one before that, a thought he found a bit depressing.

Traditions were important, there was no doubt. Traditions gave a sense of continuity and connection with the past, and even the future. But in a situation like this there seemed a fine line between tradition and just plain rote behavior. Where was the spark of imagination or even inspiration that could set this fair apart, he wondered.

"Now we always put the cake sale on the far wall of the Fellowship Hall, and then the table with the wooden crafts is set up to the left," Sophie noted, showing a chart of the room setup. "Can we have a show of hands for volunteers to build the crafts? We'll do the wooden boats, birdhouses, and pinecone centerpieces again. Those always sell well."

Sophie glanced at Fran Tulley, Tucker's wife, who was waving her hand frantically, nearly falling off her chair.

"Yes, Fran? Did you want to say something?"

Fran stood up. "I don't mean to criticize, Sophie, but those craft items are getting a little tired. Everyone in town must already own one of those centerpieces. Can't we do something different this year?"

Bravo, Fran, Ben seconded silently.

Sophie looked taken aback. "Well, I don't know. We always do boats, birdhouses, and centerpieces. What do the rest of you think?"

"I saw some very pretty painted boxes at a fall fair in Hamilton," Lucy Bates called out. "They looked easy to make, too. All you do is use a stencil and some ribbon."

"That sounds nice," Sophie said. "But ribbon can get tricky . . ."

Ben shifted in his chair, feeling weary. He was eager to bring up Wood's Hollow but couldn't see how he would ever work it into this meeting. The whole Christmas Fair discussion was starting to seem petty and silly to him, and he struggled to hold on to his patience and not be so judgmental.

Grace Hegman, who sat with her father, Digger, in the front row, stood up to speak. "People like our items. I don't see that we should change, especially now. Why, it's December second, only three weeks to the fair, and we've already ordered the kits." She glanced at Fran, her voice a bit sharp and agitated, then sat down, smoothing the front of her brown cardigan.

Grace was usually in charge of the handcrafts assembly. She was quite good at it, Ben recalled. But she did get a bit anxious when volunteers didn't show up, and then she felt obliged to do it all herself. It was understandable that she would veto the idea of taking on something new.

"Yes, we have ordered the kits." Sophie flipped her papers. "Let me see . . . they should be delivered this coming week. Doesn't give us much time, I guess."

"Three weeks is long enough," Fran argued. "I don't see why we can't do some stenciled boxes, too."

Grace stood up again, looking stricken. "It will take time enough to put together what we've ordered. We were here all hours last Christmas. I don't think we should try to take on even more. And stenciling besides . . ."

Ben considered offering a conciliatory word, but before he could speak, Sophie called a vote, and it was decided by a narrow margin to skip the new craft items this year.

Sophie then suggested the group take a coffee break. There were several more items on her agenda, Ben noticed. He wouldn't be able to talk to them about Wood's Hollow tonight; he'd have to save it for some other meeting. He decided to make an early, inconspicuous departure. It was almost ten o'clock. He wasn't sure if he was tired, bored, or simply frustrated.

"DID YOUR MEETING END EARLY, DEAR? I DIDN'T EXPECT you home so soon."

Carolyn stood in the living room, surrounded by boxes of Christmas ornaments. They had bought the tree the other night and he promised to help decorate over the weekend. But Carolyn had been determined to get started on her own. At least Mark had strung the lights before he went out to meet friends.

"I decided to leave at the coffee break. It's been a long week." They all seemed long lately, Ben thought.

He sat down in the armchair next to the sofa, picked up the TV remote, then put it down again. He wasn't in the mood for television. And he certainly wasn't in the mood to decorate a tree now. "I guess I'll go straight up to bed. I'm beat."

Carolyn hooked an ornament on a pine branch, then walked over and sat on the sofa beside him.

"Do you feel all right? You look as if you might be coming down with something."

"I'm okay. I feel a bit guilty, ducking out like that on Sophie. There was a debate about what type of craft items to sell, but she handled it well. She didn't need me."

"I'm sure she didn't mind you leaving. She's been running that fair so long, she could do it with her eyes shut."

"Yes, and that's both a blessing and a problem. I was sitting there tonight thinking that the fair is getting so . . . predictable. Every year, the same tables of gifts and foods and the same pageant. Maybe it's unfair to say, but it all started to sound very trivial to me. What I mean is, there are more important things to worry about than whether we sell birdhouses or stenciled boxes, don't you think?"

His words trailed off, Carolyn's concerned look distracting him. "Yes, of course there are, Ben."

"Oh, I don't know. It just seems to be getting under my skin this year. I don't know why it should, after all this time. I don't think this year is any different, and I don't think the congregation has changed. Maybe I have. What kind of minister has no patience for his flock?"

"You're only human, Ben. You're allowed to occasionally lose your patience, just like the rest of us," Carolyn reminded him. "The holidays are hard on you. There's so much going on at church, you're exhausted by Christmas. Maybe we ought to plan a vacation for January—go somewhere warm and sunny for a week?"

Ben forced a small smile. "It might help to get away for a while. But I don't know. I don't think I need a real vacation. I'm feeling unproductive enough as it is. Sitting on a beach somewhere will only make me feel worse. I feel as if I've just lost the thread at church somehow. Does that make any sense?"

"You're an excellent minister, Ben. You know that. But you sound as if you're losing perspective. You sound depressed, dear," she said finally. "I'm concerned."

Serious words coming from his wife, who had battled that demon long and hard during her thirties and forties.

"I don't think we should just ignore it," she went on. "Maybe you should speak to somebody, a therapist. It might help to talk to someone and sort out your feelings."

Good advice, as always. He had thought of that himself, of course. But it was different hearing it from Carolyn.

He'd prayed about it, of course, asking God for some direction, some insight into these feelings. But so far, no insight had come.

"Maybe some counseling would help," he allowed. "I'm not sure what I need right now," he added honestly. "Perhaps a spiritual retreat of some kind."

Carolyn's warm gaze remained on him. "That sounds good, too. Just promise me you'll look into it. You won't just brush this aside?"

Ben nodded. "Don't worry. I'll find someone to talk to. Maybe another clergyman who understands my situation."

It was hard to admit that he had come to that point, that this mood was more than just the result of a bad day or a bad week. It was, he thought, due to growing frustration over feeling his message wasn't being heard. Or perhaps heard, but not heeded, which was even worse. He felt a little better admitting his feelings to Carolyn.

"It's good to talk to you about this. I should have told you sooner."

She leaned over and took his hand. "You're always there for everyone else. You always give so much. I'm here for you, Ben."

"Yes, you are. I ought to be counting my blessings instead of complaining."

Carolyn smiled, her easy, winsome smile that had won his heart so long ago. "You can always complain to me if it makes you feel better."

He felt better just holding her hand, as always. She was right, though. He couldn't let this go too far. He had to face it squarely and find someone to help him sort things out. There was a minister up in Princeton he could talk to, an old friend. He would call tomorrow and see when they could visit. The thought lifted his spirits just a notch or two.

Carolyn leaned over and suddenly shut out the lamp. The room was dark, except for the lights twinkling on the Christmas tree.

"Look at the tree. It's lovely, isn't it?"

"Oh, yes, we picked out a good one this year, nice and full."

"I like the way it looks with just the lights on."

"I do, too. Why don't we skip the ornaments? That would save you some work."

"That would be something different." Carolyn laughed, though she didn't sound at all convinced it would be better.

Maybe that was all he needed in his life right now, Ben thought. Just something different.

CHAPTER FIVE

～

SARA WALKED INTO THE BEANERY, DEEP IN A CONVERSATION on her cell phone with her editor, Lindsay Forbes. "I think I got a good shot, too, right while he was waving the canceled checks."

In the midst of a routine meeting of the county building commission—a meeting Sara dreaded covering since it was usually so deadly boring and devoid of any interesting news—a longtime commissioner was accused of assigning contracts for road repair to his brother-in-law and taking kickbacks.

It was a scandal in the making and certainly worthy of the front page in tomorrow's edition.

If she wrote the story up quickly.

"I'm just picking up some lunch. I'll be back in five minutes," she promised Lindsay before ending the call.

It was already past three. Another gobbled meal at her

desk. Such was her lot in life these days. But she wasn't complaining; a front-page byline was more important than food any day.

Sara snapped her cell phone closed and dropped it into her cavernous leather knapsack. She'd already made her way to the take-out counter and now faced a waitress ready to take her order.

"Sara! Over here!" She turned quickly at the sound of Luke's voice. He was sitting at a table near the back of the café. He waved her over, and she walked toward him, smiling. But she felt the expression freeze on her face when she noticed a woman sitting at his table, an extremely attractive woman with sun-streaked blond hair cut in shaggy layers and large brown eyes that pinned her with an interested stare. Forget extremely attractive; the woman was flat-out gorgeous.

Sara approached warily, wishing she had run a comb through her hair and freshened her lipstick when she had had a chance.

"Hey, Sara, what are you up to?" Luke greeted her.

Sara felt like smacking him. How dare he sit there with that bombshell and sound so perfectly casual?

"Just picking up some lunch. What are you up to?" She tried to keep the sarcasm from her tone but somehow couldn't.

"Just visiting with my friend Christina. She called the other night, remember?"

"Sure, I remember." Sara looked directly at Luke's old friend. "Nice to meet you. I'm Sara."

Christina smiled slowly. Not unkindly but in a somewhat patronizing manner, Sara thought.

"Nice to meet you, Sara. Luke tells me you're a reporter at the local paper."

"Yes, I am. Luke tells me you're writing a book."

"Trying to. It's sort of miserable at the beginning, like

pushing a rock uphill," Christina said with a self-deprecating laugh. "But every time I write one, it does get a bit easier."

Every time? How many books had she written? Well, she was older, about Luke's age, Sara guessed. That was some comfort, or not, depending on how you looked at it.

Sara resolved to Google Christina Cross as soon as she got back to the office.

"I was just showing Christina around," Luke explained. "Want to sit down and have some lunch with us?"

From the look of the table, it seemed they were just about finished. Sara didn't want to join them anyway.

"No thanks. I've got to get back to the office. Lindsay wants my copy right away. Seems some commissioner awarded his brother-in-law lots of juicy contracts. There could be an investigation."

"That's a good story. I guess you have your little scandals here, too, don't you?" Christina sounded surprised, as if she'd found some otherwise well-behaved children fighting in a sandbox.

"Yes, we do," Sara said evenly. "But the crooks are usually shorter than the ones in the city. I mean, on average."

Luke stared at her a minute and then laughed. Christina smiled mildly but didn't reply.

"Well, sorry to run. See you," she said, meaning Luke. She had little desire to see more of Christina Cross.

Luke met her gaze a moment and waved. He had a rather dopey look on his face, she thought, as she turned and headed for the door.

Sara was halfway to the newspaper office when she realized she never got to order her lunch. Oh . . . bother. She'd have to call out for something and starve in the meanwhile.

Another reason to be mad at Luke. He had some nerve sitting there so smugly with that—that Christina. He probably planted himself there just hoping Sara would run into them so he could make her jealous. That's what it was,

Sara decided. Just because she told him she wasn't ready to get engaged.

And he jumps on the first log that floats by!

Couldn't he see through that Christina? She was about as sincere as the blond streaks in her hair. How dumb was Luke, anyway?

Fuming, Sara stomped into the newspaper office, nearly walking right into the editor in chief.

"There you are. I was just about to call you again."

Eager for Sara to start her article, Lindsay was practically breathing down her neck as she followed Sara back to her desk.

"So, tell all." Lindsay perched on the edge of Sara's desk, her arms crossed over her chest.

Sara related the events of the meeting and the accusation and argument that had taken center stage. "So this commissioner is denying flat out that he's taken any kickbacks and then this other county official, an attorney, pulls out copies of canceled checks. You should have seen the guy's face. I thought he was going to have a heart attack or something."

"Sounds good. But watch the editorializing. The guy isn't even officially charged with anything yet. Did you get any statements when the meeting broke up?"

"I tried, but they cleared out pretty quickly. Ducked out, more like. I'll make some calls, see if anyone will talk to me."

"See what you can get. But start the piece right away. We don't want to be here all night."

Sara felt the same way. She had tentative plans with Luke that night. On Friday evenings they usually got together late, after her art class. But Luke had looked pretty busy in the Beanery. Maybe he had forgotten. Or maybe his dear old friend was staying on into the evening. They had a lot of catching up to do, Sara was sure, feeling upset and annoyed all over again. She would wait and see if he called.

She stared at her computer screen, momentarily forgetting what she was supposed to be writing about. Then she pulled out her notepad and forced herself to settle down.

Covering news like this was tricky business. So far it was only a lot of accusations flying around. If she wasn't careful in her reporting, the paper could get in trouble. Lindsay would go over her article, of course, but the real responsibility rested with her. She wasn't going to let Luke and that Christina person mess up her story. She had to focus.

Several hours later, Sara and Lindsay were the only ones left in the office. Lindsay was going over Sara's story for about the third time. It was getting to be a long day.

Despite Sara's efforts to be careful, Lindsay had found more than a few errors. Sara took it on the chin and kept returning to her desk. She wasn't about to explain what had thrown her off track.

"All right, this is better. I think that's everything." Lindsay looked up from the copy. "Good job, Sara. You should go home and get some rest."

Grateful for the reprieve, Sara went back to her desk and gathered up her knapsack and belongings. Her cell phone rang. It was probably Luke, she guessed, trying to catch her at the last minute.

"Hello?" she said curtly.

"Hi, honey. Are you coming to class tonight? I just wanted to check," Emily asked.

Sara took a class in watercolor painting with Emily on Friday nights. They were both so busy, it was usually the only time they got to see each other. Sara felt beat but knew their time together meant a lot to her mother. She glanced at her watch. She was already late.

"Yes, I'm coming. I got stuck at work. I'm just leaving now."

"Were you working on a good story?"

"A doozy. I'll tell you all about it later."

"All right. Don't rush. Did you eat anything?"

Sometimes Emily sounded so motherly, Sara practically laughed at her. But it felt good to know she cared so much. "I'll pick something up on the way," she promised.

Emily would appreciate the story. She wouldn't think it was "cute and small town."

Sara grabbed her jacket and called out a last good night to Lindsay before she headed out the door. She was looking forward to seeing Emily. Her mother was a good listener and wise about relationships, too. She'd surely say something that would make her feel better about Luke and this Christina episode.

THE PAINTING CLASS WAS HELD IN AN OLD SCHOOL building that had been turned into a community center. At night the classrooms were filled with adults studying everything from yoga to car repair.

Sara normally enjoyed taking a break from real life—work, Luke, and even the writing she did for herself. But tonight she felt tired and out of sorts, not in the mood to focus on the bowl of yellow pears on a blue satin scarf set up for a still life. She quietly slipped into the class, spotted her mother, and headed across the room. Emily was busy at work, blocking out her page with broad strokes. She looked up at Sara and smiled.

"Another fruit bowl." Emily's tone was hushed. She glanced over her shoulder at the instructor who stood a few aisles away. "I'm not sure if my painting talents are improving, but at least I'm getting some intellectual fiber."

"That's about all the fiber I've had all day," Sara quipped in return. She took a to-go cup of tea and a container of yogurt out of a paper bag and set them on the table, then set up her paints and easel. She stared at the fruit bowl, not sure where to start.

Emily dabbed at her painting with quick strokes. "Tell me about your story."

"You're going to like this one. Looks like a scandal is brewing in the county building commission."

What Sara really wanted to tell Emily about was meeting up with Luke and his old girlfriend. That was the biggest story on her mind. And he hadn't called her tonight either, she realized. He always called at night to check in, even when he knew she was working late or had this class.

Before Sara could go further with her story, their instructor, Sylvia Cooper, appeared. In her mid-sixties, Sylvia was a former high school art teacher and now a professional artist. Her specialty was watercolor landscapes, mostly beach scenes. She'd won a number of awards and her pictures were exhibited in galleries throughout New England. She was dressed tonight in a long, loose tunic top and skirt in deep purple tones that made a striking contrast to her pure silver hair. She wore several large silver rings on each hand; strands of bright beads around her neck and an array of silver and copper bracelets made a jangling sound as she moved through the room.

Sylvia was always very encouraging. Overly so in some cases, Sara thought. She now cast an appraising glance over Emily's picture.

"I like the way you've outlined the fruit. Nice and bold. The paint is getting too opaque in here, though." She pointed to a section on the bowl. "Keep it transparent, fluid," she coached. "Remember the light."

Her usual warning. Sara suppressed a smile.

"Oh, by the way. I read about your episode with the abandoned baby. What an experience."

"It was pretty unbelievable." Emily cast a quick look at the instructor.

"What's become of the child? Is she in an orphanage?"

"She's been in the hospital the past week, being treated for a respiratory infection."

"Oh, that's too bad. Is she better now?"

"She's coming along. She won't be placed with adoptive parents until the county completes an investigation. But Dan and I have applied to be her temporary guardians."

Sara had been half listening as she started her painting, but at that last sentence her head turned toward Emily. She could barely hide her shocked expression.

"That's wonderful of you and Dan to step forward like that and help the child," Sylvia said.

"It's something we really wanted to do."

Something Emily wants to do, Sara decided. She knew Dan wasn't interested in taking on a baby, not that he didn't like children: he was great with Darrell and Tyler. But once Jessica and Sam's kids had come along, Sara had heard him comment often enough that he was glad his child-rearing years were behind him.

"Well, best of luck." Sylvia glanced at Sara's blank canvas and shot her a puzzled look.

"I had to work late," Sara said apologetically.

"That's all right, dear. I'll come back and check at the break." She touched Sara's arm as she walked past to the next student.

Sara turned to Emily. "So you applied to be guardians? I didn't realize—"

"It's all happened very quickly. We just decided to go ahead with the paperwork on Wednesday and had the home visit last night. I just didn't get a chance to tell you," Emily explained. "We don't even know for sure if it's going to work out."

"That's great. I hope it does."

"So do I," Emily said.

For some reason, it hurt a little to hear the excitement and anticipation compressed in the simple reply.

Sylvia called for attention and gave the class some pointers. A welcome interruption to the conversation, Sara thought. She turned to her blank sheet of paper and dabbed some paint on. She wasn't sure why, but she didn't think

Emily's news was so great. She was certainly surprised, though.

Emily was going to take in a baby. Her birth mother was going to care for another child.

The last time she'd seen Emily with that look of excitement and particular glow was when Sara had finally agreed to stay in Cape Light so they could get to know each other better.

You're jealous. That's the problem. You're jealous of a poor, homeless little baby. Sara felt a wave of guilt.

No, I'm not. That's not it at all, she argued with herself.

No? Then what is it?

I just think it's a bad idea. Emily's too old and too dedicated to her job to take on a baby. Dan will freak. She might even end up messing up her marriage over this. But who can tell her that? Look at her. She's on cloud nine.

Exactly. You're not going to be Emily's number one anymore. You're not going to be her "can do no wrong" princess. You've been dethroned, the little voice pointed out.

Sara plunked her brush into a container of water and turned to the snack she'd brought along in lieu of dinner. She flipped the lid off the yogurt and took a spoonful. She should have skipped the art class and gone straight home to eat a real meal, crash in front of the TV, and go to bed early.

She had come to see Emily, seeking some comfort from her problems with Luke, and now she felt even worse.

Then again, she would have heard the news sooner or later.

Sylvia began circulating around the room again. "Finish whatever you're working on, and we'll take a ten-minute break," she announced.

"So, when will you find out?" Sara asked Emily.

Emily, who was swirling her brush in a long curvy line, didn't look up for a moment. "Tomorrow," she said finally.

"The social worker said she'll call early if it's a go. We may have to pick the baby up right away. I don't think I'll be able to sleep tonight," she confessed.

Sara forced a smile. "Get used to it. I hear babies keep you up all night."

Emily nodded and turned back to her work. "We'll see," she said wistfully.

Sara felt suddenly ashamed of her snide comment, though Emily hadn't seemed to notice. She should be more supportive, more positive. Emily was doing a good deed, an admirable act of charity.

And Sara fully understood Emily's motivation. *She never mothered me as a baby, so she needs to make up for it this way. She's never gotten over having to give me up.*

How ironic that she would be the one who begrudged her own mother the experience.

Sara made another halfhearted try at starting her painting and grimaced. She had exactly two brushstrokes on the paper and they were all wrong.

"Having trouble focusing tonight?" Emily asked kindly.

"Looks like it. Those pears aren't inspiring me much," Sara admitted.

"You never told me about your story," Emily reminded her.

"Oh, right." Sara paused. "It's pretty good stuff. You'll see it tomorrow though." She sighed and cleaned off a brush.

"Sara, is something wrong? Did you have a problem at work today?"

Sara shook her head. "No, but Luke and I have been arguing. Things are sort of shaky between us right now."

"What did you argue about?"

"He wants to get engaged for Christmas," Sara confided. "He had me trying on rings and everything. I guess I shouldn't have been so surprised. We've been together forever, as he kept reminding me. But I really thought it over and I had to tell him I wasn't ready. We had a fight. I think I really hurt his feelings."

Emily looked surprised, Sara thought. Then her expression turned serious again.

"I'm sure it was hard to tell him you weren't ready. That took guts. But if that's how you feel, Sara, you did the right thing. I'm proud of you. Most young women your age would have seen the ring and said yes automatically."

"It was a nice ring," Sara admitted with a small smile.

Emily patted her hand. "All good things come in their own time. Marriage is a huge commitment, honey. You can't afford not to be honest with each other right now. Luke is being honest with you about what he wants. Just don't stop talking to each other. It takes time to work these things out."

"If Luke can fit me into his schedule. There's this old friend of his who's come to town. An old girlfriend," Sara corrected herself. "I ran into them in the Beanery. They were hanging out the whole day together and she's probably still here now. Luke never called me and he promised he would."

"Why would he get in touch with an old girlfriend?" Emily asked curiously.

"She found him. She's writing a book about police officers who have left the force and how their lives have turned out. She came to interview him. I think it's more like she came to check him out again."

"Come on, Sara. Don't jump to conclusions. You only saw them together once. She might have gone back to wherever she came from by now. You might never hear about her again."

"I doubt that very much. She looked to me like she was . . . digging in," Sara said honestly. *Digging her hooks into Luke,* she wanted to add.

Emily cast her a concerned look. "Don't worry, honey. He may be just trying to get your attention, make you jealous."

"Well, it worked."

Emily laughed. "Luke loves you. He wants to marry you. You just told me that. You're not going to lose him in one day to some old girlfriend."

"You haven't seen her. She's tall, thin, blonde, and sort of all-around gorgeous . . . although the hair is definitely chemically enhanced," she added.

Emily shook her head. "You're all-around gorgeous, too. A total knockout, with brains and talent to boot. So there."

"Thanks, but you have to say that. You're my mother," Sara pointed out, only a tiny bit cheered by the reinforcement.

"Yes, I know. It's in my contract." Emily gave her a tender look. "I'm also the mayor, don't forget. Maybe I can figure out some way to run her out of town. Too much flirting with other women's boyfriends? We have laws against that sort of thing around here," Emily said firmly. "Or we can . . . if it's convenient."

Sara finally had to smile. "Thanks. That would be a help."

"I'll put Officer Tulley on it right away." Emily glanced at Sara's mostly blank page. "Want to pack up and go over to the Beanery?"

"You don't mind? Your painting is coming out pretty good tonight."

"That's all right. I can finish some other time. I only come here to hang out with you, you know."

Emily's admission was touching. Sara sighed. "I guess that fruit bowl is making me hungry."

"Let's go then," Emily said. "If we run into Luke and his old flame, I'll give that upstart a piece of my mind."

Sara knew that if the circumstances should arise, Emily would be perfectly polite and would never embarrass her.

But it was nice to know Emily sympathized and was in her corner. Of course, Emily always was. Sara had come to rely on her gentle counsel and unflagging encouragement.

Tonight, of all nights, she appreciated it even more.

CHAPTER SIX

"HERE SHE IS." NADINE PRESTON STEPPED CLOSER and handed Emily the baby. Jane wore a pink velour onesie and was wrapped in a white blanket, both of which Emily had brought from home. Emily was sure she'd never seen anything sweeter, cuter, or more beautiful in her life.

She had worried and fretted nonstop until Nadine called late Friday night to tell them that they would be Jane's temporary guardians. She and Dan had jumped out of bed Saturday morning and driven as fast as they dared up to Southport. They'd met Nadine and signed the final papers in the hospital waiting room. Now they stood together in the hospital nursery. The big moment had arrived.

"Isn't she beautiful?" Emily glanced at Dan and then back at the baby.

"That she is," Dan agreed, peering over her shoulder. "Look at her little outfit. How cute."

"I bought it yesterday, just in case," Emily admitted.

"It's nice and warm. I have her snowsuit, too, in this bag."

She showed them a big blue bag filled with all sorts of baby necessities she had picked up.

Nadine smiled at her. "She's all yours now. You can put it on whenever you want to."

"Yes, of course." Emily smiled nervously. She was sure she seemed in a state of shock. She did feel overwhelmed, more than even she expected. She looked up at Dan, who seemed subdued, though she could tell he was making an effort to be enthusiastic and say all the right things.

"Well, I'll leave you three to get acquainted. I'll be in touch. Call me if you have any problems, though."

"Thank you, Nadine. Thanks for everything," Emily said.

"No thanks necessary. I think you'll be fine," the social worker added.

Emily watched her go, then turned to Dan. "Hold the baby a minute and I'll get her snowsuit out."

Wordlessly, Dan took the baby. Emily thought he looked a little nervous and held Jane a bit stiffly, but it would take time for them to get acquainted. He wasn't a natural at this.

The baby fussed a bit and Dan bounced her in his arms. "There, there. It's all right. You're coming home with us. How do you like that?"

Apparently, Jane wasn't thrilled at the idea. She immediately crinkled up her face and started crying. Dan stared at Emily with a "What now?" look.

Emily restrained her instinct to rush in and take over.

"Try talking to her some more. She's just a little fussy. She doesn't know us yet. Babies need to get accustomed to your smell," she added, repeating something she'd read last night in one of Jessica's baby books.

Dan turned back to the baby. "Come on, Jane. Stop crying now. It's okay," he soothed her.

He put the baby up on his shoulder and patted her back. Jane's cries rose in intensity and volume. Emily thought she saw him actually wince, though he kept on pacing around the room, patting the baby's back.

"It's all right. I'll take her. Let me put this snowsuit on and we'll go."

The suit was more like a down-filled sack that, luckily, went on easily. Dan grabbed the rest of the baby's belongings and they headed out of the hospital.

Once in Emily's arms, Jane stopped crying. Emily hoped she would fall asleep. It wouldn't be a good start to things if she cried all the way from Southport to Cape Light.

In the parking lot, Dan opened the back door of Emily's Jeep. Emily leaned inside and checked the car seat. They had bought it at a Shop-Mart on the way up to the hospital, and Emily wasn't sure they had put it in the car correctly.

"I don't think this is right. It shouldn't shift around so much. Maybe the seat belt goes through a different spot?"

"Honey, I read the directions. It's in right," Dan insisted. He leaned inside the car and yanked on the seat. It came free of the strap in his hand.

Emily hid a grin. "Where are the directions? Let's take another look."

Dan rubbed his forehead. "I think I threw them out."

"You threw them out? What did you do that for?"

"Now, now. Don't panic," Dan said, an edge to his voice. "It's just a car seat, Emily. We'll figure it out."

Emily was about to reply, then stopped herself. She didn't think it was good for the baby to be out in the cold like this.

"Here, you take the baby. I'll fix the seat," she said in a calm but firm tone. "I think I remember how to do it. It's just like Jessica's."

She handed Dan the baby so that he had no choice. Jane stared around, looked at Dan, and started crying again. Dan took a deep breath and tilted his head back, staring at the sky for a moment. Emily knew he wasn't a praying man but had a feeling he'd resorted to making a heavenly appeal for patience.

They hadn't even had the baby an hour yet. *Not a good sign*, she thought.

She got into the Jeep and started working on the seat. It took a bit longer than she expected to figure it out, and she had to rethread the straps. But finally the seat seemed secure.

"Okay, it's good now. Hand her over." Dan quickly handed the baby back. Emily gently placed Jane in the seat, fastened the straps, and got in beside her.

"Why are you riding back there?" Dan asked.

"She has to face backwards. It's safer. I want to see her while we're driving, make sure she's okay."

"Oh, all right." Dan sighed and got into the front seat. "I'll be the chauffeur, I guess. Where to, madam?" he joked halfheartedly.

"Home, James." Emily ignored his tone. She was bringing Jane home, and the thought filled her with happiness.

The baby slept most of the ride home, as Emily had hoped. When they finally got back to the house, Emily gave her a bottle while Dan looked on. Emily invited him to have a turn feeding the baby, but he said, "I think I'll pass this round. You can show me later. I'm sure she'll be having another meal soon."

True enough, Emily thought. She had a head start bonding with the baby while visiting at the hospital, and now Dan needed to catch up. But she sensed it was wiser not to force him. Emily took Jane into their bedroom, changed her, and then walked back and forth with her, humming a vague little tune. She felt the baby's body grow heavy, her head falling limply on Emily's shoulder. When Jane was sound asleep, Emily carefully put her in the portable crib she had borrowed from Jessica.

Emily stood by the crib a moment, watching the baby sleep. She lay on her side, her cheek pressed flat against the white sheet, her fist curled to her mouth. Emily thought she could stand that way for hours, watching her. But she pulled herself away and returned to Dan, who sat in the living room reading the newspaper.

"How's it going?" he asked.

"Everything is under control. So far, so good," Emily reported. "She ate, dirtied a diaper, and is now fast asleep."

"Sounds about right," Dan said approvingly. "Babies are programmed on a loop, as I recall. I think you'll be seeing a lot of that routine."

"You'll" be seeing, he said, not "we." Emily ignored the distant tone and smiled at him.

"It's going to be fun having her around for Christmas, don't you think? It makes me more excited for the holidays."

Dan glanced at her. "Yes, Christmas. It will be here before we know it. Didn't the social worker say their investigation would be over about that time?"

She knew what he was hinting at. The baby might be released for adoption by then, which wouldn't make for a very happy Christmas at all. Emily didn't want to think that far ahead and ruin her happiness here and now. "I think we should just take it one day at a time," she said.

He nodded. "Good plan."

The doorbell rang. Dan looked over at her. "Expecting company?"

Emily shrugged and stood up. "No, I wonder who it could be."

She glanced out the window as she walked to the front door and spotted Betty Bowman's white Volvo in the driveway. Emily's step quickened and she pulled open the door.

Betty peered inside curiously. "I hope I'm not being a pest, but I was passing by and I just wondered if I could see the baby. Just a peek," she promised. "I won't stay long."

"Don't be silly. Come in, please. What a nice surprise." Emily hugged her best friend and stepped back, smiling. "I just put her down for a nap, but we can sneak in. I don't think she'll wake up."

"Sounds great." Betty smiled at Dan as she walked through the living room.

"Hi, Betty. Did you come to meet our new houseguest?" Emily cringed at his terminology but let it slide.

"I couldn't resist," Betty admitted. "How's it going?"

Dan shrugged. "Seems to be going fine. Emily's doing all the work so far."

"We just got home about an hour an ago. There's not much to report," Emily said honestly.

"Here, I brought her a little something." Betty handed Emily a small pink gift bag with a big chiffon bow. Emily peered inside and found a beautiful hand-knit outfit made with pale yellow fine-gauge yarn, pants and jacket and matching hat, all trimmed with white. The tiny buttons on the jacket looked like daisies.

"Betty, this is beautiful. You shouldn't have gone to all that trouble."

"No trouble. I hope it's the right size."

"Seems perfect. She'll look adorable in this."

Emily led Betty back to the bedroom, noticing that Dan was already sunk deep behind his newspaper again.

Inside the darkened bedroom, Betty quietly crept up to the crib and peered inside. She gazed at the baby a long moment.

"Oh my. She's beautiful." She took hold of Emily's hand but didn't seem able to say more.

Emily and Betty had been friends since high school. Betty knew everything and understood everything.

Emily stepped closer to the crib and adjusted the blanket, tucking it up over the baby's shoulder again.

"It's not forever. But it's something," she said softly.

"You never know," Betty said. "How is Dan doing with all this?"

"Keeping his distance. He can do that pretty well when he wants to," Emily confessed, even though it hurt a bit to admit it. "I'm not sure what I expected," she went on ruefully. "Maybe I had some fantasy that he would take one look at the baby and just flip head over heels. That hasn't happened so far."

"Give him time."

"As much as I can," Emily said, again hoping that Jane wouldn't be taken from them quickly. "I think it's just going to be harder than I realized. But I was willing to take the risk. So here I am."

"Yes, here you are." Betty sighed and looked down at the baby again. "Whatever happens, you're doing the right thing."

Emily looked up at her friend. "Do you really think so?"

Betty nodded, still watching the baby. "Yes, Emily, I really do. Besides, you know how Dan is. It may take him awhile, but when he does fall, he falls pretty hard."

She knew that too. Dan didn't bestow his love easily, but once he gave his heart to a person or even a project, he gave it completely. Irrevocably. She knew that for a fact.

It was some comfort, some hope, Emily thought. But it wasn't only Dan's doubt she had to worry about. Taking in this child was complicated, maybe more than she'd allowed herself to consider. It was all just hitting her now.

Had she rushed into this too quickly?

Closing her eyes, Emily sent up a quick, silent prayer that she had done the right thing and not just acted on the selfish, impulsive whim of a middle-aged woman who had missed out on an important path in life.

SATURDAY MORNING, SARA CLEANED HER APARTMENT IN a frenzy, trying not to watch the clock or listen for the phone. There hadn't been any message from Luke on her answering machine last night, and he hadn't called all morning. Sara had been on the phone twice, talking to Emily about the baby. She had made plans to go over there for a quick visit that afternoon. She wondered if Luke had called and found the line busy. She knew he would call back if that was the case. He would call here and then try her cell phone. But he was sure taking his sweet time about it.

They always went out on Saturday nights unless some emergency came up. It was simply understood. But they usually spoke to each other by now to catch up and figure out their plans. She often called him; she wasn't one of those women who had a "rule" about men doing all the calling. That was silly. It didn't matter.

But this morning Sara felt odd each time she picked up the phone and started to dial his number, as if she were checking up on him. All things considered, she felt he should call her. Maybe it was silly and immature, but she couldn't help it.

She finished cleaning and jumped in the shower, wondering if she should make plans with a girlfriend. What was Luke's problem anyway? One minute he's begging her to get married, and the next minute he pulls this disappearing act.

Get a grip, Sara; you just saw him yesterday. He's not exactly a candidate for the FBI missing person's list.

She just hated waiting like this. It was annoying, like being in high school again. She had thought they were well past that "Will he call?" stage. *If he doesn't call by the time I get home from Emily's house, I'm going to do something drastic—like make plans with my grandmother.*

She was turning off the shower when she heard the phone ring. *Finally! Let him talk to the machine. I'll call back,* she decided. But once she stepped out of the shower and heard Luke's voice rambling on for what seemed like the longest message in history, she couldn't help herself. She wrapped a towel around her middle and skidded across the wooden floors on wet feet, risking life and limb, until she reached the phone in her bedroom.

"Hello? I'm here," she interrupted him.

"Oh, I thought you were out. I've been talking into this machine for about an hour."

"I was in the shower."

"Sorry. I just wanted to say hello. How was your art class last night?"

"I got there late and Emily and I left early. We just hung out at the Beanery." *Why didn't you call me at work, like you promised?* she wanted to demand. But she held her tongue, waiting to hear what he had to say for himself.

"Skipping class, Sara? How are you ever going to learn to paint vegetables, or whatever?" he teased.

"Emily had some big news. She and Dan applied to take in the baby, as temporary guardians."

"That *is* news. I guess you had a lot to talk about."

"Yeah, we did." *Mostly about you*, she wanted to say.

"When will they know?"

"They found out late last night that they were approved. This morning they picked her up at the hospital. They got home a little while ago. I'm going to stop over later and say hello."

"Wow . . ." Luke didn't say anything more, but his simple expletive summed up Sara's feelings exactly. "I'd offer to go with you, but I'm sort of tied up at the center today."

"Oh? What's going on?" She braced herself, imagining the worst, then immediately chided herself for her overactive imagination. *Don't be silly. Christina Cross is long gone, back to Boston. She was here for an interview, not a vacation.*

"Well, Christina's still here," he said blandly, as if he had gorgeous former girlfriends hanging around all the time. What a bore. "I'm not sure what to do with her. We might go out to the beach or something. It's chilly but clear, not too windy either. Should be a nice day for a walk."

A winter beach walk! Sara immediately pictured the two of them strolling along the shore, their arms around each other. The image was totally infuriating. How dare he take Christina for a walk on the beach? That was their special thing to do on a Saturday afternoon. She knew how cold it got out there, and how Luke had a positive talent for keeping a girl warm.

She felt so hurt, she was speechless.

"I guess some of the kids and counselors will come. We can play Frisbee or touch football."

Sara took a breath. They weren't going to be alone. That was a little better.

"Want to meet us out there?" Luke added.

"No thanks. I promised Emily I'd go see the baby." Sara didn't need to tag along on that outing. She knew it would feel awkward, even with others there. "So what's with Christina?" she couldn't helping asking. "Doesn't she have a life?"

Luke laughed softly. "She needs to hang out and get material for her book. She stayed in one of the empty cabins last night. She'll probably go back to Boston Monday or Tuesday. I'm not really sure."

He wasn't sure? Was this woman going to move in? That just proved her theory. This Christina was unattached and looking up Luke as a possible rekindled relationship.

No wonder he hadn't been in touch all this time; he'd been too busy hanging out with Christina. Sara struggled to keep a grip on her temper. She didn't want to sound like a jealous shrew, at least not any more than she already had.

"So what about tonight?" she asked. "Are you busy being interviewed?"

"Of course not. Don't be silly." His tone was warm and reassuring, and Sara felt a little silly for sounding so snide. "I thought we could take Christina up to Newburyport. She hasn't been there yet. It will be fun to show her around, right?"

Sure, loads of fun. Like getting a double root canal.

What was he thinking? Was he thinking at all?

Sara squelched an almost uncontrollable urge to tell him what a turkey he was being. But what would that accomplish, besides making her feel a whole lot better? They'd end up in a big fight and he'd go off and have a romantic dinner with Christina.

"So." He seemed uncomfortable with her silence. "Where should we take her?"

How about down to the waterfront? We can push her off the dock . . .

"I was thinking about that French bistro," he went on. "I think she likes French food. Or she used to."

The French place? Not the French place! It was way too romantic.

"I'm in the mood for sushi myself," Sara said quickly. The pleasant, well-lit Japanese restaurant in the same neighborhood was ideal for a fast, no-frills meal.

"We'll see. Let me think about it."

Since Sara wasn't sure what time she would get back from Emily's house, they arranged to meet in Newburyport at seven. Sara finally hung up, feeling totally exhausted. How would she ever get through this? It was going to be pure torture.

But what were her alternatives? Begging off with a headache or some preposterous ailment and letting Luke take the woman out alone? No way. She was *chaperoning* this outing if it killed her.

While talking to Luke, Sara had slipped on her bathrobe. Now she stood in front of the mirror, combing out her wet hair. She needed a haircut; her split ends were terrible. And what should she wear tonight? Her good black pants were at the cleaners, and she hadn't bought anything new for the winter yet. All her sweaters and tops looked so last year.

She and Luke were at that comfortable stage in their relationship, after that point when you know the person so well, you don't fuss over your appearance anymore.

She winced at her reflection. Just when she thought the beauty pageant had ended, she was strolling down the runway again. And this time, the competition was serious.

Sara glanced at the clock and pulled on jeans and a cotton turtleneck. She could run over to the mall, look for a new outfit, and get her hair trimmed and blown out. She would have to put off her visit to the new baby. She honestly had mixed emotions about that outing, anyway, and was relieved to postpone it a day or so. When she explained the situation, she was sure Emily would understand.

As Sara tugged on her sneakers and set off for the mall, the wise words of Henry David Thoreau, her favorite New England philosopher, came to mind. "Beware of all enterprises that require new clothes."

Sara was wary of this outing. She was also determined to arrive in Newburyport looking jaw-droppingly fabulous.

"WOW, YOU LOOK GREAT." LUKE STARED WIDE EYED AT Sara, then leaned over and kissed her soundly. "What did you do to your hair?"

"I just had a trim," she said as he helped her off with her coat.

"That sweater looks great on you. Is it new?"

"Not at all. I've had it awhile," she fibbed. At least two or three hours.

She had wanted to grab his attention, but Luke's reaction made her feel as if she must look pretty ragged the rest of the time. Besides, she hadn't wanted Christina to think she had made any special effort. *By now she must be thinking I had a complete makeover*, Sara mused.

Luke politely pulled out a chair, and Sara took the seat next to him at the small table. He had decided on the French café and it was just as lovely as she remembered from their former dates, an elegant setting with French country decor, low lighting, and a romantic ambiance.

Christina sat on the other side of the table, opposite Luke. She wore a black cashmere sweater with a low, shawl collar that swooped across her neckline, revealing flawless skin and rounded shoulders. Her large topaz earrings complemented her golden hair and sun-kissed complexion. She looked tasteful, stylish, and quite sexy. *Is this what she usually packs for her research outings?* Sara wondered.

Maybe it was a good thing that I made such an effort with my appearance, Sara decided. *This is serious competition.*

"So how are you enjoying your visit, Christina?" Sara asked pleasantly. "Did you guys go out to the beach today?"

She had worked hard to come up with several neutral conversation openers. She even practiced them while getting dressed. She wanted to sound cool, confident, unruffled. That was Emily's advice. When Sara had called to explain her situation, Emily had been totally understanding, cheering Sara on like a coach in a boxer's corner.

Don't let her get under your skin, honey. Remember, you're with Luke. She's the guest. She's on your turf. You have the home-field advantage.

"We had a great afternoon. The shore is beautiful up here. We had a lot of fun, didn't we?" Christina glanced at Luke; a warm, intimate look, Sara thought.

"It was great. Too bad you couldn't join us, Sara," Luke said. "But I guess you were pretty busy with your hair."

Sara felt a jolt of embarrassment. He made it sound as if it had taken a team of stylists, working around the clock, for her to look this good.

"No, not at all." She struggled to change the subject. Next question. "How is your research going, Christina? What do you think of Cape Light?"

"It's going great. Luke's story is so compelling, so inspiring. I knew him way back when. I had no idea what he'd been through since then."

Now it was Luke's turn to look embarrassed and self-conscious. "Everybody faces challenges and hard times. My life isn't that different from anyone else's."

Sara was about to contradict him, offering an admiring comment about how he had not only faced his challenges courageously, but in finding his own way, found a way to help so many others.

Christina got there first. "He's so modest," she said with a warm smile. "He's put together this fantastic learning center that helps so many kids, and fought your entire town to do it."

My town? How is it my *town?* Sara wanted to blurt out. She had stood by Luke's side every step of that battle, even at the risk of her personal safety.

"It wasn't the entire town," Luke corrected Christina. "More like a small, very vocal group. You want to get your facts straight, right?"

"Sorry." Christina smiled at him. "I don't mean to exaggerate. It certainly isn't necessary for your story, Luke. It's already the most amazing one in the book. In fact, I think I might block it out and submit it as an article somewhere. It's great copy."

Luke looked embarrassed again, Sara thought. He also looked pleased with all the attention and compliments.

"There's the waiter. Maybe we should order," Sara suggested, picking up her menu.

Someone had to keep this dinner moving along. She wasn't sure how she was going to last through the meal. If she could just suffer through it, hopefully she would never have to see this woman again.

She felt her stomach churn as Christina turned to her with that brilliant smile. "So, Sara, you must tell me. What's it like working on a small-town paper?"

At some point during the main course, Sara gave up trying to be cool, confident, unruffled and settled for plain old quiet and boring.

Christina did most of the talking anyway, so no one seemed to notice. *She* wasn't at all boring, though, which was part of the problem. She had led an interesting life and had lively, funny stories about her adventures as a reporter in several major cities—New Orleans, Denver, and

Miami—before returning to Boston, where she was raised.

Christina seemed able to talk about any topic, from the Red Sox's chances of winning the World Series again this year to the hole in the ozone layer. She was widely published and had written several books of nonfiction that were well reviewed. Sara knew all this because she had researched her rival on the Internet.

While Sara knew she was bug eyed with jealousy, she was thoughtful enough to realize that it was partly because she admired Christina and her accomplishments.

If they had met under different circumstances, Sara thought, she might have even liked the other woman and sought her friendship. They had a lot in common. It wasn't surprising, when you considered it, that Luke had been attracted to both of them at different points in his life.

The question is, Sara realized, *which one of us is he attracted to now?*

"So I heard from Luke that your mother took temporary custody of the baby she found. That's a great story, especially since she's the town's mayor," Christina noted. "Do you think she would give me an interview? I thought it would make a great piece for the *Globe,* or even a magazine."

She wanted to squeeze a publishing credit out of Emily? Did the woman have no conscience? No sense of boundaries? Who did she think she was talking to?

Any sense of admiration or even toleration Sara had been musing about quickly evaporated.

"She can't give you a story. Sorry." Sara gave her rival a tight smile. "I've already started it, an exclusive."

That was an out-and-out lie. Sara had given a moment of vague thought to the idea then gotten distracted by her own conflicted feelings. But she had to take a page from Ace Reporter Christina Cross's handbook and go for the jugular.

"She's a public figure, fair game. Anyone can write

about her." Christina sounded perfectly cool and unruffled. "Let's see who can get it into print faster, okay?"

"I don't think so," Sara said, trying to laugh off the challenge.

"Why not? It will be fun. Like the *Iron Chef* cook-off. Two chefs, same ingredients. Ever see that show?"

"This is my mom we're talking about," Sara reminded her, "not some stranger."

"Look, I don't mean to step on your toes, but it's a little naive to think you have a patent on that idea just because Emily Warwick is your mother. We both might open the newspaper and see it in print tomorrow." Christina met Sara's infuriated glare with a bland smile, then glanced at Luke, as if sharing a joke at Sara's expense.

Sara knew that what Christina said was true, and that made her even madder. "Right, someone might be tapping it out as we speak, and we might both lose your little contest." She stood up abruptly and grabbed her bag. "Be right back."

Her voice was deadly calm. Even Luke noticed the ominous note. He stared up at her but she ignored him and stalked off towards the ladies' room. She faced the door, but didn't push it open.

Instead, Sara made a sharp turn toward the front of the restaurant. She retrieved her coat from the coat check, pulled it on, and walked out. Maybe leaving this way was a bit dramatic, but she knew that if she had to sit through another minute of Christina Cross, she couldn't be held responsible for her actions.

Outside the cold air cleared her head a bit. She walked with her hands jammed in her pockets and paced up and down the street, wondering if she should just leave or go back inside. She half expected Luke to come running out after her.

But he didn't.

She didn't want to go in again, she decided. *If I'm going to lose Luke to that woman this way, I never really had him to begin with.*

Feeling desperately sad and defeated, Sara trod down the hill to her car and started the drive back to Cape Light.

"GO AHEAD, GO AFTER HER. I'M SURE SHE DIDN'T GET too far." Christina took a sip of her water, gazing at Luke with her large, liquid brown eyes.

Luke had an impulse to get up and follow Sara, just as Christina advised. But for some reason, he remained in his seat, gazing across the table at the other woman. He was always chasing after Sara, it seemed. That was the story of their relationship. He didn't feel like it tonight. She would be all right, he told himself.

"I'm sorry . . . I think I upset her," Christina apologized. "It's all my fault."

Luke waved his hand at her. "It's not your fault. Sara can be sensitive about Emily, though. You had no way of knowing that."

"I should have realized. I need to watch what I say sometimes. I'm too honest. It scares people."

Luke smiled at the admission. Christina could be startlingly frank at times. That was one of the things he always liked about her. "So be honest," he said. "You were pouring on the compliments a little thick. If you think I'm such a natural wonder, why did you break up with me?"

Christina's smile widened. "Now the conversation is getting interesting. Want the real answer?"

"Yes," he nodded. "I do."

"I was young and stupid. Sure, you've changed a lot since you left the police force. But inside, you've always been the same. A sweet, smart, decent guy. I don't know what was wrong with me. I wasn't ready to settle down, I guess. I didn't appreciate you."

She wasn't ready. Where had he heard that before, Luke thought.

"Have you ever forgiven me for dumping you?"

"Sure I have." He laughed and shrugged. "I don't think it would have worked out anyway, for a lot of reasons. My head wasn't really together back then, either."

"You seem to have gotten it all together now," she said quietly. She traced a line on the tablecloth with her fingertip. "So here's confession number two. I did want to include you in this book when I came across your story. It's compelling, inspiring, all that stuff. But I could have interviewed you over the phone and with e-mail. I didn't have to come up here."

"I know that. I'm not that thick, Christina."

She smiled at him, her long bangs falling across her eyes. "I wanted to see you. I got to thinking about you, Luke. About the time we spent together. Guys like you aren't growing on trees back in Boston, you know."

He sat back. He didn't know how to react to that one. This woman really knew what she wanted and knew how to go after it. He wasn't used to this direct approach, not that he didn't like it.

"What about Sara?" she asked.

"What about her?"

"That looks pretty serious to me."

"It is," he said honestly. "We're having a rough time right now . . ."

"I sort of sensed that." Christina always had good insight and intuition about people. That was part of what made her a good reporter and a good writer. It wasn't hard for her to guess at the problems brewing between him and Sara.

"But we have a commitment," he said. "I'm not about to mess that up."

"I didn't think you would," she said quickly. She shrugged a smooth shoulder.

"You're terrific, Christina. You could get any guy you

want. What's so special about me?" He laughed, trying to make light of the charged moment.

"I told you. You are special. You don't realize it, though, and that's part of your charm."

Luke felt himself almost blush at her compliments.

Christina leaned toward him and her voice became softer, more intimate. "Listen, I respect your relationship with Sara. Honestly, she's a catch. But so much of life is timing, Luke. You have to meet someone on the same page, or else it just doesn't work. At least, that's what I've figured out."

Luke swallowed hard. He wanted to argue, to defend his relationship with Sara. But Christina had hit the nail right on the head.

"I think I'm on your page. That's all I'm trying to say." Christina paused, took a breath, and then met his gaze, the candlelight casting her face in a warm glow. "And maybe Sara just isn't there yet."

CHAPTER SEVEN

⌒

THE LIGHT SNOWFALL ON SUNDAY MORNING SLOWED
Emily and Dan down, but it didn't deter them altogether
from church. That morning would be their first time there
together with Jane. As they drove through the snow-
covered village, Emily realized she was feeling tired from
all the visitors the day before. They had come and gone
throughout the day, stopping by to see Jane and bring baby
gifts. First Betty, then Jessica. Next had been Molly and
Matthew Harding, her boyfriend, with their three girls all
together. "You have a stable of babysitters here, standing
by for your calls," Molly had teased her.

It was good to know. With the snowy weather that had
started yesterday, Emily was already feeling a bit house-
bound. It was good to get out, even if just to church and back.

As Dan carefully steered the car through the icy streets,
Emily knew that they'd be late.

They slipped into the sanctuary from a side door,

Emily carrying the baby. The service had already begun and Reverend Ben was making announcements about a Christmas Fair meeting and other church business. They walked in quietly and found a place in the rear row. Still, many heads turned and Emily saw the news fly through the congregation.

She spotted her sister, Sam, and their children sitting several rows ahead alongside her mother. Jessica turned and smiled at her. Finally, her mother's head turned toward her. Lillian passed a swift cool glance over Emily, as if they'd never been properly acquainted.

Emily held the baby a little closer and met her mother's grey gaze with a calm expression. She was sure Lillian had heard the news from Jessica by now—or from any number of people. Of course, her mother hadn't even bothered to call to wish her luck.

It hurt but it was no more—and no less—than she expected.

The service went by quickly. When it came time for the congregation to share their joys and concerns of the week, Emily was feeling self-conscious about announcing their news, though it was indeed a great joy to her. Reverend Ben cast her an expectant glance, but she couldn't do it. She glanced at Dan. He sat staring straight ahead, his hands folded in his lap over a hymnal. He wasn't going to do it, either, she realized.

Suddenly, Jessica stood and turned in their direction. "We have some happy news to share. My sister, Emily, and her husband, Dan, are temporary guardians of the baby Emily found outside the church about two weeks ago. Her name is Jane and she's just beautiful."

Now everyone felt free to turn and openly look at Dan and Emily. She sat and smiled, holding up the baby, who now slept in her arms.

"Congratulations, Emily," Reverend Ben said, and everyone smiled and clapped.

Everyone except her mother, who stared down at her prayer book in her lap and didn't even deign to glance Emily's way.

A short time later, when the service was over, Emily carefully made her way down the middle aisle and out of the sanctuary. It took awhile, though. People kept stopping her to admire the baby and wish them all good luck.

"What a yummy little thing," Sophie Potter said. "Look at those apple cheeks."

Emily had to smile at the compliment. Sophie, who had lived on an orchard her whole life, thought all babies had apple cheeks.

"I guess you won't have time this year to work on the Christmas Fair, Emily," Sophie went on.

Every year Emily volunteered for the fair and was usually stationed at the wreath and garland table with Jessica.

"I'll have to come as a customer this year, Sophie. Don't worry, I'll be sure to buy lots of things."

"Oh, don't be silly, dear. I'm not complaining. On the contrary, it's nice to see you with new priorities." Sophie gently patted her arm. "Now if you need any help with that baby, if you have any baby-sitting or questions about anything at all, you feel free to call on me. Maybe I can be her spare grandma. Most of my grandchildren live so far away, I don't have any little ones left to fuss over."

Emily was touched by the offer. Sophie would certainly know how to fuss over a baby. But *spare grandma* was not the term she'd use. Only *grandma* was more appropriate, considering what her own mother's interest was likely to be.

"I'm taking next week off," Emily said. "Maybe we'll take a ride out to the orchard and visit."

"That would be lovely, dear. You know me; I'm always there unless I'm over here at church. Drop in anytime."

Emily and Dan soon met with Reverend Ben, who stood by the doorway sharing a word or two with the congregants as they left the sanctuary. His smile beamed as he took in the baby. "My, my. Look at her. She looks so healthy and clean, maybe even bigger than when you found her?"

"She's a bit below average weight and height, they say," Emily noted. "I don't believe she grew at all in the hospital last week with that infection. But I think she'll catch up fast."

"She sounds like a mom already, doesn't she?" Dan remarked with an indulgent smile. He slipped his arm around Emily's shoulder.

Reverend Ben and Emily shared a private glance. He knew the worst and best of her, her torment over Sara and her joy at finding her daughter again. "Changing diapers doesn't make you a mother," he'd once told her. "Loving a child does, even at a great distance." He knew that she was already a mother and didn't have to tell her so.

"I was so pleased to hear that you and Dan had stepped in to be Jane's guardians," Ben told them. "How did all this come about?"

"I'm not exactly sure," Emily said honestly. "I went to visit her in the hospital a few times. And it evolved from there. I just feel so relieved having her with us. I was afraid of where she might end up, so I had to do something."

"I understand. Good for you, Emily. It's a big step. And you and Dan both look very happy."

Emily met his warm smile, then felt a bit guilty. She had never called Reverend Ben to tell him the news personally or even to consult him about the decision. Her minister had always been a close confidante, especially in the days when she had felt so troubled and weighed down by her feelings of loss over Sara.

She hadn't turned to Reverend Ben for counsel in a long time, she realized, not even over this question of taking temporary custody. Well, it had all happened so fast. She hadn't asked anyone's advice. She would have to let Reverend Ben know that his take on things was still important to her. She wanted him to baptize the baby. She would discuss it with it him soon, she decided, once things felt more settled.

The reverend looked down at Jane again and placed his hand gently on her forehead. "Let me give her a blessing," he said. "Dear Lord, please watch over this dear child, lend her the grace of Your divine love, and aid her foster parents in her care."

"Amen," Dan said solemnly.

Emily stood silently a moment gazing at Jane, who stared back at them wide eyed. She looked from Emily to Dan and suddenly seemed to smile, making little cooing sounds as she looked up at them and blew a giant spit bubble.

"Good job," Reverend Ben said to the gurgling baby. "That was a beauty."

Laughing, they all said good-bye. Dan and Emily moved on into the crowded sanctuary, where people were putting on coats, hats, and scarves, bundling up for the cold weather outside.

"Day two . . . drum roll," Sam said, coming up beside them. "How are you guys doing? Are you surviving the 'Invasion of the Baby?' "

"We're taking this one hour at a time," Dan replied. "So far, so good."

"Come on now, Dan," Emily said. "It's not such a big deal. Everything is basically the same—"

"Except that it's a lot more complicated," he finished for her. "Just take getting out of the house in the morning. The car seat, the baby bag, the pacifier we forgot to put in the baby bag . . . I thought we'd never get here."

"It's a different routine," Emily argued. "We'll get used to it."

"The question is not when or how, but why. Why on earth have you done such a thing? Taking in this child, from unknown origins besides?" Lillian stepped up beside them. "Have you lost all perspective? All common sense and reason?"

"Lillian, calm down. This is a temporary arrangement. We're interim guardians," Dan began to explain.

"Interim, my foot. I know how these things work. One thing leads to another. You're both too old for this. When the child is applying to college, you'll be checking out nursing homes."

"You don't seem to understand. We won't be raising her," Dan insisted. "We're trying to help out, to do a good deed."

"A good deed, indeed. You'd better not get sucked into raising her. She looks innocent enough now, surely. But this little baby will most likely grow up to have all kinds of problems, mentally, physically, emotionally. Bad genes, bad chromosomes—they used to call it bad blood in my day. Same difference. The mother was most likely a drug addict. Have you even given a thought to that reality?"

As if reacting to Lillian's insults, the baby suddenly started crying. Emily soothed her, rocking her in her arms. She wanted to take Jane away, but there seemed no place to go.

All she could do was turn her body to the side, shielding the baby from her mother's outburst.

Dan stepped forward and put himself between Emily and her mother. He rested his hand on Lillian's birdlike shoulder, towering over her.

"This isn't the time or the place, Lillian," he began in a firm tone. "You're upsetting Emily. I won't stand by and—"

Lillian shrugged off his touch. "As if either of you care what I think. She never did." Lillian raised her cane a few inches off the floor and pointed it at Emily. "She probably did this just to spite me. To shame me, more precisely."

Emily could only stare in disbelief. "Mother, this is not about you. How unbelievably . . . egocentric."

"Foolish girl, you're well on your way to fifty and you have so little insight into your own actions."

Reverend Ben suddenly came into view, obviously summoned by Sam. The two men walked quickly in their direction. Emily felt relieved at the sight. Even her mother would be mollified by the sight of her minister. Wouldn't she?

"Lillian . . ." Reverend Ben called to her from the other side, making her turn away from Emily to face him. "Would you care to go into my office for a visit? We could talk over your feelings about Emily and Dan taking in this baby. Maybe your daughter and son-in-law would like to come and explain their side of it to you."

Lillian stood up ramrod straight, her head tilted back as she peered at Reverend Ben through half-closed eyes. "I have neither the time nor the interest for such touchy-feely nonsense. I know why she did this. It's perfectly clear to me. As for my views, there's no secret about how I feel, Reverend. It seems to me my entire family has lost all common sense, all judgment. . . ."

She was going off on another diatribe, Emily feared, keenly aware of the other parishioners staring at them.

Jessica rushed up beside her mother and held out her coat, like a bullfighter waving a cape at the charging beast. She spoke in a hushed, embarrassed tone. "Mother, I have your coat. Put this on. We're taking you home."

Lillian stared at Jessica defiantly a moment, then straight at Emily. Finally, she held out one arm and allowed her younger daughter to help her put on the coat.

"I'm just an old woman. Nobody listens to me. What does it matter what I say?" she muttered as Jessica took her arm and led her out of the church. Sam followed, carrying Tyler and leading Darrell by the hand.

"Emily, I'm so sorry." Dan leaned forward and hugged her, gently enfolding the baby as well. "I didn't know what to do. I didn't know how to stop her."

She rested her hand on his arm. "I know you tried. I expected something like that, just not here. I thought she'd wait until we were somewhere private."

Dan sighed. "Well, at least we got it over with."

Emily stared at him, feeling she might laugh out loud. "You've known my mother all these years and really think that's the end of it?"

Dan's expression changed to one of amusement. "You've got a point, as always."

She forced a small smile in answer but could tell he knew she felt shaken by the encounter. He reached out and touched her shoulder. "Let's go home now."

"Yes," she said. "Let's."

REVEREND BEN WATCHED DAN AND EMILY LEAVE, feeling he should go after them but at the same time at a loss for words. He knew he shouldn't have been shocked by Lillian Warwick's outburst. It had been as easy to predict as snow in the wintertime around here. Still, the contempt and anger behind the cold, stinging words had dismayed him. This was a woman who rarely missed a Sunday service, who listened intently to his sermons each week, a woman who most likely considered herself a "good Christian."

And no matter what one might say about Lillian, Ben felt that the deeper failing lay not with her, but with him. He'd failed her as a minister. All these years, he'd failed to reach her, to touch her heart. He'd failed to even coax her into his office for some counsel.

Ben sighed and turned toward the sanctuary. It stood empty now, though the space seemed to echo with Lillian's harsh words and his own feelings of futility.

ON MONDAY MORNING EMILY FOUND FAT WHITE FLAKES that looked like feathers falling from the low grey sky. She didn't mind at all. She wasn't going to work and was in no hurry to start the day. Still wearing her bathrobe and nightgown, she sat by the kitchen window with Jane and showed her the snow.

Dan was getting ready to leave the house, driving up to Boston for the day to work in a research library. He'd made special arrangements to examine some historic documents and didn't want to miss the appointment despite the weather.

Emily wished he would skip the trip and stay home with her and the baby. She was worried about him driving all that way in the bad weather and also felt a bit apprehensive about being alone all day for the first time with Jane. She struggled not to show it, though, and kept up a calm front. She didn't want Dan to think they'd made a mistake, that she couldn't handle the baby.

"So I'm off," he said, taking a last sip of coffee. He wore his down jacket, a Red Sox baseball hat, and a scarf and gloves.

"I'll keep my cell phone on, in case you need to call me," he promised. "I'm not sure about the reception in the library, though. It might not get the signal."

"I won't need to call," she assured him. "I can handle the baby."

"I know that. I just mean, if there's an emergency."

"Well, you'll be too far away to do anything if there is one." She held Jane to her shoulder as she glanced out the window. "Honestly, I don't know why you have to go all the way to Boston in this weather. Can't you do it another day?"

"I really have to go," he insisted. "I checked the reports. It looks bad here, but it's fine on the interstate. And there isn't much snow toward the city."

She couldn't persuade him to stay, she realized, so she gave up. "All right. Drive safely."

"I'll be fine. Don't worry. I might be late, though." He leaned over and kissed her. He gazed at the baby a moment, but didn't kiss her, too, Emily noticed. He walked out the back door in the kitchen. "I'll call you later," he promised.

"We'll be here." Emily held up Jane's hand to wave good-bye. It was silly, she knew, but she couldn't help it.

The baby's infant seat was set up on the kitchen table and Emily strapped her in. Then she sat at the table and started to eat the bowl of cereal she seemed to have poured for herself hours ago. It was soggy and the milk was warm. She thought about tossing it out and starting over, then decided to just finish it. Who knew when she would get another chance?

With one eye on Jane, she began to skim that morning's headlines. She had scanned the first page of the news when Jane began fussing. Emily put everything down and picked her up again.

She checked the baby's diaper. Wet again. She took her into the bedroom for a change. Dan hadn't made the bed. She would do it later, she decided.

She changed Jane's diaper, then changed her onesie, too, which had also gotten wet. The baby's clothes drawer was ominously empty, and Emily saw that Jane's laundry had mounded up, overflowing the basket. In two short days? Babies sure went through clothing, she realized. She would have to do wash later.

Jane was still fussing, so Emily sang to her and talked to her, then waved around a few toys, seeing if any of them would interest her. No, not a bit. Emily checked her list. It was close enough to feeding time. Maybe that was it. She was hungry again.

She took a bottle out of the fridge and heated it in some water on the stove. She needed to make more bottles; there was only one left. She had to sterilize the bottles first, though, she remembered. She had a list for that somewhere that she had copied from one of Jessica's baby books. When Jane took her long nap later, she would take care of everything, Emily decided. For goodness sake, she ran an entire town. She could manage a little baby.

Then the phone rang. It was a man Dan had interviewed for his book, asking if Dan had received the deeds he faxed over; his machine indicated a problem. Emily's eyes widened as she realized he was talking about old deeds that Dan had been searching for for months. "Just a minute," she told the caller. Still holding the baby, Emily rushed up to Dan's office, saw that the fax machine's paper feed was jammed, and managed to clear it while Jane lay in Dan's big armchair, protesting the fact that she was being ignored.

Ten minutes later, back in the kitchen, Emily realized that she had left Jane's bottle in the water too long and that it had gotten too hot. Jane was crying in earnest now, she was so hungry. Emily felt bad for her. She ran the bottle under cold water, but it was taking a long while for the formula to cool down again.

This can't be all that complicated, Emily told herself. She just had to figure out the right timing for heating formula.

Finally, she had the bottle at the proper temperature and gave it to Jane. Silence was truly golden, she thought. And Jane looked so cute drinking her formula, Emily forgave her instantly for all the raucous crying.

The phone rang again. This time Emily decided to let the machine pick up. She wasn't about to disturb Jane while she was happily eating.

"Ms. Warwick, this is Carla Nickerson. I was supposed to stop by your place this morning to talk about that babysitting job? Well, all the snow has put me off. I don't drive in the bad weather. I'll call you back and maybe I can come some other day, okay?"

Carla Nickerson, Emily thought. That was too bad. She had such good references, recommended by a friend of Jessica. Emily was practically counting on the lady working out, desperately hoping she wouldn't have to go through a long search for a babysitter.

But it was definitely a problem if Carla didn't drive in bad weather. There was nothing *but* bad weather in the winter, and the other seasons weren't that reliable either. Carla would be missing work every other day.

"So you won't be interviewing Carla Nickerson today," Emily said, acting as if she were Jane's private secretary. "Let me check the rest of your schedule, dearest girl. We have a feeding, a bath, a nap, another bottle. Another diaper, I suspect. Some playtime on the baby mat—build up those muscles?" Emily tickled the baby's bare foot and watched it curl.

The phone rang again and this time Emily answered it.

"Mayor Warwick?"

"Yes?" she said, switching quickly to her dignified, official voice.

"It's Ralph Clancy, from the Public Works Department. I'm calling about those documents from the government, the grant the town was awarded. You need to sign those papers, Mayor. They have to be returned to Washington today."

"Oh, yes. I completely forgot. It's been a busy weekend . . ." Everyone in town seemed to know that she and Dan had picked up the baby on Saturday. Ralph Clancy, however, didn't reply.

"The papers are sitting right on my desk," she told him.

"Well, can you come in a minute and sign them? It's important."

"That would be . . . difficult right now." The baby had fallen asleep on her lap. It wasn't her nap time, Emily thought with a quiet panic. What now? Was she supposed to let her sleep or keep her awake awhile?

Could she take her out in the snow? That didn't seem wise. Emily glanced out the window. It was still snowing, and Dan had taken her Jeep because it had four-wheel drive. She only had Dan's little compact, which she didn't trust in the snow, even for the short distance to Village Hall. "Can you have someone bring them over? I'll sign them and they can bring them right back."

"I suppose so. Wait, you need to be witnessed by a notary. I'll have to find one who'll come." He sounded annoyed at her now, but it couldn't be helped. She had expected to go in to her office for a few hours on Saturday; then the call about Jane came, and she had dropped everything.

"I'll see what I can do, Mayor. I'll call you back," he said curtly.

"Yes, please do," she said and hung up the phone.

She suddenly realized she was still in her bathrobe. She really should shower and dress before someone from Village Hall showed up. But what to do with Jane? Put her in her crib? Or maybe her infant seat, just outside the bathroom door?

They never mentioned this kind of dilemma in the child-care books, she realized.

Emily put the baby in her infant seat again, and Jane started to cry. Emily knew she wasn't wet or hungry, so she had to assume she just wanted to be held. Sure enough, the moment she lifted the baby into her arms, the crying stopped. But how could she get anything done around the house if she had to hold Jane all day?

She didn't want Jane to be upset, so she decided to put off the shower until the baby slept. Resting the baby against one shoulder, Emily walked through the house, trying to get a few chores done. She hauled the laundry basket one-handed into the laundry room, then filled the washer with Jane's clothes and started up the water.

But there was no soap. Now what was she going to do? Jane didn't have that many outfits yet. If she dirtied this one, which was only a matter of time, she would be down to a diaper and an undershirt.

"We can't go shopping, so I guess I'll have to rinse out a few things by hand," she told the baby.

She fished out some necessary items and took them to the kitchen sink. Still balancing the baby on her hip, she hand washed the clothes with some dishwashing liquid, wrung them out, and tossed them in the dryer. They would likely take all day to dry, considering that she wasn't able to squeeze that much water out. But what could she do? She had all day to wait, she realized.

It was only nine thirty. Emily felt as if she had been up for hours, but nothing around the house was done. The breakfast dishes were still on the table, the living room was littered with newspapers, and the bed upstairs was still unmade.

The phone rang again, and a familiar voice said, "Hi, honey, how's it going?"

Emily felt a surge of happiness go through her. Had he decided to turn around and come home? She hoped so.

"Fine, it's going fine," Emily told her husband. "Everything's great. How are you doing? How are the roads?"

"The roads are clear as soon you leave our area. No problem at all," he said in an annoyingly cheery tone. "I'm making good time."

"Oh. That's good."

"Listen, I'm sorry, but it looks like I took the car seat by accident. I didn't even notice it. You weren't planning on going out today, right?"

"Well, if I was, I can't now, can I? Unless I take her out in her stroller."

"The snow is too high for a stroller. You won't be able to roll it. You'll get stuck, Emily."

"Oh, of course." She hadn't been planning on leaving the house, but now that she couldn't, she felt caught. Trapped, actually. "When will you be back?"

"I don't know. Depends on how my appointments go. I'll call you later, when I have a better idea."

"All right. I'll be here."

"Sure you're okay? Is the baby doing all right?"

"Oh sure. She's just fine. She wants me to hold her all the time, though."

Dan seemed to think that was sweet. He didn't understand the implications. "Well, you enjoy your time with her. You'll be back in the office soon enough."

Yes, she would be, Emily realized. She considered the comment with mixed emotions.

They both hung up, and she tried to settle Jane in her infant seat for what seemed the umpteenth time. This time, however, she set the seat near a mobile so Jane would have something distracting to grab at. The mobile did the trick, and Emily actually managed to clear the table, get the dirty dishes into the dishwasher, and clean out the sink. Jane seemed content to sit in the infant seat, with an occasional bounce from Emily as she passed to and fro.

Emboldened by this success, Emily decided she would tackle the bottle situation. She gathered up all the empties and filled a big pot of water to sterilize them. She knew she could be using disposable plastic bottle liners, but Jessica had insisted that the plastic was bad for babies—too many chemicals leaching into the formula. You certainly didn't want that.

Jessica had turned out to be a bit extreme in her precautions, Emily thought, making her own baby food for Tyler from strictly organic, unprocessed foods. Well, that was very healthy, Emily was sure, but it certainly took time. She wasn't sure she would have either the time or the motivation to make organic baby food.

Jane was still so young. The only solid food she ate now was a little cereal, so it wasn't really a question. Yet.

Emily glanced in the cupboard, searching for more cans of Jane's formula. She didn't see any and felt slightly panicked. Dan had probably put them in some other closet. She pulled open one door after another, searched above and below, behind boxes and cans that hadn't been moved for years. Still no formula.

Now she felt really panicked. What would Jane eat all day? She only had one bottle left that the baby would take in a short time. Dan wouldn't be home until late tonight, and she had no car seat to go out to the store. She would have to find a place that delivered.

The idea almost made her laugh. None of the markets or drugstores delivered in Cape Light. More likely, she needed to call someone to help her. Emily wasn't used to calling on anyone for help, even friends. She was used to being the one people in trouble called up to help them.

The pot of bottles bubbled and boiled away. Emily wasn't sure how long it took for them to be officially steril- ized. She found one of Jessica's baby books in the living room, one with yellow Post-its on critical pages, but couldn't find the page she marked about bottle boiling.

She smelled something funny and rushed back into the kitchen. The water boiling in the smaller pot that held rub- ber nipples and bottle caps had all but boiled away. The nip- ples were scorching and melting at the bottom of the pot!

Oh . . . bother! Emily grabbed the pot, nearly burning her hand, and tossed it in the sink, then ran cold water over the mess. A huge mushroom cloud of steam erupted in her kitchen.

Startled by all the excitement, the baby started wailing. Emily ran over and picked her up. She had nearly forgotten poor little Jane was sitting there all this time.

"Oh, sweetie pie. Don't worry. It's nothing . . ." Emily ran into the next room to escape from the smell in the kitchen.

Now what would she do about nipples? She hoped she hadn't ruined all of them. Nipples, formula, and she still needed laundry detergent. And if she didn't sign those fed- eral documents today the village might miss out on the funds for road repair.

Jane continued crying fiercely as Emily cooed and soothed, waltzing around the living room. She hoped the baby hadn't breathed in too much of that awful smell in the kitchen. Could it have hurt her? Emily bit her lip. One lit- tle baby seemed to generate at least a hundred new worries.

The sound of the ringing phone penetrated her thoughts and Emily ran to answer it, shifting the crying baby to one hip, away from the receiver. It was hard to hear who was on the other end over the sound of Jane and the water still running in the kitchen.

"Yes? Who is it?" Emily called out over the noise.

"Emily? It's me, Sara. Can you hear me?"

"Sara! Where are you?" Emily felt instant relief at the sound of her daughter's voice.

"I'm on my cell, driving back to the village from a meeting in Peabody. I wondered if I could swing by and see the—"

"Come right over! That would be great. I'll make you lunch. Listen, could you pick up a few things for me on the way? Dan took my car this morning and forgot to leave the car seat and I'm sort of stuck here."

"No problem. What do you need?"

Emily gave Sara a quick list, talking over the crying baby. Simultaneously, she ran back into the kitchen and shut off the running water, but realized she'd now left the bottles to boil too long. She shut off the stove and pushed the pot back on another burner.

This baby business wasn't as simple as it looked, not by a long shot. Thank goodness Sara was coming over. Her call felt like a gift from above.

"Thanks," Emily said quietly, looking heavenward. "Looks like I need all the help I can get around here today."

Sara arrived a short time later. By then Emily had managed to put Jane on the bed for a few minutes while she changed into real clothes, foregoing a shower. When the doorbell rang, she picked up the baby and ran through the house to answer it. She gently placed Jane on her play mat, then quickly passed through the living room, realizing the place was still a total mess. She had had no chance to pick up. She never entertained company this way but, as they say, a baby changes things.

Sara walked in holding the grocery bags and a gift box wrapped with pink paper and a big bow.

Emily hugged her and took the bags. "I'm so glad you

called. I was having a rough morning. You really rescued me."

"Good timing then. I've been dying to see the baby. Where is she?"

"Right over here on her play mat." Emily led the way to Jane, who was set up on the floor surrounded by baby toys.

"Oh, she's adorable!" Sara walked over and sat down on the floor beside the baby. "Hello, Jane!" Sara picked up a plush toy lamb and waved it in Jane's direction. The baby gurgled and kicked her feet, grabbing at it. "Oh my, you're so cute. Can I take you to work with me?"

"Would you? I mean, just for an hour or two?" Emily laughed at her desperate admission.

Sara looked up at her. "You don't really mean that?"

"No, of course not. But this baby care hasn't been as easy as I thought. It's not the baby. It's all the routines and equipment. I can't believe we ran out of formula. I feel like such an airhead. But we used it up much quicker than I thought over the weekend. I just didn't realize."

Sara picked up the baby and held her in her lap. "It's all new," she reminded her mother. "You never did all this before."

"No." Emily's voice was barely audible. "No, I didn't." She smoothed her hands over her jeans and stood up. "Want some lunch? I can heat up some soup and make you a sandwich."

"Sounds good, but don't go to any trouble."

"No trouble. Why don't you bring Jane into the kitchen?"

"Sure." Sara got up with the baby and followed Emily. Though the kitchen looked like a war zone, Emily found a can of soup and a clean pot and started the soup. She took out a cutting board and bread for the sandwiches, but Jane started whimpering and squirming in Sara's arms.

"Maybe she wants you," Sara said, holding up the baby. "I can fix us lunch."

Emily took Jane and gave her daughter a rueful, apologetic glance. "I didn't invite you here so you could do my shopping and make me lunch, you know."

Sara laughed. "I don't mind helping out. It's no big deal."

Emily knew that logically it wasn't. Still, it felt odd to be reversing roles with Sara like this. Sara didn't seem to mind, yet Emily sensed a certain disquiet in her daughter's demeanor. Did she feel displaced by the baby? It was possible. Emily thought she and Sara should talk about things, but this didn't seem the right time.

Sara set out the bowls of soup and sandwiches for each of them and then sat at the table across from Emily, who held Jane in her lap, feeding her a bottle.

"So what's new with you and Luke? Did that old flame of his finally leave town?"

Sara rolled her eyes. "I don't know and I don't care. Well, I do care," she admitted. "But everything is such a mess now with Luke and me. We all went out together on Saturday night and it was just awful."

Emily felt alarmed at Sara's tone. She could see Sara trying to speak reasonably but quickly melting down, her eyes on the verge of tears.

"Oh, honey . . ." Emily wanted to get up and give her a hug, then realized she had Jane in her lap, firmly attached to her bottle. "What happened, exactly?"

Sara nodded bleakly and wiped her eyes on a paper napkin. "It went all right at first and then that woman went too far. She was pushing my buttons all night, and I finally just lost it. I got up to take a break in the ladies' room and I just kept going."

"You walked out on them?" The baby squirmed and Emily lifted her up to her shoulder, patting her for a burp.

"I couldn't help it. I was so mad, I didn't know what to do. It wasn't just Christina. She was just being her fabulous, condescending self. I was so mad at Luke for putting us together like that. I think he wanted to sit back and watch two women fight over him or something. It was really twisted."

Jane began whimpering and wiggling on Emily's shoulder. Emily tried to set her upright in her lap and pat her lower back, but the baby wasn't having any of it.

"Don't think the worst, Sara. Luke isn't like that. Maybe he just didn't realize."

"He knew," Sara insisted. She waited, watching Jane. Emily could tell she wanted to say more. She really needed to talk to someone about this but now felt short-circuited by the baby's fussing.

Emily stood up and paced around the small kitchen with the baby, who was now whimpering fitfully. She couldn't figure it out. Maybe Jane ate her food too quickly and had a gas bubble. The pediatric nurse said that could be painful. If only babies could talk and tell you what was going on. Meanwhile, she had a grown daughter sitting here who wanted to tell her what was wrong, and she could barely give her three minutes of attention. Emily suddenly felt stretched like a rubber band between Sara's needs and those of the baby.

"Have you and Luke talked at all? Did he call you?"

Sara nodded. "He called yesterday. I wasn't home. I haven't called him back yet. I just didn't feel ready to talk." She glanced at the baby, raising her voice to talk over Jane's sharp, fitful cries. "I guess I might see him tonight. I tutor at the center, so I might run into him, but I'm not going out of my way . . ." Sara suddenly looked up at Emily, as if wondering if her mother heard her at all.

"I'm listening," Emily insisted. "Go on."

"It's all right. We don't have to talk about this right now. Why don't you just take care of the baby?"

Emily didn't answer for a moment, feeling torn in two. The baby squalled and she had no choice but to focus on her. "I'm going to take her into the bedroom. Maybe she needs to be changed or something. Wait right here. Finish your lunch," she said.

Emily took Jane into the bedroom and changed her diaper. She should have realized that was the problem. After she did, the baby still fussed a bit but more or less stopped crying. Emily carried her back to the kitchen where Sara had finished her lunch and now read the newspaper.

Sara looked up and offered a thin smile. "Is she feeling better now?"

"Just a dirty diaper . . . duh. I'll catch on sooner or later. There really aren't that many choices."

Sara laughed. "It's pretty simple at that stage."

"Just let me finish giving her this bottle and then she'll go down for a nap. We'll be able to talk. She's just tired. That's why she's so cranky. She's really not like this normally. She has a beautiful temperament. Even the nurses at the hospital thought so. One of them said—" Emily cut herself off as she realized she was going on about the baby.

Sara nodded encouragingly, but there was something else in her expression, something at odds with her mild smile. "I'm sorry, Emily. I can't stay. I have to get back to work."

"I wish you didn't have to go."

"Call me if you need anything else, okay?"

"I'll be fine. Dan can stop for me."

Sara leaned over and kissed her good-bye and then lightly kissed Jane on the forehead. "I'll come by and visit again soon," she promised.

"I'm sorry we got sidetracked. I'll call you tonight and we can catch up some more."

Sara nodded. "Sure. Don't get up. I'll let myself out."

Sara waved good-bye and moments later Emily heard her go out the front door. She sighed and sat back in her chair, watching the baby finish her bottle.

"I'll call her later, when you go to bed, young lady," Emily told the baby. She looked up and noticed the pink gift box on the table. She hadn't even opened Sara's gift to the baby. She hoped Sara's feelings weren't hurt by that slight, too.

Emily felt sad. She'd disappointed Sara, failed to be there at a moment when her daughter needed her. But she didn't know what to do. She hadn't anticipated this.

She would make it up to Sara somehow.

CHAPTER EIGHT

❧

REVEREND WALTER BOYD JONES WAS A RETIRED
minister of the same denomination as Ben. He lived in the
small town of Princeton, just northwest of Cape Light. It
was an easy drive up to Princeton on Monday afternoon,
when Ben usually took a few hours to visit members of the
congregation who were in nursing homes or the hospital.
Today he took the time to visit Reverend Jones, to minister
to himself a bit.

The older minister had been a great support years ago
when Ben was just starting out in Cape Light with his first
congregation and Reverend Walter was leading a large,
thriving congregation in Princeton. *Time passes so quickly*,
Ben thought as he drove down the reverend's street and
picked out the small saltbox-style colonial that dated back
to the late 1700s.

The Reverend Walter's wife had died a few years ago
and he now lived alone. He had been pleased to hear from

Ben and eager to meet. Ben realized that he had neglected his old friend lately; he really should be more attentive to him, not just calling when he needed advice or help. That wasn't being a very good friend. Though it was very much the way many people related to God, he reflected, calling only when they had a problem.

Reverend Walter greeted him at the door and led Ben into the small living room, which was lined with bookshelves and filled with old, comfortable-looking furniture. A small dog was curled on one armchair, an old tabby cat on another. A fire glowed in the hearth beneath a mantel covered with framed photos.

Reverend Walter was a short, stocky man, bald on top with a fringe of white fuzzy hair. He wore an old grey cardigan, leather slippers, and black pants that appeared to be left over from his clergy days, though Ben didn't think that could be possible.

Walter took Ben's coat and brought him some coffee. He settled back in a wing-backed armchair while Ben made himself comfortable on the couch.

"Thank you for seeing me, Walter. I hardly know where to start."

"It's hard to talk about these things. Ministers are expected to be superhuman. It's hard to admit we have problems and setbacks and flaws just like everyone else. We can forgive and accept all types of human frailties except our own."

"True enough. I also feel so . . . disloyal to my congregation, admitting how I really feel lately."

"Which is?"

Ben looked up at him. "Unmotivated. Uninspired. Distant, as if it's all happening on a stage far away, and I'm just going through the motions. The same old events, the same old sermons, more or less. I have nothing new to say to them, nothing new to offer. And they have nothing new to offer me, which is perhaps not only irrelevant to our work but also unfair."

Walter listened to him thoughtfully, then said, "Let's not worry about being fair or unfair right now, Ben. Just tell me what's in your heart and in your soul. I'm not here to judge. I want to help."

Ben knew that was true. "Maybe I've gotten too comfortable, Walter, too complacent. I've thought and prayed a lot about this lately. Maybe God has set this as a challenge for me. And if that's the case, I don't think I'm meeting it very well."

"Is this a crisis of faith, Ben? Questions are only natural, you know. They're actually essential. There is no real faith without questions."

"It's not my faith in God that's been shaken, Walter. It's my faith in myself, to carry out His work, to energize my congregation with His word and His spirit with my own example."

"I see."

"Everywhere I turn lately, I feel frustrated, blocked. I'm starting to wonder if God is trying to send me a message. Maybe my time in Cape Light is drawing to a close. Maybe I am being called to move on, to serve someplace new, in some new capacity."

He watched Walter's expression carefully. His friend frowned, considering the idea. "I suppose that's possible. But we need to be very careful about how we interpret messages from above."

Ben heard the echo of his own advice to Emily Warwick. "Indeed. I'm only saying it's a possibility. Do you remember that young missionary who was at my church last year?"

Walter nodded. "Yes, I do. He's gone back to mission work, you say?"

"Yes, I got a letter from him about two weeks ago. He's

out in Wyoming on a reservation. He took his new wife and their baby along, too. Nothing holds James back. He's always got a goal for the greater good.

"That letter from him seemed almost like a sign to me, a sign that I should at least start asking myself, what are my larger goals?" Ben stared at his friend, knowing full well that he was posing questions Walter couldn't answer. "I mean, aside from delivering a spiritual message each week in my sermon and serving the congregation when there's sickness or a death or other hardships."

"Aren't those all important and meaningful ways of serving them, Ben?"

"Yes, of course. I didn't mean to say that they weren't. But after so many years, I wonder what it all adds up to. Is this place changed in any way, improved in any way, after I've passed through?"

Walter rose and stirred the fire with a metal poker. Sparks danced and orange-yellow flames shot up from the heart of the fire and licked the white-hot logs.

"What about Joe Tulley, your church steward? He was a lost man, Ben, a homeless man with no hope. You saved his life.

"I didn't save his life, Walter. I just helped him get back on his feet."

"You reunited him with his brother; you gave him a job. You believed in him when everyone else was accusing him of being a thief. Even when he ran away to Portland, you were the only one he trusted enough to contact."

Ben nodded. "I'll chase after the wandering sheep whenever possible, but that's part of the job description, too, Walter. And a man like Joe is really the exception. Most of the congregants I counsel have more ordinary problems."

"Not enough challenges for you, is that what you're saying?"

"I suppose. Mostly I've been wondering: Am I even really helping them anymore? Am I giving my best to the congregation, or would they be better served by a new pastor—someone who can see them with a fresh perspective, wake them up on Sunday morning with a new voice?"

"Do they need waking up, Ben?"

"Yes, I think so," Ben said honestly. "So, in a way, that seems my failure or shortcoming. They're a generally kind, good-hearted group. People are willing to help each other out when there's a need, most of the time. But I feel so ineffectual lately. I've been trying to interest them in doing some outreach in a poor neighborhood in our village, Wood's Hollow—"

"Yes, I know the place." Walter nodded.

"A few families from the area have come to church lately. I thought it would be good for our congregation to get more involved there, lend some support. I tried to start with something simple, a coat drive." Ben shook his head. "I can't even get one congregant committed. They're all too busy now, baking cookies and making birdhouses for the Christmas Fair."

He swallowed hard—swallowing back his anger, he realized.

Walter glanced at him. "What did you do? Did you read them the riot act, like Moses scolding the Israelites?"

Ben laughed. "Hardly. Don't get me wrong. They're all good people," he added quickly. "There's genuine fellowship and goodwill. But are they really spiritually committed? Is there any real difference between the church gatherings and the gatherings at the boat club down the street from us?"

Walter laughed at the comparison. "I know what you mean. I often wondered the same thing. But we can't lose sight of the big picture, Ben, our higher role. You make it sound as if we're recreation directors on a cruise ship."

"Sometimes that's how I feel."

"Well, that's honest." Walter stared into the fire. "Did you ever read Dante's *Inferno*?" he asked. Ben nodded. Of course he had; it was required reading for divinity students. "Maybe you're just reaching the dark wood of middle age, Ben. It can be a frightening place."

"Yes, it is, and that might be part of the problem."

"Maybe these issues have existed in your church for a while, but you're just now noticing them. You've come to a certain point in your career as a minister when it's normal to ask, 'Is that all there is? What's next? Is there more?' "

Ben pondered that. He did feel as if he had reached a spiritual crossroads. "I think you're right. But what *is* next? Do I pick up and plow on, or is it time for something different?"

"I'm not saying I agree with your message-from-above theory, but maybe a change of scene would do you good. A sabbatical—you must be long eligible for one. Consider your options. You could get involved in a mission opportunity that will really renew you spiritually and give you something to take back to your congregation when the time comes. Sounds to me as if you need renewal, Ben. You need to have your spirit recharged. Some hard work, digging wells, building a school—some hands-on service you can step back from and take pride in. That might be just the cure."

Ben shook his head. "I thought of that, a temporary assignment someplace. I even tried to bring it up with Carolyn, but she doesn't want to budge. She thinks we should take a vacation to Florida." It was hard to keep the dry, sarcastic tone from his voice.

"Have you really talked to her about it? Maybe she doesn't understand what it means to you, what you're going through."

"Maybe not. We talked more the other night, when I thought of coming to see you. I think she's starting to see that I need more than a vacation. But how can I expect her to understand what's going on with me when I don't know myself?"

"You're working on it. You're not just brushing it under the rug. That's important. Talk more with Carolyn," Walter urged him. "Ask God to grant her greater understanding. And continue your own prayers. Maybe some insight will come to you. I'll be praying for you, too."

"Thank you, Walter. And thanks for seeing me today, for hearing me out."

"No need for thanks. I hope it's helped."

"It has," Ben said. "It's helped me a lot."

Though he still didn't see a clear solution, he felt the relief that comes from unburdening oneself of honest feelings. And he trusted Walter's advice. As his friend had reminded him, he needed to have more faith, to show greater trust in God.

Maybe he was in the dark wood of middle age and had to take some drastic steps to find his way to the other side. With the Lord's help, he would find his way.

"Roxanne's knees shook under her desk. Mrs. *Newton was going to call on her next. She just knew it. She stared down at her math workbook, wishing she was in . . . vi . . ."*

Sara's student, Shania Watson, looked up from her paperback as she stumbled over the word. Sara suddenly snapped to attention.

"Try to sound it out, Shania. You can do it."

Her expression doubtful, Shania looked back at the book. "In . . . vi . . . zi . . . ball? Invisible!" she said.

"Very good." Sara nodded. "Keep going."

Looking proud and pleased, Shania continued. Sara tried hard to focus, but her eyes kept moving to the big clock on the wall of the New Horizons study center. Only five minutes to go, and then she could run to her car and go home, hopefully avoiding an encounter with Luke.

She still didn't feel ready to see Luke or talk about what

had happened on Saturday night. That is, talk to him reasonably, without losing control.

But she couldn't disappoint Shania. That was part of the program, showing these kids that adults could be consistent and counted on, building trust.

Sara had always trusted Luke, but now she wasn't so sure. Maybe her disappearing act at the French restaurant had pushed him right into Christina's arms.

"*. . . Roxanne had to sit with Zachary Oster, who was always tapping away on a big cal . . . kool . . .*"

"I know it's a tough one," Sara said quickly. "Let's break it down by syllables."

With a few prompts from Sara, Shania finally said, "Cal-cu-la-tor."

"Good job. That was a hard word. Why don't you read to the end of that page and then we'll be done."

"Okay." Shania took a breath and started again.

As she listened to Shania reading, Sara heard the sound of singing coming from some other part of the building. She felt a little melancholy, recognizing the tune of "Deck the Halls." She always went out caroling with Luke and the students. This year, he hadn't even called to let her know they were practicing. She wondered if he was part of the group, merrily singing along, not giving her a thought at all.

"*. . . Roxanne walked toward the bus. Something gooey made her sneakers stick to the ground, but she didn't care. It had been a terrible day and she could not wait to get home.*"

Boy, can I ever relate to that, Sara thought. She smiled at Shania. "Sounds good. Why don't we stop there for tonight? You worked very hard. I'm proud of you."

Shania glowed but seemed partly embarrassed by Sara's praise. "Are you coming back next week?"

"I wouldn't miss it," Sara promised.

She walked Shania to her dorm and then turned down a path to the parking lot. She was just about to congratulate herself on escaping without meeting up with Luke when she saw his SUV pull into the lot. He got out, carrying bags of groceries.

Nice. He knows I'm here tonight so he runs out and goes grocery shopping. What does that tell you?

She stood by her car, her arms crossed over her chest, and waited for him to walk up to her.

"So you had your tutoring tonight. How did it go?"

"Fine."

"I had to go into town this afternoon. I'm glad I didn't miss you." When Sara didn't say anything, he added, "I think we should talk."

"About Christina, you mean?"

"About everything. Want to come back to my cottage?"

Sara considered the offer for a moment. "No, I have to get home. I have work to do."

"Okay. We'll talk right here then."

Sara shrugged. "Do you want to get back together with Christina? Because if you do, that's fine. I just want to know."

Luke pulled back as if slapped across the face. "Wow. You get to the point, don't you?"

"Just answer, yes or no."

"No. I don't want to date Christina. I'm dating you. We have a relationship, remember?"

"You seem like the one who forgot," Sara prodded him.

"I love you. I want us to get married. How much clearer do you want me to make it?"

"It's not very clear to me at all lately. You weren't with me Saturday night. You were with Christina!"

"You were the one who ran out and left us alone together," Luke reminded her. "Maybe you expected me to run after you, like always. But I just didn't feel like it."

"Obviously. With Christina sitting in your lap, how could you? Do you want to start seeing other people now?"

"No, I don't." Something like understanding flickered

in Luke's dark eyes. "Maybe you do. Maybe that's what this is all about."

"Don't turn this around on me, Luke. You're the one acting like you want out. It seems as if you've already started something with your old girlfriend."

Luke straightened, his body tense with anger. "Is that what you really think? I thought you had a little faith in me, Sara, a little more trust."

Sara looked down at the icy ground. She had thought she trusted him, but now she felt so upset and jealous, she wasn't sure what to think.

"So where is Christina?" she finally asked. "Did she go back to Boston yet?"

"She left yesterday, but she's coming back. She likes it around here," he added.

"Yes, I'm sure she enjoys the scenery." Sara turned, pulled open her car door, and then got inside. "I'll see you."

"So long, Sara." Luke watched her pull out of the parking lot and drive away. She saw him in her rearview mirror. His expression was bleak, exactly the way she felt inside.

She wanted to believe that he had no special feelings for Christina and had been faithful to her. But she didn't feel reassured by anything he just said. Why was Christina coming back here if there was absolutely nothing going on and if she had no hope of winning Luke back?

Christina didn't strike Sara as the type of person who wasted her time or got swept up in unrequited love affairs.

Sara drove toward the village on the dark, empty road. The woods were covered in snow; the bare branches, coated with silvery ice, arched over the narrow road, glittering against the black sky. The passing scenery looked magical and mysterious. She recognized its beauty while at the same time feeling lost inside. She felt empty and adrift now that she didn't know where she stood with Luke.

* * *

"Yes, I'll be there, one way or the other," Emily promised.

She ended the call with Warren Oakes and sat for a moment, wondering who would be available to watch Jane on such short notice. She had interviewed a few sitters during the week, but here it was Thursday morning, and she still didn't have any solid prospects to take over on Monday, when she was due back at work.

Meanwhile, an emergency meeting of the village zoning board had been called. A legal challenge to the zoning in Wood's Hollow had been filed and the board had to meet.

As Emily understood the story from Warren, a local developer had a pending deal to buy the land where the old hotels stood—only to knock them down, of course, and build luxury minimansions on the lake. The firm, Acorn Development, couldn't go ahead unless the zoning was changed from multiple- to single-unit housing. Acorn Development had backers in town, Emily knew. They'd once tried to build condos on the Cranberry Cottages property.

A request to change the zoning would normally be considered at the regular monthly meeting. But Lionel Watts, who was in favor of development, had called an impromptu emergency meeting, hoping to force it through behind her back, Emily suspected. Luckily, Warren had figured out the scheme and alerted her in time.

She paced back and forth in the living room, bouncing Jane gently in her arms. The meeting was at ten, and it was already five past nine. She still needed to shower and dress in real clothes, not just her sweats or jeans. And worst of all, she didn't have a sitter.

She picked up the phone and dialed Dan's cell. He was off at another library doing research. This one was a private collection but it was fairly close, in Newburyport. He could definitely get back in time if he hustled.

"Hi, it's me," she began when Dan picked up. "I have a little problem."

"What's wrong? Is the baby okay?"

The concerned note in his voice was encouraging. "Jane's fine, but they've called me in for a meeting at ten. It's a zoning vote, and I have to be there. Could you come home and watch Jane—just for an hour or two?"

She heard Dan take a deep breath. "I'm sorry, Emily, I really can't. I've waited four months to get this appointment with the curator. If I leave now, it could take four more months before I get another crack at viewing this collection. And I'm on a deadline. I have to finish this research and get out the outline by next Friday."

"Yes, I know. But it would only be for a few hours."

"I'm sorry, but I warned you that this wouldn't be easy. I told you I wasn't going to baby-sit while you went in to the office."

Emily sighed. He had said that. Dan had made it very clear that he wasn't going to be Mr. Mom and that working out child-care arrangements was her responsibility. That had been the deal.

"How about those sitters you interviewed this week?" Dan suggested, sounding sympathetic. "Maybe one will come over."

"There were only two and I didn't like either of them." Carla Nickerson never did find a day when the weather was clear enough for her to drive. And the other two, one too old and one too young, hadn't filled Emily with confidence.

"Well, don't wait for Mary Poppins. I hear she's already taken."

"Thanks for the tip."

"I'm sorry, honey. I would help you if I could. But I think you need to figure this out yourself."

"Okay, I will. I'll talk to you later." Without waiting for him to say good-bye, she hung up the phone. She didn't have time for editorial comments today, and, though she couldn't say he hadn't warned her, she was annoyed at him for not dropping everything and helping her.

She picked up the phone and dialed Jessica next, the closest thing to Mary Poppins in the neighborhood.

Jessica picked up on her tone at once. "Anything wrong? You didn't melt the bottles again, did you?"

"Nothing like that. But I need to run in to work this morning. There's a zoning-board meeting that I can't miss. Do you think I could drop Jane with you, just for an hour or two?"

"I'm sorry, Emily; that won't work out today. I have to be at the bank and I'm bringing Tyler to Sam's mother. She's taking him for a checkup, so I don't think she could handle two little babies in the doctor's office. That would be a bit much, even for Marie. I'm sorry. Any other time I would do it for you."

"Sure, I know you would." Emily sighed. "I'll find someone; don't worry."

"How about Betty or Molly?" Jessica suggested. "Maybe Molly will come over if she's not in the store."

"Good idea, I'll try them next."

Emily quickly made another call to Betty, but her secretary said she was out, busy showing properties to someone from out of town. Emily left a message on Betty's voice mail, then called Molly. Just about the same story—Molly was off with a catering client; no telling when she'd return.

Emily considered trying Sara next, but knew that even if her daughter could come for a little while, her time was too tight. She didn't even want to ask and put her in an awkward position. Then her mother came to mind, and she nearly laughed out loud at the thought.

"Don't worry, sweets. I wouldn't leave you with her for a million dollars," she promised Jane.

Sophie Potter was her last resort. Hadn't Sophie offered to take the baby if Emily needed help? Maybe she was just being polite, but Emily was going to take her up on it. Besides, Sophie was perfect. She was great with children, kind, gentle . . . and she worked at home, Emily thought, picturing Potter's Orchard, where Sophie lived.

But there was no answer at the Potter house despite Sophie's promise that she never left except to go to church. The answering machine picked up, and Emily left a half-hearted message.

It was half past nine. Time was up. She had to get cleaned up and get out of there.

"Practice that big smile, honey pot. You're going into politics."

Jane gurgled at Emily, looking pleased at the idea.

For the next half hour, Emily ran around frantically, getting showered and dressed in record time. She wore a navy blue suit with pants and a fitted jacket that looked appropriately serious, she thought. With no time to blow dry her short, auburn hair, she did her best fluffing it out with her fingertips and hoped the heat vent in the car would do the rest. She skipped all extras, like makeup and jewelry entirely.

She spent far more time on the baby's appearance, she realized later, dressing Jane up in one of her cutest outfits and gathering her wisps of baby hair into a tiny ponytail on the top of her head. There was also considerable packing to do—diapers, formula, wipes, rattles, toys, blankets, a change of clothes in case there was an accident.

Finally dressed and ready, she scooped up the baby and bag and headed for the door, turning back briefly to snatch up her briefcase. Luckily, the stroller was in her trunk and the middle section popped out into a portable infant seat. Emily planned to wheel Jane, kit and caboodle, into the meeting and then use the infant seat later in her office.

"Maybe you'll take a nice nap in that boring meeting for me, won't you, Jane?"

Emily breezed into the Village Hall and headed for the meeting room, wheeling Jane down the corridor. She was already nearly ten minutes late, but that was her usual style and couldn't be blamed on the baby.

She looked for Helen, her secretary, who sat at a desk outside her office, but she was nowhere in sight. That was a snag in her plans; she had hoped Helen would watch Jane for a bit.

With no help for it, Emily opened the door to the meeting room and entered backward, tugging in the stroller and big baby bag.

"Good morning, everyone. I couldn't find a sitter on such short notice and had to bring Jane along. Hope you don't mind."

The zoning board was made up of older men, mainly retired engineers and businessmen, and one woman who had been on the school board. They took themselves and their jobs on the board very seriously. None of them had a great sense of humor, or much humor at all, come to think about it.

Lionel Watts was the chair and called the meeting to order. He didn't even glance at the baby, though Emily sat right next to him. "Let's begin, shall we?"

Emily reviewed the pile of handouts that sat on the table at her seat. She reached into her bag for her reading glasses, but came up with a baby thermometer, which she quickly stuck back inside. It seemed she had forgotten her glasses altogether. Well, she had to remember to pack nearly everything else in the house. It was only the law of probability that she would forget something.

She tried not to be too obvious as she leaned back and forth in her seat, trying to bring the important memos into focus.

The meeting went from bad to worse. Just as the discussion started, Jane began whimpering and squiggling around in her seat in the stroller. Emily leaned over and tried to distract her with a rattle toy. The sound made everyone stop talking and stare at her.

"Oh, sorry." She put the rattle down on the table next to

her pile of memos. "Go on, Lionel. I didn't catch that last part. You were saying?"

Lionel Watts gave her a chilly stare and continued his lugubrious commentary. ". . . and the fact that most of the residents in that area are not property holders and not paying taxes to our town supports the position that the land-use definition should be altered so that the village can reassess and thus collect a higher revenue . . ."

Jane started crying. Something about Lionel's droning tone upset her, Emily was almost sure of it. She leaned over and peered at the baby, realizing that she had better check her diaper, just in case. "So sorry for the interruption. She's fine. She'll stop in just a second. I just want to check . . . something."

All clear in the diaper area, thank goodness. Emily unclipped Jane from the stroller and picked her up. She held her in her arms and patted her back, trying to quiet her. Twelve impatient stares fastened on her, making Emily feel a little nervous. Gosh, it was just a baby. More important, it was just a meeting. *Get over yourselves already*, she nearly said out loud.

She paced back and forth near her chair, trying to soothe the baby and get her to fall asleep. Jane seemed to like it when she sang "You Are My Sunshine," so Emily started off in a whispery tone. Then realizing that everyone was watching her with raised eyebrows, she stopped, too self-conscious to finish the song in front of her audience.

"I think she's just tired," Emily explained. "She needs a nap."

George Gunther, a crusty old man in his eighties, made a disgusted face. "So do a lot of us here. But we're managing not to cry about it."

This brought a few reluctant smiles from the others.

Lionel cleared his throat very loudly. "Well, then . . . as I was saying . . ."

The baby's cries were growing louder. Emily quietly

started the song again, singing in a whisper, ". . . my only sunshine . . ."

Martha Dodge heard her and sat back with eyebrows raised haughtily. "Maybe you ought to see if your secretary can sing to her, *Mayor*," she suggested. She put special emphasis on Emily's title, as if to remind her of it.

"Yes, of course. I'll just be a minute." Emily ran outside with Jane, tugging the stroller behind her. Fortunately, Helen had returned to her desk and was sitting at her keyboard, typing.

"Helen, could you help me out just for a few minutes? I couldn't find a sitter, so I brought Jane in with me this morning to the zoning meeting. It's not going well. Could you watch her, just until the meeting is over?"

Helen held out her arms with a smile. "Sure thing. Here, let me have the little doll." She folded Jane in her soft embrace and the baby seemed calmer instantly. "Just go on to your meeting," Helen said. "She'll be fine with me."

Emily gave Jane one last gaze, then went back to the meeting room. Helen, who was in her mid-fifties and had raised three children, did seem to have a good touch with her. Too bad she was such a great secretary and liked her job. She would make a terrific babysitter, Emily thought.

From then on, the meeting proceeded without interruption, and arguments for both sides were heard. Those who favored a change in the zoning argued that the area of Wood's Hollow would suddenly triple in value, becoming a builders' bonanza. Many in the town would be in favor of a pocket of luxury real estate replacing the dilapidated apartment buildings that now bordered the lake. If nothing else, the town would get far more revenue in taxes from the area.

"And what would become of the people who live there?" asked Warren Oakes. "There are families with children, not to mention seniors who've lived there their entire lives."

"Exactly," Emily said firmly. "I don't see how we can

just toss people out of their homes because other people want to 'clean up' the area. You're talking about people who don't have other options, who wouldn't have another place to go."

The discussion grew more heated until, finally, a motion was made to table the vote. It seemed that some legality in the petition had to be researched and clarified. Emily was relieved. She didn't think the important question should be voted on so quickly. She really wanted to find some way to bring the issue to the town council and the villagers themselves.

Just as windy Lionel Watts was winding up the meeting with a long, windy summation, Helen poked her head in the room. "Sorry, Emily. There's an important call for you."

"Oh, sure. Sorry, everyone, I have to run. Thanks for your patience."

Emily ran out of the room, following her secretary down the hall.

"It's the baby. I didn't want to say," Helen admitted. "She needs her diaper changed and I couldn't find any spares."

"Oh, thanks. I'll take care of it." Emily had had a feeling the important call was something along these lines. Not for the first time, she found herself glad of Helen's discretion.

She had just finished changing Jane's diaper, using her desk for a changing table, when Warren knocked on the half-closed door.

"Come on in." Emily picked up Jane and rested her on her hip. Jane was all dressed again, but the desk was littered with diaper-changing paraphernalia. Emily hurried to clean it up.

Warren came in and closed the door. He surveyed the scene and frowned.

Emily sat down in the chair behind her desk with Jane on her lap and took a bottle out of the baby bag. "What's on your mind, Warren?"

Warren looked unnerved. "Do you have to feed the baby right now?"

Emily looked up at him, surprised by his tone. "Well, she's hungry and it's time for her bottle. Yes, I do." She looked back at Jane, making sure she was eating all right. "Don't worry, I can give her a bottle and listen to you at the same time."

Emily and Warren had a special relationship. Warren had worked in town government for ages, and she owed a lot to him. Although they had their differences, he was one of her biggest supporters and had even run her last campaign. He was a canny and trusted confidante who always managed to watch her back. Warren was prickly, though, and sometimes a little too concerned about her image.

"Is this going to be a usual thing now?" he asked. "The baby in the office? Because if it is, Emily, you're going to have some trouble on your hands. It's not going to fly around here. This isn't a movie on the Lifetime channel."

Emily had to laugh at the last remark. "Do you really watch that station, Warren? I would never have guessed."

"You know what I mean," he said. "They weren't very happy in there. You should have heard the comments when you left."

"I'm glad I didn't."

"They don't find this baby thing so adorable. I don't either. Now you tried it out once, on a small board. Let's not push our luck with another meeting."

"I've been interviewing sitters this week, Warren. It's harder than you think to find somebody reliable."

"Well, you'll have to by next week. You were elected to do a job."

"Yes, I know that, Warren," she said evenly, though she was starting to get angry. She didn't need to be lectured. "Is that all you wanted to talk about?"

"Yes," he said curtly. "That's it. I'm going to lunch. Will I see you here later?"

"No, I'm going home now. I just came in for the meeting." She picked up one of the memos from the meeting. "We have to fight this rezoning, Warren. We can't let them tear down those old buildings to make way for minimansions. I don't care how much it will up the town's real estate value."

He nodded but avoided her gaze. "Yes, I know. It's a complicated question."

"It's not complicated; it's very simple. It's wrong to just toss people out so other people can make money. The people who live in those old buildings can't afford to go anyplace else. I want you to look at the legal grounds for this petition."

Warren shifted in place a moment, then turned and headed for the door. "I'll let you know what I find."

After Warren left, Emily finished feeding Jane, then dressed her up in her snowsuit and strapped her into the stroller. She left Village Hall with all her bags and stowed them in the car outside. Then she wheeled Jane down Main Street and stopped at the Clam Box.

As she opened the door and started to maneuver the stroller inside, Lucy Bates rushed up to help her. "Here she is! Here she is!" Lucy announced in a singsong voice. "I've been dying to see this little baby. I couldn't really get a close look in church," she added, peering into the stroller. "Oh, she's beautiful. Look at those eyes."

She looked up at Emily. "How's it going? Did you come out for a little stroll around town today?"

"I had to go in to work, a meeting. I don't have a sitter yet, so I had to take Jane with me. It didn't work out very well," Emily reported, rolling her eyes. "Don't tell Charlie, but one more visit from Jane at my office and I could get impeached."

Lucy laughed. "Don't worry, I won't tell him. Don't

want to get his hopes up. Now, come sit down. What can I get for you?"

Emily knew the menu so well she didn't need to look. She ordered a turkey sandwich on rye toast with lettuce and tomato. Lucy put her order in and brought a cup of coffee.

The baby was perfectly calm now and content to sit in the stroller, gazing quietly out at the world around her. Emily loved to watch her. She was such a wonder.

"You know, it's really funny how you never hear a man say he's having trouble juggling his family and his job," Lucy said with a wry grin.

"Isn't it," Emily replied. "Dan isn't any great help. He likes the baby, but he's keeping his distance. I think he's afraid of getting too attached because the arrangement is only temporary."

"And you aren't afraid?" Lucy asked.

Emily couldn't answer that question. "How do you do it?" she asked instead. "You have two kids, work here, and go to school."

Lucy shrugged. "Some days I feel certain I'm going to wind up in the hospital, either in the emergency room or the psych ward. But it all works out. The boys are big now. I can even leave them on their own now and again. My mother was a big help when they were little. I could drop them off there anytime."

Emily knew she didn't have that safety net available to her and never would. "I'll find a good sitter sooner or later. It's going to take time."

"Why don't you ask around church? You might find somebody to help you out there."

Lucy's suggestion was a good one. Emily wondered why she hadn't thought of it herself. "Good idea. I'll post a sign on the bulletin board."

Charlie wasn't on duty that day; it was the part-time cook, Jimmy. He rang the little bell on the service counter, and Lucy left to retrieve an order.

A short time later, after Emily had finished her sandwich and was on to a second cup of coffee and a slice of lemon meringue pie, she spotted her friend Betty coming toward the diner. Betty was walking and talking in her usual animated fashion with another woman whom Emily didn't recognize. Emily realized this must be the client Betty had taken out to view properties. She always brought them over to the Clam Box. Newcomers to Cape Light found the diner quaint and charming, until they got to know Charlie Bates, of course.

Betty swept in with her client and spotted Emily at her table near the window. "Emily, how are you? My secretary said you called this morning. Why didn't you try my cell?"

"Oh, that's all right. I didn't want to bother you while you were working." Emily glanced at the other woman. She looked to be in her early thirties, strikingly attractive, dressed in a golden brown suede jacket and a colorful striped scarf, with jeans and neat brown leather boots.

"Did you take Jane out for lunch today?" Betty peered into the stroller and gazed down at the baby, who was dozing off.

"I had to run in to work for a while. I couldn't find a sitter, so I took her along."

Betty's companion bent to look into the stroller, and her sun-streaked hair fell forward, gleaming. "What a sweet little baby," she said, then glanced up, her expression curious. "Are you Emily Warwick?"

"That's me," Emily said easily; she was used to strangers recognizing her.

"Oh, I'm sorry," Betty said. "Let me introduce you. This is Christina Cross. She's writing a book and wants to rent a cottage for some peace and quiet."

"It's the perfect town for peace and quiet," Emily said amiably, but the name Christina had snagged her attention. Wasn't that the name of Luke's old girlfriend? Emily realized in a flash she'd come face-to-face with Sara's rival.

"I can't believe I've lived in Boston so long and never knew about this place. It's just so . . . perfect." Christina's praise sounded sincere, but Emily suspected that if Luke didn't live here, the little village that lacked stylish stores, good restaurants, and any nightlife except movies might seem inconvenient, dull, and rather provincial.

"Guess who's going to be in Christina's book? Luke McCallister," Betty said, answering her own question. "He's getting an entire chapter."

"I heard something about that," Emily admitted.

"I guess Sara told you. You're her mother, right?" Christina said. "She mentioned that her mother is the mayor. It must be fun being mayor here."

"Most of the time," Emily answered carefully. "It's not all parades and tree-lighting ceremonies, though."

She didn't mean to sound defensive, but something in Christina's tone suggested Emily's job was about as demanding as presiding over a doll's tea party.

"I'm sure every little town has its intrigue," Christina said. She leaned down and looked at the baby again. "It's just amazing about you finding this baby and taking her in. I'd love to do an article on you sometime. It would be a perfect feature for the *Boston Globe*, or even one of the big women's magazines."

"Oh, wouldn't that be great, Emily? I could just see a picture of you and Jane on the cover of some magazine," Betty said. She leaned a bit closer. "Let's see Charlie Bates try to beat that publicity," she added in a laughing whisper.

Emily smiled, unswayed by the prospect of Christina Cross making her a star of the supermarket magazine racks.

If anyone is going to get a publishing credit out of this experience, it's going to be Sara, Emily thought. She had a good mind to stroll right over to the newspaper office this afternoon and have her get working on the story right away. Before this blonde barracuda scooped her.

"That's a very nice idea," Emily said diplomatically.

"I'm very flattered. But Dan and I would rather be low key about all this. We're only temporary guardians right now, and I don't think I'd feel right drawing such attention to the situation."

"Sure, I understand." Christina shrugged and smiled. She really was very pretty, Emily thought. Not as pretty as Sara, but a formidable contender.

Lucy walked over with menus. Finally, Emily thought.

"I'm sorry to keep you waiting, ladies. Can I show you to a table?"

"Thanks, Lucy." Betty turned to Emily. "See you later. Call me at the office if you get a chance."

"Yes, I will," Emily promised. "So long, Christina."

"Very nice meeting you, Emily. See you around town."

Emily just nodded. She couldn't honestly say, "Looking forward to it," or any of those other niceties.

She put some bills on the table and slipped on her coat, then made sure the baby was properly bundled up. She tugged the stroller out the door and headed down Main Street toward the village green, church, and dock. She wanted to show Jane the place where they first met, even though it seemed a little silly.

She thought of dropping in at the newspaper office but decided not to disturb Sara at work. She needed to be low key about this Christina woman and not run over there, sounding alarmed after meeting her. That would just reinforce Sara's fears about the situation. She wondered if Sara even knew Christina Cross was moving into town. If not, she didn't want to be the one to tell her. Not just yet.

Still, Emily couldn't help but feel a wave of concern. Sara wasn't exaggerating. This Christina was a formidable adversary: intelligent, attractive, poised, and confident. Closer in age to Luke, too, she was the kind of woman who knows what she wants and isn't afraid to go after it.

"Poor Sara," Emily murmured to Jane. "She'd better watch out. That woman is trouble."

She pushed the stroller around the paths on the village green. It was a sunny, windless, cold day. She'd heard fresh air was good for babies. Way back when, during her own babyhood, mothers would leave their babies outside in their carriages for hours to "air" them, like rugs getting a spring cleaning.

People didn't do that anymore, thank goodness. But there was some value to the fresh-air theory. She had a feeling Jane would sleep well tonight, and then so would she.

When they reached the crèche, Emily paused to gaze at the manger scene, particularly the empty wooden cradle where she had found Jane that frosty, momentous morning.

She lifted Jane up out of her stroller and showed her the scene. "Two weeks ago tomorrow," she whispered to the baby. "Can you believe it?" She turned Jane in her arms to look into her clear blue-grey eyes. "Seems as if I've known you forever. I suppose in my heart I have."

As Emily stood murmuring to the baby, she noticed Reverend Ben coming out of the church. He looked distracted, deep in thought until he noticed her. She smiled and waved as he walked over.

"Are you here to teach Jane the true meaning of Christmas before she gets corrupted by toy commercials?" he inquired.

"Not really," Emily admitted. "We were just reminiscing. It will be two weeks tomorrow that I found her, right in this very spot."

Ben finally smiled. "We ought to commemorate the spot with a plaque or something."

"Perhaps." Emily's tone was cautious. So many remarks about the baby, kindly meant, only served to remind her of their temporary situation.

Ben seemed to sense her thoughts. He placed his hand

gently on her arm. "You've taken quite a risk. You're out on the high trapeze without a net."

"Yes, that's what it feels like sometimes," she admitted.

"I'm proud of you," he said. "And I'm praying for you, too."

"Thank you, Ben. I think I need the prayers."

He shook his head. "No thanks necessary. You didn't ask my advice on this, I noticed. Were you afraid I'd be against it?"

"No, not really. It all happened so quickly, I didn't ask anyone. It was something I just felt I had to do . . . almost as if some power I didn't have any control over was pushing me forward." She met his gaze. "That sounds silly, doesn't it? I mean, we always have a choice over our actions."

"It doesn't sound silly. Not to me anyway." He looked at Jane again, touching her lightly under the chin with his fingertip until she smiled back at him. "We can't ignore our inner voice, our intuitive feelings. Some people might say that's the way angels advise us."

Emily was surprised. She had rarely heard Reverend Ben talk of angels or intuition.

Finally, he looked back up at Emily. "How will you make it home with that stroller? The side streets are still snowy. Do you need a lift?"

"My car is parked down the street. We'll be fine, thanks."

"All right then. See you soon, Emily." Ben dug his hands in his coat pockets and started off.

Emily watched his determined stride as he crossed the green. He had been in a thoughtful, subdued mood lately. She hoped everything was well with his family. He had been through so much in his private life the past few years. Their minister was an inspiring example of a man who navigated life's perilous seas with a compass of faith and a sail of solid character. She wondered if he knew how im-

portant he was to the congregation, how much he was respected and needed.

BEN DROVE HOME, HIS MIND NOT ON THE MEETING HE
had just had with Emily but on the call he had received that
day confirming that he was eligible for a sabbatical. He had
spent the rest of the day researching his options: where he
might go and what he might do. The notion of hard, meaningful mission work still drew him. He couldn't focus on
much else.

It was the right time to tell Carolyn, he decided, while
he still felt the urgency to take some action, before self-
doubt and conflicted feelings set in.

He entered his house and shrugged off his coat and
muffler, hanging them up on the rack in the foyer. He heard
the piano in the living room. Dvořák, he thought, and not
too bad—an advanced student, though not Carolyn's fluid,
knowing touch. It had taken her some time to get back to
giving lessons after her stroke, but she loved to teach and
had been much happier once she returned to work.

Could she teach piano students if we lived in Tanzania?
he wondered. Well, of course she could. Sharing her knowledge of music would be a rare and great gift under those
circumstances. He just hoped she would see it that way.

Ben drifted into the kitchen and made a cup of tea for
himself, listening for the sounds of voices in the hallway
and the front door opening. Ten minutes later the student
was gone, and Carolyn came into the kitchen. She looked
energized and cheerful, pleased with the student's
progress, he thought.

"I thought I heard you come in." She walked over to him
and kissed him on the cheek, then looked up at the clock.
"You're home early," she said, turning on the kettle and putting a tea bag in a mug for herself. "Do you feel all right?"

"I feel fine, better than I have in a while," he told her. "I had some good news today. I looked into my eligibility for a sabbatical. I definitely qualify, so I started the process to apply."

Carolyn turned, her expression halfway between surprise and alarm. "A sabbatical? Really? I didn't know you were thinking of that."

"I told you I was thinking of something like that, dear. Remember the other night when we talked, the night the kids came over? I asked if you ever thought about moving away for a while, doing something different with our lives."

"Yes, but I thought you meant . . . oh, I don't know, finding a new church maybe. You never said anything about a sabbatical."

He realized now that he hadn't. Not those exact words. He'd been carrying all this around so much in his own head, he needed to give Carolyn time to catch up a few steps.

"You're right. I never used the exact word, but Walter suggested the idea. And once I thought it over and prayed about it, it seemed like a good solution."

She stared at him. The kettle's shrill whistle sounded. She turned suddenly, shut off the stove, and then poured the water for her tea. "Have you made out an application?"

"The paperwork should be coming in the mail in a day or two. I expect I'll be approved without any problem."

Carolyn brought her cup to the table and sat down across from him. "Then what?"

"Well . . ." He hesitated. This was the hard part—persuading her to move away from here for a while. "I've looked into mission opportunities, some in Africa and Asia. I've also written to James, asking if he needs help on the reservation."

Carolyn didn't reply. She sipped her tea, avoiding his gaze.

"Well?" he asked finally. "What do you think?"

"I'm surprised. I'm shocked, actually." She met his gaze, the bright look gone from her eyes.

"I'm sorry, Carolyn, but I thought you realized that I've been unhappy lately and thinking about making some real changes."

"Yes," she said slowly. "I know that you've been troubled, Ben. I've prayed that you would find some answer to your questions, some peace of mind and a new direction." He could see that she was trying hard to soften her reaction, to show him sympathy and understanding.

"Thank you, dear. It looks as if your prayers have been answered."

"You know what they say, 'Be careful of what you pray for. You just might get it.'" She forced a smile. "I never dreamed you would come home early one day and announce you want to move to the other side of the world." She took a sip of tea, as if needing the pause to organize her thoughts. "I've heard you, Ben. I really have been listening these last few weeks, and I've been concerned about you. I definitely think something serious is going on. But this idea seems . . . impulsive to me."

Impulsive? He sat back, at a loss for words. *Am I asking too much of her, Lord? Or is she not trying hard enough to understand?*

"Is this really the solution, Ben? Is there no other way?" she asked quietly.

Ben knew he couldn't soften the truth; he had to be completely honest. "I'm dissatisfied, unfulfilled," he said carefully. "I've fallen into a rut and I feel as if I've led the congregation into a spiritual rut, too. I've lost my sense of purpose, the sense that I'm making a difference. I feel as if I'm failing them, Carolyn. Even worse, I'm failing to keep the promises I've made to God."

"I don't agree. I don't see you as a failure at all. But I can see how the job might wear on you—the same events one season to the next, the same problems."

He nodded. At least she understood and acknowledged that much.

"But the idea of such a big move, Ben . . . it frightens me," she said plainly. "It seems as if our lives have just gotten back on track. First Mark leaving us, and then my stroke. It's taken awhile to recover, to get our wind back. We have a lot to be thankful for, Ben. So much really."

"I'm not denying that, Carolyn. I am thankful. But that doesn't seem to mitigate or compensate for what I'm facing now. Do you understand at all?" he appealed to her.

"I think I do," she said, her words also carefully chosen. "But life isn't lived all at one speed or one level; there are peaks and valleys. You even told me that once. Maybe you're just in a valley right now. You may even be there for a reason, I don't know. But I do know it will pass. Something will happen and things will change. They always do."

It was hard for Ben to hear his own reasonable counsel tossed back at him. He had told Carolyn that once, and he did believe it.

He tried again. "I am in a valley, Carolyn. And I believe there's a reason for it. I believe God is directing me to some other place, at least for a while."

She didn't answer, but gazed at him levelly, her expression still and unreadable.

"I've been thinking about this a lot." He forced himself to go on, to say the words that were so difficult. "If you don't want to leave here, maybe I should consider going on my own."

She stared back as if he had struck her across the face.

"You would go anyway. Without me." It wasn't really a question. She said the words as if to clarify, as if the idea was so unbelievable she had to say it out loud to fully understand.

Ben felt sad. He knew he had hurt her, which was the last thing he wanted to do. But this was a serious moment in his life and he needed to help himself, or he knew he wouldn't be any good to anyone else.

"I can see all the reasons why you want to stay," he assured her. "If that's your choice, I'll understand and accept it. I just thought . . . well, that you would want to come with me. We've never really been apart more than a night or two our entire married life," he reminded her. "I need to do this, Carolyn. I wouldn't take such a step if I didn't feel so strongly. It's not just a whim."

She nodded quickly, staring down. "Yes, I know it's not a whim, Ben. Still, I feel a little hurt that you could really go without me."

She looked up at him, his dear wife and life's companion. He forced a small smile. "I haven't left yet," he reminded her.

He reached across the table and took her hand. Neither spoke for what seemed a long time.

Finally she said, "When you asked me to marry you, I didn't know what to do. I loved you with all my heart, but I didn't think I had what it took to be a minister's wife. Do you remember?"

He nodded. "Yes, I do."

"But you talked me into it. You persuaded me that I would be just fine, that our family would be just like everyone else's. You said I didn't have to be some model of female perfection." She laughed, remembering. "And I wasn't."

He smiled, but didn't interrupt her.

"I knew when I married you that our lives would be different. No matter what you said, your job is . . . unusual. It's not even a job really. Not like some husband who's an accountant or a plumber. Your stock-and-trade is with the spirit; it's with God. If you believe you've been called to leave here, then I can't dig in my heels like some suburban housewife upset about a job transfer."

He nodded thankfully and squeezed her hand, too moved to speak.

"I knew what I was taking on when I married you," she

said. "I made that promise. If you go, I'll go with you. Your ministry is more than your job; it's you having dedicated your life to God's work. It's your heart and soul. I can't hold myself apart from that. What kind of marriage would that be?"

Ben gazed at his wife, his vision blurred with tears. His heart was filled with love for her. More than love, he thought. He felt they were as close at that moment as two people could ever be.

"What about Rachel and Jack, and little Will? I know you'll miss them."

"Oh, of course I will. But they'll be all right. They'll appreciate us more when we come back." She sighed, a little teary, too, he noticed. "When do you think this will all happen, Ben? Very soon?"

"I was thinking I would leave the church in February, if I can find an interim minister by then. But I don't want to tell anyone yet, not until the plans are firmer. I have to go to the church council first, then the congregation. I'd rather not say anything about it before Christmas, until I send in all the paperwork and the request is formally approved."

"I understand. I won't mention it. Not even to Rachel," she added.

He knew that would be hard for her, especially with Christmas coming. Carolyn was already having a hard time with the idea of Mark leaving; now an even greater cloud had drifted overhead.

They would get through the holidays as best they could, Ben decided. The season didn't seem nearly so oppressive to him now, having made this plan.

CHAPTER NINE

"THIS IS MY OFFICE NUMBER, THE DIRECT LINE, AND this is my secretary's. And this is my cell and Dan's. And here's my sister Jessica's number, though I think she's working today, but you can call her if you have a problem. And this is the number for the doctor, Dr. Harding; he's right in town. And here's the phone number for the fire department, too."

Emily felt breathless, having worked her way down the list taped to the refrigerator door. The new babysitter, Liz Barrow, nodded, her expression calm and pleasant. She wasn't very old, Emily thought, only in her mid-twenties. But she'd come from an agency and had lots of experience, and all her references had checked out well.

Dressed for work in a black wool suit and black heels, her makeup done right and her hair blown out, Emily looked all business again. But she felt as if she were wearing a costume. It was funny how just one week away from the office and spending time with Jane had changed her perspective.

The only thing that felt right was the baby, balanced on her hip. She hated now to hand her over and wished there were some way Jane could come along with her. But she'd tried that last week and it hadn't gone over very well, she reminded herself.

Emily wasn't even going to be at the Village Hall for most of the day. She had a meeting at the county seat in Southport, more than an hour away. She wished that she could run home during lunch and check on the baby, but it just wasn't to be. Tomorrow for sure, she promised herself, she would try to find some way to come home early.

Dan had already left. He was going to a shipbuilding museum in Essex to interview the town historian. He wasn't very far, he reminded her. He would stop in at some point and make sure everything was going all right.

"Don't worry; the baby will be fine. Lots of kids are left with sitters every day," he had said as he set off that morning.

Emily hadn't answered. It wasn't the same for him. He didn't understand.

Now she sighed, looking down at Jane, who seemed so content in her arms. Emily kissed the baby on the cheek and handed her over to the sitter, feeling a pang in her heart.

"All right. I'd better go. Make sure you lock the doors." She forced herself to put on her coat and grab her briefcase. "I'll call later when I have a break. And you can call me anytime. Don't even hesitate."

"No problem." The sitter followed Emily to the door. "I'm sure everything will go fine, but if I have any questions, I'll be sure to call." She turned to the baby and smiled widely. "We're going to have fun today, Janie. Aren't we?"

Emily took one last look at the baby, then turned and

headed out to the car. For a few moments she sat in the driver's seat, letting the engine warm up. The car smelled of the baby, of hand wipes and formula. She felt that little twist again and tried to ignore it.

It was a good sign that Dan had offered to come home and check on the sitter, she thought. He was kind to the baby, if still a bit aloof. At least he was showing an interest. She hoped that in time, Jane's charm would wear down his defenses. But she had to admit, Dan was good at keeping up his "force field" when he wanted to.

How much time did they have? She wasn't sure. The social worker had said the investigation would take about four weeks. That meant only two weeks more.

She hoped Dan's feelings would soften. The past week of caring for the baby had only confirmed her initial impulse: she was convinced they needed to apply to be Jane's adoptive parents if a relative didn't come forward. But she didn't dare mention it to Dan yet. It was just what she had promised not to do, argue for that next step. It would be going back on her word to him.

I'll bring it up when and if the time is right, she told herself, then added a quick prayer. "Oh, Lord, please let there be a right time and let us do the right thing for Jane."

DAN WRAPPED UP HIS RESEARCH AT THE MUSEUM IN ESsex much earlier than he'd planned. Just as he promised Emily, he called the sitter to check up three times, but had gotten an endless busy signal. He even called the operator to see if the phone was off the hook. No, someone was using it, she said.

That annoyed him. They weren't paying this young woman to talk on the phone all day. Emily must be apoplectic if she had been trying to call, too. He wondered why Emily hadn't called him yet, but then realized she must still be hung up in her meeting.

The drive from Essex back to Cape Light didn't take long. Dan pulled into the driveway and walked in through the back door, which had been left unlocked, he noticed.

He was hungry and wanted some lunch. The kitchen was a mess, looking even worse than when he had left that morning.

"Hello? Anybody home?" he called out. "It's me, Liz . . ."

He walked into the living room, the sound of the TV growing louder. Jane was in her portacrib, set up near the sofa. She was lying on her stomach, surrounded by toys and screaming her lungs out. The sitter was watching TV and talking on the phone, a bowl of popcorn in her lap.

No wonder she hadn't heard him come in. Dan walked right up to her and tapped her hard on the shoulder.

"Ahhh!" She screamed and jumped up, dropping the phone and spilling the popcorn in all directions.

Dan leaned over and picked up the receiver. "Liz has to go now. So long." He hung up and looked at the sitter, eyes narrowed.

"Mr. Forbes . . . I didn't hear you come in." She took a step back and started toward the baby. "I don't know why she's crying all of a sudden. Maybe she's teething or something."

"Don't bother, I'll get her." Dan literally pushed the young woman aside to reach Jane first. He leaned over and scooped up the baby, who was red faced and gasping.

"Now, now. It's all right, little girl. I'm here," he whispered. He held her close, tucking her head to his shoulder. She felt so hot, he thought. Her skin was on fire. Was it right for a baby to feel so warm? She never felt this way before when he held her. "She's so hot," he said to the sitter.

Liz peered at the baby. "She has a lot of clothes on. Maybe she's overdressed."

Dan stared at her. "You're fired. Don't come back here."

The young woman glared at Dan for a minute, then

turned on her heel and picked up her purse and coat, which were tossed on a chair. "Fine. Watch your own stupid baby."

She stalked out of the living room and slammed the door. Dan barely noticed. He clicked off the TV with one hand and carried Jane into the kitchen.

"Dr. Harding, Dr. Harding . . ." he mumbled nervously as he scanned Emily's endless list of phone numbers. Finally, Harding. Dan grabbed a phone and punched in the numbers with his thumb.

Busy signal. He dropped the phone and paced around the kitchen. Jane was crying fiercely. The sound of the child wailing and the mounting anxiety threw him back, way back to the days when he was a young father and this was Lindsay, in his arms. His little Lindsay, who was now running the newspaper. His wife, Claire, had gone somewhere, overnight to see her mother who was ill. She couldn't take the baby and she didn't trust Dan to watch her. Dan had never watched Lindsay on his own before, but he was willing to give it a try.

Claire had left angrily, as if daring him to take care of his daughter alone. And the baby had gotten sick, a high fever. By the time he noticed, she was going into convulsions. He didn't know what to do. He felt so helpless. He called Claire to come home. She told him to meet her at the hospital. She had been so angry, saying he should have noticed Lindsay was sick. That it was just like him—in his own world, never thinking of anyone else.

But Claire had been strangely pleased to have been proven right, Dan realized later. In her mind, all her accusations had been validated. He wasn't a good father. The newspaper always came first, even before his own children. He was cold and selfish. So egotistical.

Dan sat down in a chair, trying to soothe the child, feeling overwhelmed by the wave of dark memories, of failures and disappointments. He was successful in his professional life, an award-winning publisher of a small-town paper, but he was a failure as a husband and a father. No wonder he had been a workaholic. Putting out a paper was the only thing he ever felt truly good at.

He glanced down at Jane, who had stopped crying, finally. Her eyes were glassy, her cheeks red. He had to do something; he would take her to the doctor. Right away. "Come on, little girl. Come with me. We're going to get you some help and make you better."

He found a big blanket and her baby bag and had her in the car moments later. When they reached Dr. Harding's office, he found a parking space right in front. He ran into the doctor's office, Jane wrapped in a blanket and held close to his chest.

"My little girl is very sick. She has a high fever. I tried to call but the line was busy," he explained to the woman at the desk.

She barely glanced up. "Your name, please?"

"Dan Forbes. This is Jane. I'm not her real father. I'm her guardian . . ." Dan swallowed hard. He was trying not to scream. Couldn't this woman see this was an emergency?

She started typing on a computer keyboard. "I can't find anything under Forbes. You've been here before, you said?"

"Warwick. Try Warwick, then," he said through gritted teeth.

"Is the name Forbes or Warwick? I'm sorry, I don't understand."

"It's Forbes. My name is Dan Forbes. My wife's name is Emily Warwick. Ring a bell?" he asked tightly.

"Oh, of course, the mayor. Is she a patient here? I'm rather new." More typing on the keyboard. Dan nearly screamed in frustration. He wasn't trying to buy an airline ticket; he just wanted to see the doctor.

"Why don't you take a seat over there, Mr. Forbes? I'll call you when—"

"You don't seem to understand . . ." Dan could hear his voice getting louder. A woman reading a magazine in the waiting room frowned at him, her brows drawn together in disapproval.

Dan was about two seconds from exploding when Matt Harding stepped out from one of the exam rooms and came toward him.

"Dan, what's up?" He looked down at the baby swathed in the plaid blanket.

"She has a high fever. Emily is up in Southport. I didn't know what to do so I brought her here."

"Bring her right in. Let's have a look."

Dan followed Dr. Harding into an exam room. The doctor took the baby and gently placed her on the exam table. He unwrapped the blanket and opened her outfit, then listened to her heartbeat and felt her neck and abdomen.

"She has a rash on her stomach," he said. "Was this here this morning?"

"I'm sure it wasn't. Emily examines every inch of her. She would have stayed home from work if she saw anything like that."

The baby looked so small and helpless, Dan's heart went out to her.

Matt stuck an electronic thermometer in Jane's ear, and it quickly started beeping. "One hundred four. That's high, even for an infant. How long has she been crying like this?"

"I don't know. I came back home about an hour ago. This nightmare of a sitter we hired had Jane stuck in her crib while she watched TV. The poor thing was screaming her lungs out."

"I see. Don't worry . . . we'll figure it out," Matt promised as he continued to examine the baby.

Finally, he pulled off his stethoscope and turned to Dan. "She has an ear infection. Her head is all clogged up. These things can come on suddenly, especially in babies this age. It's very painful for her, though. That's why she's crying every time you put her down."

"That sounds awful. Can you give her something for it?"

"Absolutely. I'm going to give her a shot, and then you'll need to give her some antibiotics. The medicine should work quickly. The rash is a symptom of the infection. That will go away, too. She can have some Tylenol for the fever, too. Watch her temperature. Don't let it get too high. She should have a tepid bath if it spikes up tonight, and plenty of fluids around the clock, as much as she'll take."

"All right." Dan nodded. "Can you write this all down?"

"Yes, of course I will."

Matt called in the nurse, who helped him give the baby her shot. Dan could hardly watch. Jane cried so hard afterward, he thought he might cry himself. Finally, she was dressed again, and the nurse placed her back in his arms.

"She's all tired out. She'll probably fall asleep right away," the nurse said gently.

Dan didn't answer. He rocked the baby awkwardly, to and fro, as he'd seen Emily do. Then he dipped his head down and kissed her softly on the forehead. Her soft hair tickled his nose.

Jane looked up at him a moment, wide eyed and silent, then slowly closed her eyes, as if she recognized who was holding her now and knew she didn't have to cry anymore.

DAN TRIED EMILY'S CELL PHONE ON THE RIDE HOME. HE couldn't believe he had waited so long to call her. But he only got her voice mail, so he left a brief message telling her to call him.

Jane slept peacefully in her car seat all the way home. She continued to sleep even when he brought her inside and put her to bed. Her forehead felt cooler and he felt deeply relieved.

He meant to go into the kitchen to grab something to eat and call Emily, but instead he lingered in the dimly lit room, watching the baby sleep.

He thought of the episode with Lindsay and his ex-wife again. Claire had rarely missed a chance to remind him that he wasn't a very good father. Well, he was a good father in some ways, Dan told himself. Both his kids had told him that, now that they had grown up and gotten out from under his wife's thumb. He just wasn't good when they were very little. He hadn't known what to do. He left too much to Claire and then felt inept even trying to make a peanut-butter sandwich.

That was partly Claire's doing, though. She had shut him out, acted as if helping with homework or serving a bowl of cold cereal was rocket science. It was mainly his fault, of course. He could see that now. He was always at the paper, practically slept there some nights, dedicated to a fault. Then he came home late one night and realized he had entirely missed out. His kids had grown up while he was chasing a big story. In the years since then, he had tried to make it up to them. But he never really could.

"I didn't do too badly for you today, did I, Jane? We got through it all right," he whispered to the baby.

He wondered what kind of father he would make now. He sensed that Emily, for all her talk, was headed in that direction, determined to tug him along, too. She didn't really understand his hesitation. You don't want to take on a job as important as fatherhood when you believe you failed at it, screwed things up entirely. It was different now, though. He was different.

The question was, was he different enough to do this? It was so hard. He had gotten through today by the skin of his teeth. Maybe the answer was, he just wasn't sure. He didn't want to think about it now, anyway. He was just relieved to have handled the crisis.

The phone rang and Dan picked it up in the bedroom.

"Dan? You're home already? I didn't think you'd be getting back until three."

"I came back early. I couldn't reach the sitter so I got worried. I had to fire her, Emily. She was a total disaster."

"What happened? Is Jane all right?" Emily was not quite in a panic, but Dan could tell from her voice she was getting there.

"She had a fever. I took her right over to Matt, and it seems she has an ear infection. She's much better now. She's got some medicine and some Tylenol to take—"

"An ear infection? Poor thing. I'm coming right home."

"If you want to. But she's sleeping now. Everything's under control," he promised. "I can take care of her."

It felt good to say the words, he realized. He meant them, too.

Emily didn't answer right away. "I know. I would just feel better if I came right away. I'll see you soon."

Emily ended the call, and Dan hung up. Then he left the room, but only after taking one last peek at the baby.

Emily came in about an hour later, which gave Dan time to relax and compose himself. He greeted her at the door, then took her coat and briefcase while she rushed back to see Jane.

"She's still sleeping," Emily said when he quietly entered the room. Emily reached into the crib and touched the baby's forehead. "I don't think she has a fever anymore."

"That's good." Dan stood next to Emily and put his arm around her shoulder.

"I feel awful," Emily confessed. "I should have been home. I should have noticed that something was wrong with her this morning. She's been with us less than two weeks, and I'm flunking out already."

Emily sounded as if she was about to cry. Dan knew what she was feeling. He hugged her closer to comfort her.

"It's okay, honey. Matt said these things come on very

quickly. You can't be everywhere at once. I was here. I took good care of her."

Emily glanced up at him. "Yes, I know. Thank you, Dan. I don't know what would have happened if you hadn't come home when you did."

"Let's not think about that. And you don't have to thank me. I'm her guardian, too."

Emily didn't answer. She leaned up and kissed his cheek; then she reached down and smoothed the baby's blanket.

"I know she must have been screaming bloody murder before, but she looks like an angel now," Emily said softly.

"She is an angel." Dan's voice was quiet, but emphatic, his gaze still fixed on the baby. Emily glanced at him. He rarely sounded so sentimental.

"So are you. Lucky for me I have a husband who can handle these things so well without getting rattled."

SARA HAD TO SPEND A FEW HOURS AT THE NEWSPAPER office on Saturday, finishing up a story for Monday's edition. Afterward, she found herself with nothing to do. She didn't want to go home to her empty apartment and hang around waiting for Luke to call. That wait would be in vain, she knew. They hadn't spoken or seen each other all week. It was one of the longest stalemates in the history of their relationship. Did they even have a relationship anymore, she wondered?

She did some errands and some halfhearted Christmas shopping. A few hours later, she found herself climbing the steps to her grandmother's house on Providence Street.

The mansarded Victorian was a historic treasure, at least architecturally. It wasn't the type of house, though, that people pointed out and admired. Painted slate grey with black shutters and white trim, its only ornaments were two cement urns at the top of the walk that held dark green ivy.

It could really be something, Sara thought, if her grandmother cheered it up a bit. It was the type of house that would look spectacular trimmed with Christmas lights, the kind that cling to the roof edges and look like icicles.

But her grandmother's house was bare of all holiday decorations. Sara held the only possibilities forever in her hand—a large pine wreath with a red satin bow and a small tabletop Christmas tree. She also carried a shopping bag with gifts for Lillian.

From her first year in Cape Light, Sara had brought her grandmother a wreath every holiday season along with an amaryllis bulb that eventually sprouted a huge, trumpet-shaped red flower. Lillian's husband used to buy her one each year, so she accepted the amaryllis as tradition. The tree was a new idea, though, a sudden impulse. Sara fully expected that Lillian would complain about it at length, and also secretly prize it.

Sara sometimes wondered why she went to so much trouble for her grandmother, who rarely seemed to appreciate the effort. Yet there were things about Lillian that she not only respected but also enjoyed—her sharp intellect, for one thing, and her quick, surprising wit. Her audacity, too. Lillian was her only grandparent and despite her prickly nature, they had managed to forge a genuine relationship.

Sara rang the brass doorbell. The place looked deserted as usual, the windows dark except for one small light up in the bedroom. Sara waited a long time, then rang the bell again. She knew Lillian was in there. Her grandmother did need extra time to get to the door, but it was also her particularity about accepting visitors that made her reception so slow.

The corner of the curtain in the living room window shifted slightly, and Sara took that as an encouraging sign. "It's me—Sara," she said forcefully. "I know you're in there, Lillian."

She waited a few more minutes, thinking she might just

leave everything on the doorstep. Finally a light clicked on in the foyer and the big door opened.

"What are you doing here? Did your mother send you to see if I was still breathing?"

Sara ignored her grandmother's play for sympathy. "Yes, exactly. I figured the wreath could be used either way," she said lightly, hiding a small smile.

"Touché, young lady. You may enter," Lillian said grandly. She opened the door all the way and Sara stepped inside.

"What do you have there? Is that pathetic stalk of greenery supposed to be a Christmas tree?" Lillian reared back, taking in the tiny tree. "I hope you didn't pay much for it. And I don't want a tree in the house, for goodness sake. What a pagan tradition. They make a huge mess, and who's going to clean up those pine needles and do all the decorating?"

"Calm down, Lillian. It's hardly a tree. More like a Christmas . . . branch."

Sara brought the tree into the living room and looked for a good spot to set it up. The rooms in Lillian's house were spacious but crammed with furniture, large antique pieces that had come from the Warwick family estate—a real mansion that was now a historic site owned by the town.

When Lillian's husband, Oliver, was caught in a business scandal, they had been forced to sell everything. Lillian had kept the family together and courageously pulled them through the crisis, though not without a cost to her spirit, Sara knew.

"How about right here, by the window?" Sara held the tree up over a small table that was covered with bric-a-brac. "I'll just move some of these photos and things. Then you can see it when you come in the room."

Lillian had followed her at a snail's pace, walking slowly with her cane. She waved her hand at Sara and sat in her favorite high-backed armchair, the one that made her look like an ancient queen on her throne, Sara thought.

"Why ask me? I only live here. You seem determined to plant that thing in my house, no matter what I say. You pick the spot. It clearly doesn't matter what I think about it."

"Okay then," Sara said brightly. She rearranged the table, making space for the tree.

"For goodness sakes, don't break anything," Lillian called out sharply.

"Don't worry." Sara placed the tree in the middle of the empty table. It looked cute, but too bare.

"Don't you have any ornaments, Lillian? I thought a few years ago you put up a tree in here."

"Of course I have ornaments. Very fine ones, hand-blown glass. They don't make ornaments like that anymore." Lillian shifted in her chair. "They're up in the attic, though. I have no idea where."

"I'll go up and get them," Sara offered. "It won't take long."

Sara had ventured into Lillian's attic on a few other occasions and actually liked exploring up there.

For once Lillian didn't object. "All right, you know the way. Just don't get lost up there. The boxes are marked Christmas, of course. Just bring down one or two. I don't want to turn this place into Santa's workshop, for goodness sakes."

"No chance of that," Sara said dryly. She ran up the three flights to the attic and pulled on the string that controlled the light. A weak light bathed the shadowy space; it was just enough to help her find her way around. Sara was tempted to peer inside the trunks of old clothes and cartons that held the history of the family. But she knew Lillian was waiting impatiently and would start calling if she took too long.

She found a dusty old box marked Christmas. Inside were ornaments wrapped in yellowed tissue paper. The tree was so small, a single box would do, she decided, and carefully carried it down the stairs.

"What took you so long? Did you get lost up there?" Lillian watched her as she came down the last few steps into the foyer.

"It's a mess up there. You really ought to find someone to put it all in order for you, Lillian."

"Hire someone, you mean? Why should I? There will be plenty of volunteers when I'm dead and buried; you'll see."

Sara shook her head but didn't laugh. Her grandmother could connect the most innocent comment to her imminent demise. Reminding everyone of her fragile mortality seemed to be one of her favorite pastimes.

You're so stubborn, you'll probably outlive all of us, Sara often wanted to say.

Sara could have made short work of trimming the tiny branch of pine, but Lillian watched closely, micromanaging the placement of the antique ornaments and relating some long story about each one.

"Those round red balls with the reindeer design come from Switzerland. We spent Christmas there one year, when your mother was just a baby, in a chalet on Lake Lucerne. My husband, Oliver, was a great sportsman, loved to ski. I couldn't stand it—foolish sport, sliding around the snow with planks of wood strapped to your feet. Ridiculous." She sighed, remembering. "The Alps are spectacular, though. You really ought to travel, Sara. That's what you should be doing at your age. I can show you some pictures someday."

Sara stood up and brushed off her hands. "I'd like to see them, Lillian. You know how I love your old photographs."

Lillian had made them some tea while Sara was working on the tree and served it on a silver tray alongside a dish of tea biscuits. Sara was familiar with the dry, hard cookies, which lived in a little tin in Lillian's kitchen. They must have taken up residence there about the year that she herself had been born.

There should be some music and a fire in the hearth,

Sara thought, but the little tree had definitely brightened up the room and made it feel more like Christmas.

"I have some gifts for you in that bag, but you can't open them until Christmas," Sara teased her. "I'll put them under the tree."

"I have one for you, too . . . somewhere. Oh yes, over there on the dining room table. I wrapped it today. A premonition of your arrival, I suppose. It's not much," she warned Sara. "You know how I despise holiday shopping, all the expense and fuss. It's just a big swindle that the shopping malls manage to put over every year. People are like sheep. They have no common sense."

"I agree there's too much commercialism this time of year, Lillian. But I wouldn't call the entire holiday a big *swindle*."

"Of course it is, silly girl. Open your eyes. This Christmas malarkey is about as genuine as the beard on a department store Santa. It's a corporate conspiracy. Conscienceless lot, too. The way they use the children, it's shameful. Making the parents feel guilty if they aren't buying their kids everything under the sun. My children were never spoiled at Christmas, I'll promise you that."

"I believe you." Sara couldn't even imagine Lillian spoiling a child.

"So." Lillian smoothed her skirt over her boney knees. "I hear your mother still has custody of that foundling. I hear she disgraced herself, too, carting the child into a very important meeting at Village Hall."

Lillian was obviously keeping a close eye on the situation despite her distant perch. Sara wasn't surprised. Lillian acted aloof but was actually quite interested, always fishing for news.

"You should have been a reporter, Lillian. Sounds like you have some good sources."

"Nonsense. Your mother is being gossiped about all over town, and not in a very kindly way. One more stunt like that and she'll be up in front of the town council. Then what? Is it worth losing her office over this . . . baby?"

"Lillian, you exaggerate. She's found a full-time sitter now, an older woman from church, Blanche Hatcher. I'm sure Emily can figure out how to be mayor and have a baby."

Lillian grunted with disapproval. "So she's going through with this then? I thought it was only temporary."

"The social service agency should be concluding their search for relatives soon, maybe by the end of the week," Sara explained. "Then the baby will be free to be adopted."

Sara paused. She didn't know how much she should share with Lillian. Since the scene at church, Emily hadn't spoken with her mother at all, though she did get reports from Jessica that all was well.

"I'm sure my daughter wants to proceed with this madness," Lillian said. "Though I'm not so sure about her husband. He seems too settled in his ways for such an adjustment." A keen observation, Sara thought. Lillian was actually paying more attention than people realized.

"I know everyone thinks this is all so warm and wonderful, but it's not. For one thing, Emily is likely to get hurt," Lillian insisted. "There are probably a lot of younger couples who have been on these lists, waiting for a baby. Rich husbands with stay-at-home wives who are a far better bet than middle-aged newlyweds with a workaholic streak. What makes Emily think she's going to get this baby anyway?" Lillian asked. "Why is she so obsessed with the child?"

Sara put her teacup down and looked at her grandmother squarely. She had considered this question herself and could come to only one conclusion.

"Maybe because she had to give me up."

Lillian glared at her. "Because I made her. Isn't that what you mean to say?"

Her grandmother didn't seem the least bit rattled. She sat back in her chair, squared her shoulders, and lifted her chin. "That's the family legend anyway. Well, I won't apologize. I've said it before and I'll say it again. I did what I thought was best for her. For everybody. It wasn't easy for me. When you have a child, you'll see. You'll have to make some hard calls," she said knowingly. "Emily might find she has to give this baby up, too. And she won't be able to blame me this time, thank goodness."

For all Lillian's anger, she did have a point. It would be ironic if that happened, Sara realized. Despite her own mixed feelings about the baby, she didn't want Emily to be hurt again.

"Let's hope it doesn't come to that," Sara said, wanting to put the subject aside.

"When will they know? By Christmas, do you think?"

"Probably," Sara answered.

"Well, it might not be such a happy holiday on that side of town," Lillian observed. "Where will you be? Will you stay here or visit your *other* family?"

The ironic note at the mention of her granddaughter's adoptive parents was not lost on Sara, though she pretended not to notice it.

"I'll be down in Maryland. My parents have asked me to come for a visit. I'm looking forward to it, actually."

She was looking forward to being back in her old house where she could have some distance from her problems with Luke.

"And what about your boyfriend? Will he go with you?" Lillian asked curiously.

"No." After her initial invitation they hadn't talked again about Luke visiting Winston for Christmas. There's no way he was coming with her now, she realized.

"He'll probably just hang around here then," Lillian said, "looking to crash our family party with that hangdog expression of his."

Sara had to laugh. Luke didn't have a hangdog expression, but he had appeared uninvited at Lillian's doorstep more than once, which drove her grandmother crazy. Lillian had enough trouble welcoming guests into her home who were actually invited.

"I doubt he'll do that," Sara said finally. "I don't know what he's doing for Christmas."

Lillian looked surprised and stared at her curiously. "Hmm, that sounds rather ominous. Are you two getting tired of each other?" Lillian paused, but Sara didn't answer. "I've never thought he was at your level, Sara. I'm sure you could do better. This isn't the worst news I've heard lately, by any means."

"Yes, I know how you feel about Luke."

Sara hardly considered herself "too good" for Luke. He was about as good as good gets. She doubted she could ever do better, though it looked as if she would have a chance to test Lillian's theory, Sara thought glumly.

The last light had faded and Lillian moved about, turning on her little china lamps. Sara had no plans for the evening. She wondered if her grandmother wanted to go out for a bite of dinner or maybe to a movie. Had Lillian ever gone out to see a movie, Sara wondered. Not since she'd known her, and probably not since *Gone with the Wind* was in the theaters.

The doorbell rang. Lillian was in the dining room, holding Sara's present.

"That must be Ezra," she said, not sounding very cheered at his arrival. "He's persuaded me to be a fourth at bridge. Some group of old fogies he plays with on Saturday nights. I told him quite clearly I wasn't interested, but he wouldn't take no for an answer."

"Oh, go ahead," Sara encouraged her. "It will be good for you to get out of the house."

"Why is that? Why is everyone always trying to get me out of my house? I like my house. I'm comfortable here. Other people's houses are not nearly as nice. I'm sure it will be a very tiresome evening with this geriatric bridge group. I'm sure half of them won't be able to remember any of the plays."

The bell rang again and finally Sara went to answer it. She couldn't stand arguing with Lillian all night while poor Dr. Elliot cooled his heels on the porch.

"Hello, Sara. Good to see you." Dr. Elliot looked neat and jaunty as usual, in a blue overcoat and a silk muffler. He put his coat and hat in the foyer on the long bench and followed Sara into the living room.

"Are you ready to go, Lillian? I thought we could stop for a bite to eat first."

Hmmm. Sounded like a real date, Sara thought with a secret smile. She wanted to tease her grandmother but didn't dare.

"I already told you, Ezra, I'm not going anywhere. I don't know why you even bothered to come here . . ."

While Lillian and Dr. Elliot bickered about the bridge party, Sara gathered her things and headed for the door.

"Good night, Lillian, Ezra. I've got to run."

"Good night, Sara. Good to see you, dear," Dr. Elliot said. "Don't worry about your grandmother. I'll take it from here."

Lillian glared at him. "Good night, Sara," she said. "Thank you for the Christmas tree. I hope you'll return in the New Year to clean up the pine needles before they ruin my Persian rugs."

"I will," Sara promised, "and I'll call before I leave for Maryland."

"Yes, do." Lillian nodded regally. "I'd like to hear from you." Which was just about her limit of showing interest and affection, Sara realized, though she did believe that in some secret place Lillian harbored a great deal of affection for her.

Sara was soon outside, on her own again. She walked quickly to her car and drove away, though she didn't quite know where she was going. It was only six o'clock—too early go home.

Even her grandmother had plans tonight and she was all alone. She wondered what Luke was up to but refused to break down and call him. She didn't want to get his answering machine, or call him on the cell phone and hear Christina's voice in the background. She'd be up all night speculating on what they were doing.

She'd be up all night speculating anyway, she realized. It wasn't a good feeling.

CHAPTER TEN

❧

$\mathcal{W}$ARREN OAKES HANDED EMILY A THICK SHEAF OF documents. "I've looked into this petition from the developers," he said. "It doesn't hold water. There are solid legal grounds to toss it out. It's a bit complicated, though. Do you want to go into it now?"

Emily skimmed the top document, her sight blurring at the dense lines of legalese. "It's all right, I believe you. I can look at this later." She leaned back in her chair and glanced at the clock. The hands were creeping toward twelve, when she would be free to run back home and check on Jane.

The hours away from the baby seemed to grow longer and longer. She found it especially hard this Monday, after she had spent all weekend with Jane. She and Dan had enjoyed themselves, just puttering around the house, finally putting up the Christmas tree and decorations. While

Emily knew the baby couldn't tell one way or the other, it just seemed much more fun preparing for the holiday with Jane around.

"The thing is," Warren continued, "do you really want to take on this fight? It could hurt you and undo all the good work we've managed so far. It's not only the zoning board who wants this. Go out and talk to anyone on the street. They'll all say they're in favor of knocking down those old hotels."

"Anyone who doesn't live there, you mean." Emily sat back in her chair and pulled off her reading glasses. "I'm all for getting after the landlords to improve those buildings, Warren. I'm all for reassessing the property taxes, too, if that's valid. Every neighborhood in this town should be clean, safe, and secure for our residents. But I won't sit by and watch a few greedy people profit while hundreds of others, who don't have any power or influence, get pushed right out of their homes."

Warren stared down at the yellow legal pad balanced on his knee and jotted something down.

When he didn't say anything, she added, "If that makes me unpopular, I'll live with it. I don't think I could be very happy with myself if I didn't try to stop this, even at the risk of losing support in the town council or the nomination next term."

"All right then." He sighed and stood up. "Don't say I didn't warn you."

Emily shrugged. "You knew where I stood. I don't think you expected me to change horses on this situation, did you?"

"No, I really didn't. Just thought I should warn you. Your pony is headed over a cliff, Emily." His tone was discouraging, but his smile strangely affectionate.

"Yes, Don Quixote's old horse. Or did he ride a donkey?"

Warren laughed quietly as he left her office. The phone

light was blinking on her private line, and Emily quickly picked up, worried it might be the new sitter, Blanche Hatcher. They had spread the word through church and found the perfect candidate, a woman in her early sixties, energetic and sharp but a warm and loving grandmother type.

Emily answered the phone to find it wasn't Blanche at all, but Nadine Preston, Jane's social worker. Nadine had visited the house twice so far to check on Jane's progress and often called for updates. Emily was starting to feel close to Nadine, as if they were longtime friends. Nadine was certainly an intimate witness to an emotionally challenging moment in her life.

"Sorry to bother you at work, Emily," Nadine began.

"That's all right. I'm just out of a meeting. What's up? Oh, before I forget, Jane had a doctor's appointment yesterday. She's gained two pounds and grown almost an inch since Thanksgiving. And Dr. Harding says the ear thing is totally cleared up."

"I'm glad to hear it. She looked very well cared for and alert when I saw you last." Nadine paused. Emily sensed she had something specific to talk about. This wasn't just a casual call.

"I have some news. We may have located a relative. We're not certain yet if this is so, or what it might mean for the baby. But I thought you and Dan should know."

Emily felt stunned, the breath knocked right out of her. She couldn't speak for what seemed like an endless moment.

"Is it Jane's mother? Have you found her?"

"No, there's no sign of Jane's mother. That seems to be conclusive. But there may be some family connection."

"I see." Emily took a breath; her pulse was racing. "Is this relative someplace nearby?"

"I'm sorry, Emily. I'm not allowed to say."

"Yes, of course. I understand. When will you know for sure?"

"It will take awhile to see how this all sorts itself out.

Then with Christmas coming, the office closes and everything stops. You know how that is."

"Yes, I do," Emily said glumly.

Christmas Eve was this coming Saturday, but offices would slow down for parties; many people would leave town for the holidays by midweek. She and Dan would be left in the dark, waiting and worrying all through Christmas. Emily had been enjoying such sweet fantasies of the holidays, with Jane free to be adopted and she and Dan somehow in agreement to do it.

"I'm sorry, Emily. I know this is a shock for you. I'll try to do all I can to get some definitive answer quickly."

"Thanks. I know you will, Nadine." Her tone subdued, Emily said good-bye and hung up the phone.

She turned in her chair and stared out the window. It was a clear, sunny day, remarkably mild for a few days before Christmas. Emily turned back to her desk, began clearing up paperwork, and then abruptly stopped.

What was she doing sitting here when she had so few hours left with Jane? She wasn't going to waste that precious time sitting in an office.

Let the town fire me if they want to, she decided in a misplaced, stormy huff. *I'm going home for the day to be with my little girl.*

My little girl—the thought caught her short. When had she started thinking of Jane that way? Well, at some point between the moment she found her and now. It was a foolish and dangerous way to be thinking, especially in light of Nadine's call. But Emily knew she couldn't help it. She was in love, plain and simple.

A short time later, Emily had Jane all to herself. Blanche was happy to have the rest of the day free, eager to finish her Christmas shopping. Emily knew the feeling. All of last week had been a frenzy of shopping and decorating, and she still wasn't finished. But today she wanted to devote her full attention to Jane. It was hard to put her down even for a moment, Emily thought, as she snuggled the baby close and fed her a bottle.

She leaned over and softly kissed the baby's brow. *Dear God, please let Jane stay with us,* she prayed silently and quickly. *Please don't take her away like this.*

She wasn't in the mood to hang around the house, looking at all the boxes that needed to be wrapped and cards that needed to be written. So she dressed Jane in some warm clothes and her snowsuit and set out with the stroller.

She pushed the stroller down to the village and walked slowly along Main Street, admiring all the beautiful Christmas displays in the shopwindows. When they came to an educational toy store, Einstein's Toy Chest, Emily picked up Jane and went in. She picked out a few scientifically designed baby toys to help sharpen Jane's hand-eye coordination and "stimulate her nerve activity for enhanced neurological development."

She also picked out a stuffed dog that had totally captivated Jane's attention. Emily knew she was in a state of denial, going on a shopping spree as a bulwark against the bad news. It wasn't going to change anything, but it made her feel better for just a moment.

She paid for the purchases and hooked the shopping bag on the stroller handle. Dan would really lose it if he saw one more gift under the tree. She might have to hide these last few gifts or maybe stick them in the baby's stocking.

If she was still around on Christmas morning to get a stocking . . .

Emily's vision went suddenly blurry with tears, but she kept walking, afraid that if she stopped she would break down altogether. She pushed the stroller to the village green and sat down on a bench facing the water. She turned the stroller so that she could see the baby and so that Jane would be out of the wind.

Jane was sound asleep, snug as a bug in her many protective layers. Emily tucked the heavy stroller blanket around her even though she knew the extra fussing wasn't necessary.

"Well, look who's here. That little girl gets out and about more than I do," Reverend Ben joked in greeting.

Emily looked up at Reverend Ben and forced a smile. She could tell from his expression, though, that he immediately saw her distress.

"Emily . . . what is it? What's wrong?" He sat down on the bench beside her.

"Jane's social worker called me a little while ago. They may have located a relative. We may have to give Jane up."

"Oh dear. That is difficult news for you."

Emily pulled a tissue from her pocket and wiped her eyes. "The social worker warned us that they might find somebody. But I guess I was just wishing so hard, I practically convinced myself they wouldn't . . ."

Ben reached over and patted her hand. He waited a few moments until she was able to stop crying. "What did Dan say?"

"He doesn't know yet. He's up in Maine today. It would be hard to tell him this over the cell phone. I wasn't ready yet anyway," she admitted. "I think he'll be disappointed, too. He's grown very fond of her."

"I'm sure he has. I saw the way he handled her in church on Sunday. It's been a good experience for him, no matter what happens."

"I guess so. It just seems so . . . unfair."

"Yes, I'm sure it does," Ben agreed. "But you took a great risk taking in this baby, Emily. Taking her into your home and your heart. I know it isn't any consolation, but from the moment they arrive, children are constantly in the process of leaving us, every minute, by infinitesimal but sure degrees."

Emily nodded. She had already had that feeling in only a few weeks. It was a miracle to watch Jane grow but at the same time frightening in some way. It cut her to the quick now to think of having to give Jane up.

"I don't know if I can do it," she admitted to Ben. "Even to a relative—some stranger, who might not even really want to raise her. Maybe there's some way I can fight it in court. Maybe I have some rights in the matter as a temporary guardian."

"Maybe," Ben said, sounding doubtful.

Emily didn't reply. Dan probably wouldn't want to go that route, even if they did have grounds to fight. They hadn't even discussed adopting the child. She had been waiting for things to settle down, for a "good moment" to bring it up, and there really hadn't been one so far.

"This is so hard for me, Ben. It's hard to explain why. Mostly, I just have this feeling that Jane has come into my life for a reason, that she's really meant to be with me. I know it's a long shot, but the feeling is so strong. I've been praying about it, praying very hard, trying to understand why God would send this baby into my life if I'm not meant to adopt her."

"Yes, I understand. This entire situation seems to have the fingerprints of the divine hand," he admitted. "If you really feel that way deep down inside, it's a hard thing to ignore. But sometimes it's hard to distinguish if those intimations are really from some greater source or from our own deepest longings, Emily."

She knew what he meant—her feelings of loss over Sara, the hole there that couldn't be filled or healed over. Ben wasn't accusing her, just posing the question—a question she asked herself time and again.

The reverend stared out at the harbor. The inlet was calm with small patches of ice floating near the shore. A gull dipped against the bright blue sky, out above the water.

Emily chose her words carefully. "I know what you're saying. That's certainly part of what makes caring for her so meaningful to me. But this feeling . . . I don't think it's that. Not entirely."

"All right then. There very well might be some higher

purpose to the baby coming into your care, Emily. It certainly was a strange coincidence. I'd be the last one to deny that. But the reason why this has all come about may not be at all what you or I or anyone would expect. We just don't know what God has in store for us. It's not only useless but frustrating to try to second-guess or," he added, "force our own will on a situation."

Emily smiled ruefully. "You know me, Ben. I'm the persistent type. Once I set my mind on something, it's hard to let go."

"Yes, I know that. Everyone in town knows that," he said affectionately. "It's always been a strength of yours, a key to your success. But every strong trait in a personality comes with pluses and minuses. There's a time to be persistent . . . and a time to let go. Perhaps we should pray for the best outcome for the baby, whatever that may be," he added quietly. "I know that it's hard for you to put this all in God's hands and trust Him to sort it out. It takes a lot of trust and faith and courage. And above all else, a great deal of love for this child."

"It's hard to do that, very hard." Emily took a steadying breath, not wanting to cry again. "I'll think about it. I'll try," she promised. She leaned over and gave Ben a quick hug. "Thanks for talking to me. You've helped a lot."

The reverend looked surprised, then gently smiled. "I'm the thankful one, Emily. Glad I ran into you out here. If you or Dan need to talk at all, please call or come and see me?"

"Yes, of course. I will," she said.

Ben rose and touched her shoulder then headed back to the church. Emily remained where she was, staring out at the water. She felt bleak and empty. Ben was right; she had taken a great risk, reached out for her heart's desire. Now it seemed it would end in heartache and disappointment.

Would God do this to her . . . again? It didn't seem right. She wavered between feelings of desperate hope, anger, and complete despair. She just had to try to see her way clear to the high ground, as Ben advised, and trust that God was working toward that goal as well: the best outcome for the baby . . . even if it didn't include her and Dan.

SARA SAT AT HER DESK WONDERING WHAT TO DO. SHE was already late for her tutoring sessions at New Horizons. It wouldn't be right to cancel now. Yet she just couldn't face the prospect of running into Luke there again. Or worse, seeing him with Christina.

She had heard through the grapevine that Christina had rented a cottage on Beach Road and had moved into town last weekend. No wonder there had been no word from Luke. Obviously, he had been busy helping Christina get settled in.

Sara felt awful disappointing the kids, but she just couldn't do it. There would be a break in the schedule through Christmas; maybe after that she would feel better about things and be able to go back.

She called the center and spoke to one of the teachers, Craig North, concocting an excuse that she had to work late. She did have a ton of work to clear off her desk before the holiday, mostly because she had been so preoccupied lately with Luke.

"Don't worry, I can cover for you," Craig said.

"Thanks, I owe you one." Sara felt relieved. At least her students wouldn't miss out.

"They're pretty distracted right now with the holidays. You're coming to the Christmas party Thursday, aren't you?"

"No, I can't make it. I'm going out of town—to Maryland, to see my family."

"Oh . . . that's nice." Craig sounded surprised, probably since he knew Luke wasn't going anywhere for the holidays. "Well, have a good trip. Merry Christmas and all that."

"Merry Christmas, Craig. Have a nice vacation."

Sara hung up feeling unsettled. It wasn't going to be easy untwining her life from Luke's in this small town.

She turned to her computer, ready to go back to work. There was a new e-mail in her box and she clicked it open. She recognized the address as the Philadelphia paper where she had sent her clips. She read the message quickly, a short note from the managing editor. He liked her clips and wanted to set up an interview. Sara felt jumpy with nerves. The news was exciting and stressful at the same time.

She quickly wrote back, saying she could meet with him on Thursday or Friday, on her way to Maryland, if he would let her know a convenient time.

She paused a moment before clicking the "send" command. Did she really want to do this? What if she got the job? Would she really move away from Cape Light?

Sara took a deep breath and sent the e-mail. She would do the interview, and figure the rest out later. After all, if she had plans to take a new job and move away, it would be easier to confront Luke and settle things once and for all, she reasoned. If he was going to hook up with Christina, wasn't it better to move away?

A few hours later, Sara was the only reporter left in the office. She was concentrating on a revision and hardly noticed when Lindsay passed her desk on her way out, asking her to shut out the lights and lock the door when she left.

Sara didn't mind staying alone in the office. She liked the quiet. It helped her concentrate and made the work go faster.

She wasn't sure how long it was after that when she heard the sound of voices outside on the street. She picked up her head and listened. Carolers, coming toward the newspaper office.

She stood up and looked over the edge of the partitions that surrounded her desk. A group of carolers from New Horizons stood just outside the storefront window of the newspaper office. Her heart skipped a beat as she saw Luke among them.

She briefly considered ducking down again and hiding in her cubicle, like a prairie dog going back down its hole. But that would be ridiculous, she reasoned. She had to acknowledge them.

She slung a sweater around her shoulders, walked over to the door, and pulled it open as they finished "Deck the Halls."

Sara clapped. "Thanks, that was great. We have a ton of Christmas cookies and some really stale coffee. Want to come in for a pit stop?"

"No, thanks, we've had enough free cookies for one night." Peggy, one of the teachers Sara knew well, grinned at her.

"We have to get the kids back to the center. You're our last stop," Craig added.

"Well, thanks for remembering me. Merry Christmas, everyone. Have a great holiday." Sara glanced around at the group, her gaze catching Luke's.

"I'll come in for a minute." Luke turned to Craig. "You guys go ahead without me. I'll catch you later."

Before Sara could protest or make some excuse, the group of strolling singers wandered off toward Main Street and she was left alone with Luke.

"So . . . can I come in? It's freezing out here," he added, rubbing his bare hands together.

Of course, instead of wearing a reasonable coat, gloves, scarf, and hat, like everyone else in town—like everyone in all of New England—Luke wore only a flannel shirt and his battered leather jacket. Sara didn't even bother to point out that he should have dressed more warmly. She just pulled open the door and walked inside, knowing he would follow.

"The coffee is back by Lindsay's office. Help yourself."

"I'll skip the coffee, thanks. I really just wanted to talk

to you. Craig North said you were working late so I figured you'd still be here."

"Yes, I had to miss the tutoring so I could catch up on work." She crossed her arms over her chest. "It's not really a good time. Maybe you should have called first."

Luke let out a long frustrated breath. She wasn't making this easy for him, but why should she? She had a good idea of what he wanted to talk about—how it was time to face things, how if she couldn't make a commitment, he would have to move on.

She didn't want to have that talk right now. She wasn't ready. And he wasn't going to drag her through it either.

Luke tilted his head to one side. "Okay then, why don't we make a date?" When she didn't answer, he added, "You know, that thing you do when you meet another person for a few hours. Maybe have a meal at a restaurant?"

"Sorry, I'm too busy this week. I'm going out of town."

"To see your folks, you mean? When are you leaving?"

"On Thursday morning. I have a job interview on the way down, in Philadelphia."

She wasn't sure why she blurted that out. The interview wasn't even confirmed. Maybe she just wanted to see his reaction. Would he be upset about her going, or relieved?

Luke looked so stunned, she almost felt sorry for him.

"I told you I sent out my clips. Maybe you don't remember—"

"I remember. You wanted to work on a bigger paper. I thought the bigger paper was going to be in Boston, though, where I was somehow worked into the picture."

"I sent my clips to a lot of places. This is the one that answered."

"Right. It's that simple, is it?" He dug his hands in his pockets and his gaze narrowed.

"I sent my clips to a few papers in Boston. They didn't

answer. So I need to go to this interview, if only to hear them out. It might be a good opportunity."

It wasn't the entire reason she wanted to go, and both of them knew it. Sara sighed and drifted back toward her desk.

She moved some pieces of paper around on the desktop but didn't sit down. When she looked up again, over the top of the dividers that surrounded her desk, Luke was still staring at her.

"Well, that settles that, I guess." His voice was clipped and falsely bright. "Good luck with your interview. Have a nice holiday and all that stuff. Have a nice *life* in Philadelphia," he added, not even bothering now to hide his sarcasm.

Sara nodded, just wishing he would go.

He turned away so quickly, she found herself saying good-bye to his back.

Just as well, she thought, sinking down into her chair. She hid her face in her hands and heard the front door to the office slam. She didn't know if he had bothered to look back at her. She didn't want him to see her crying anyway.

It was the only time she was ever glad that she worked in a cubicle.

"EMILY? I'M HOME." EMILY STIRRED IN HER SLEEP AS Dan softly called her name.

When she opened her eyes, he leaned over and kissed her. His cheek was still cold from the outdoors.

"What time is it?" She sat up slowly and wiggled her shoulders, which felt cramped from sleeping on the couch.

"About eleven. I called from the road. I guess you didn't get the message."

"I didn't hear it. I must have been sleeping."

"You should have gone to bed. You didn't have to wait up."

"That's all right. I wanted to." Emily watched him take off his jacket and cap.

He sat down next to her and put his arm around her shoulder. "How's the baby?"

"She's fine," Emily said slowly. "She should be up soon for a bottle."

"I can stay with her tomorrow night if you need to finish your shopping."

Emily remembered asking Dan if he would mind if she ran out to the stores tomorrow. It didn't seem to matter now, though.

She turned and looked at him. It was going to be hard to tell him the news from Nadine Preston. Telling Dan made it more real. But she knew she couldn't put it off any longer.

"I had a call from Nadine today," she began. "She told me the investigation may have turned up a relative. Not Jane's mother . . . but someone else. Someone who might take Jane."

There, she said it. Her throat was suddenly thick, her eyes watery again.

Dan's expression was instantly alarmed. "A relative? I thought they were done searching."

"Well, I guess not. Not completely."

He rubbed her shoulder, pulling her closer. "What about the timing of all this? Did she say when they would know?"

Emily shrugged. "She wasn't sure. Maybe before Christmas or maybe after. I'm not sure how quickly they would . . . take Jane away."

She couldn't stand it anymore and pressed her head to Dan's shoulder, crying freely now.

He stroked her hair and kissed her cheek. "Sweetheart, I know it's hard. But we knew she was only going to be with us temporarily. Even if they didn't find a relative, we would have to give her up at some point down the road, when she's finally adopted."

Emily couldn't answer. Didn't Dan see that if by some miracle Jane was available to them, they had to be the ones to adopt her?

But she felt too worn out and heartsick to argue about that now. She settled for saying, "It just doesn't seem fair. I thought we would have more time with her."

Dan met her gaze but didn't answer.

"Don't you feel bad about losing her?"

He hesitated just a moment, then nodded his head. "Yes . . . yes, I do. You know that."

He sighed and brushed Emily's cheek with the back of his hand. "It will hurt us both if she goes, but it might be for the best, Emily."

"That's what Reverend Ben said. I saw him today, out on the green. He said I ought to try to let this go and trust that God will figure out what's best for the baby. Do you think that's true?"

Emily knew her husband wasn't the most religious man. He hadn't set foot in a church for years before they got together. Dan was very spiritual in his own way, though. He always said his church was the open sea and the sky above, and that he and God had their best talks while he was sailing.

"Yes, I do, dear." He leaned over and kissed her. "I think we have no choice now but to just wait and see."

CHAPTER ELEVEN

❦

"SARA, YOU BOUGHT WAY TOO MANY PRESENTS AND spent much too much on us. Really, dear . . ." Emily shook her head, watching as Sara emptied out her two shopping bags of gifts and arranged them under Emily and Dan's Christmas tree.

"I found some really hip little outfits for Jane at a store in Newburyport, but I'm not going to tell you more. I want you to be surprised."

Emily gazed at her, a soft warm light in her eyes. Sara knew it was hard for her to talk about Jane, now that everything was up in the air with the investigation. It was partly the news that the baby might be leaving soon that caused Sara to run out and buy even more gifts for her.

She sat on the couch with Emily again. They had just finished dinner, and after coffee and dessert, Dan had disappeared into his study.

"The house looks beautiful." Sara gazed around at the

elegant decorations. Though Emily wasn't usually big on holiday decorating, she had gone all out this year. "Are you sure one of those home makeover shows didn't sneak in here?"

Emily smiled. "No, I did it all myself. On a spree, I guess you could say."

A happy spree, inspired by the hope that she would adopt the baby, Sara knew. She felt so bad for Emily. Her feelings of being overshadowed by Jane seemed so immature now, so insignificant in comparison.

Emily took a sip of coffee. "So you leave tomorrow morning. Are you driving?"

Sara nodded. She hadn't told Emily yet about the job interview. It was difficult to find the right words, especially knowing all she was going through right now with Jane.

But Sara couldn't hide it from her. She didn't want to. They had always had a very honest relationship. That was one of the wonderful things about it.

"I'm going to stop off in Philadelphia," she began. "I sent my clips out to some newspapers a few weeks ago, and an editor down there contacted me. I've got an interview."

Emily frowned as if she didn't understand. "An interview? Are you going to write freelance for them?"

Sara shook her head. "No, for a full-time job." She took a deep breath. This was even harder than she thought it would be. "I've been thinking about working on a bigger paper, Emily. I think I'm ready to leave Cape Light."

Emily sat back, looking surprised and dismayed. "I didn't know you were unhappy at the paper, Sara. You never complain about it."

"I am happy there," Sara said quickly. "It's a cool place to work and Lindsay is a great boss, really. I could probably stay there forever, if I wanted to. But sometimes I think I need something more challenging."

Emily was silent for a moment. Sara could see her gathering her thoughts. "I understand. I just wish you didn't have to go so far away. But I know reporters move around a lot. Maybe after Philadelphia you'll come back up to Boston or New York."

"Maybe," Sara said, grateful that Emily wasn't pressuring her to stay in Cape Light.

Emily cast her a concerned look. "It's also because of Luke, isn't it?"

"Not really. I sent all these clips out way before we started having problems. I do want to advance in my career, which means moving to a bigger paper. That was part of our argument actually . . . our first argument." Sara knew her voice sounded sad. She couldn't help it.

Emily leaned over suddenly and hugged her tight. "Oh, Sara, honey, I wish you didn't have to go through all this painful stuff. I hate to see you feeling so sad about Luke. I wish there was something I could do."

Sara closed her eyes and hugged Emily back. Emily loved her and would be there for her, always. How could she have ever doubted it? There was enough love in Emily's heart to go around, even if she adopted ten children.

They parted slowly. Sara felt a little teary but managed not to cry. Emily took her hand. "I wish you luck with the interview, honey, if this is what you really want."

"Thanks. It was hard for me to tell you."

"I know, and I'm glad you did. I can't say I like the idea of you moving away. But I know I've been lucky you wanted to stay in Cape Light as long as you did. Having you here has been a great gift to me, Sara. You probably can't realize."

"I think I do . . ." Sara wanted to tell Emily how much their relationship meant to her, too. But somehow the words failed her.

She heard the baby crying in another room.

"Jane's up," Emily said. She started to get up from the couch.

"I'll get her," Sara said, and before Emily could argue, she rose and left the room.

Emily's bedroom was cast in soft shadows, lit by a small nightlight on the baby's changing table. Jane was lying on her back, wearing one-piece pajamas with covered feet. She was tangled in a blanket, but stopped crying as soon as she saw Sara.

Sara lifted her up and checked her diaper. All dry. Maybe she's hungry, she thought. Or just wants some company.

The baby felt so soft and smelled so good. She hugged her close and kissed the top of her feathery head.

She was such a dear. Maybe it wouldn't be so hard to have a baby if she had one as sweet as Jane. Sara felt shocked for a moment at the thought, but she knew it was true.

She held Jane close, the baby's head resting on her shoulder. She wondered if this would be the last time she'd see Jane, or hold her like this. The realization took her breath away, it was so stunningly final.

"Little Jane. You little sweet potato . . . I hope you don't go," Sara whispered. "I could have been your big sister. I would have loved that," she said honestly. "I really would have."

IN THE DAYS AFTER NADINE PRESTON'S CALL, EMILY knew she was hard to live with. She was depressed and distracted, jumping out of her skin every time the phone rang. When Christmas Eve arrived and they still hadn't heard from Nadine, she decided that she didn't feel up to her sister's big Christmas Eve party. There would be so many people, so much revelry; besides, she couldn't imagine facing all the questions about Jane.

Emily sat at the breakfast table with Dan, feeding Jane a bottle. "I hate to disappoint Jessica and Sam, but I don't think I can handle it," she admitted.

"Don't worry," Dan said. "Your sister will understand."

"Yes, she does." Jessica had been a great support ever since Emily had taken in the baby. She had already told

Emily not to give it a thought; she and Sam would understand if Emily and Dan didn't make the party.

Emily lifted Jane to her shoulder with a practiced motion. "What if Nadine calls today? She might, you know."

"I don't think we'll hear anything more until after Christmas. So many offices are closed," he said reasonably. "But I understand. I don't feel much in the mood for a party either. Let's have a quiet night here, just the three of us."

"I'll make a nice dinner," she promised.

"Where are you going to get takeout from, hon? Willoughby's?" he teased.

Emily made a face at him, and he laughed, then pulled her close for a comforting hug.

Emily appreciated Dan's understanding. She had been trying to prepare herself for the inevitable call, but she knew that no amount of preparation would make her truly ready.

This is all my doing, she realized. *Everybody warned me, and I went ahead and set myself up for all this heartache.*

But when she held Jane in her arms, she knew that, given a chance to decide all over again, she would have done exactly the same thing.

The phone rang late that afternoon. Emily, who was sitting in the kitchen with Jane in her arms, nearly jumped out of the chair. It rang once, twice. Emily couldn't decide if she should answer it or let the machine pick up. Where was Dan? Couldn't he be the one to get the bad news first?

Finally, not able to stand it a second longer, she got up and grabbed the receiver.

"Hello?" she said, her heart hammering.

"Jessica? You don't sound yourself. Are you coming down with a cold? I really need to know because I can't afford to be catching all kinds of germs at my age, Christmas or not."

Emily reeled back at the sound of her mother's voice

then forced herself to speak. "It isn't Jessica, Mother. It's Emily."

"Emily? What are you doing over there? I thought you weren't coming to the party."

Emily sighed and shook her head. She hadn't spoken a word to her mother since their scene in the church sanctuary almost three weeks ago. Now, being greeted by this "Who's on first?" routine felt absurd, but somehow not surprising.

"I'm at home, Mother. *My* home," Emily said with a calmness she didn't really feel. "You apparently dialed the wrong number."

"Oh, I see. It must be that new phone you picked out for me with the autodial. It doesn't work right, never did."

Naturally, Lillian couldn't even admit to having dialed a wrong number. It had to be the phone.

There was a long silence. Emily felt she should say something. After all, it was Christmas Eve; she ought to at least try to make amends with her mother. She had felt guilty not speaking to her these past few weeks, though she had kept up on her through Jessica's reports. Lillian hadn't called and Emily hadn't called her. Even though Lillian was the one at fault, Emily knew she ought to now turn the other cheek. That was the right thing to do.

Somehow, though, she just couldn't.

The baby squirmed and let out a little whimper.

"What was that?" her mother said. "Oh right, the *abandoned* baby." She gave a slight cough. "Your sister told me a relative may have been located. You might have to give the child up."

"Yes, we're waiting to hear," Emily said honestly.

"Well, I won't say I told you so. No good deed goes unpunished, though. Did you ever hear that expression?"

"No, I don't think so," Emily said.

"Well, think about it. The next time you try to run out and save the world, I mean." Her mother paused. Emily was about to say good-bye and hang up. "I'm sure you've done a good job caring for her, but the child should go to family if possible. It's only natural and logical."

Logical perhaps, Emily thought, but somehow not entirely right.

When Emily didn't reply, she heard her mother noisily clearing her throat. "I'm sure it will be hard to give the child up, after all the time and emotion you've invested."

"Yes, it will be. Very hard." Emily knew her words sounded thick, but she fought very hard not to cry.

She waited again, wondering if her mother was going to apologize for her outburst at the church.

Her mother sighed. "There's a price for loving, Emily. Sometimes it's very steep. But you know that already, I imagine." Her mother's voice trailed off, sounding as if she was talking mainly to herself. "Well, I won't see you tonight. I won't wish you a Merry Christmas. I'm sure you won't be having one. Try to be realistic. Face the situation bravely," she advised.

"All right, Mother. Thanks for the advice." Emily's tone was edged with irony, but she also knew her mother was sincere, trying to offer some support. What she could, at any rate.

"Have a good time tonight," Emily added.

"Good time? With all that noise? All those children? You should see the way they go at the gifts, like a pack of piranhas in a feeding frenzy. That's hardly my idea of a relaxing holiday get-together."

As Emily well knew. Lillian's notion of celebration was so refined, it was hard to tell there even was a holiday going on.

"Good night, Emily. Give my regards to your husband," Lillian said. Emily thanked her and said good night, then hung up the phone.

She looked down at Jane and slowly rocked her in her arms. It wasn't the call she expected, and her mother hadn't even come close to apologizing. Then again, Lillian never would. At least Emily and her mother were on speaking terms again. That was one less worry hanging over her head as Christmas quickly approached.

ON CHRISTMAS MORNING, EMILY AND DAN GOT UP EARLY and opened some of their gifts. Emily opened Jane's packages, too, oohing and ahhing with delight over all the beautiful presents so many friends and relatives had given her.

Sara had picked out a box full of clothes—amazing, arty creations. Tiny purple leopard-skin stretch pants and a purple and black tunic top. A hot pink hooded sweater, trimmed with white fur, with little white ears on top. And most amazing of all, matching hot pink high-tops.

"Look Dan," Emily held up the sneakers. "Jane can shoot baskets with you now."

"As soon as the snow clears," Dan said, laughing at the fantastic little shoes.

They dressed quickly for church and made it right on time. They were getting better at this, Emily observed, noticing how they packed up all the necessary equipment without too much fuss and bother.

The sanctuary was crowded, with just about every pew filled. The choir was singing a lively carol, their voices blending in harmony. Emily felt her spirit lifted by the music as she and Dan found a place in a rear row. Looking up front, she saw her sister and Sam, along with her two nephews and her mother, sitting with Dr. Elliot, who only came to church on Christmas and Easter.

"Merry Christmas, everyone," Reverend Ben greeted the congregation. "It's a wonderful day, Christmas Day. A day of miracles and fresh, new beginnings. Let us come together now and worship, rejoicing in God's word."

Emily tried to pay close attention to the service, but her thoughts kept drifting. She had been praying long and often the past few days, trying to give her problem up to God and asking only for the best outcome for Jane. It had been difficult though—nearly impossible.

Deep in her heart she felt she wasn't being totally sincere. Couldn't God see that? Did her prayers still count? She hoped they did. She hoped God was at least seeing that she was trying to do the right thing.

Ultimately, though, she couldn't change her real feelings about giving up the baby, not even for God, it seemed.

Reverend Ben was partway through his sermon. She realized she had missed some of the beginning. He was talking about the miracle of Christmas, about spiritual rebirth and renewal.

". . . and if you have ever been around small children—and most of us have at one point or another—then you know what I mean. Children have a way of making you feel new. Especially small children, babies, who are experiencing everything in this beautiful world for the first time. And watching them, we vicariously do, too. We rediscover and relearn. We lose our skepticism, our cynicism, our malaise. We see everything with new eyes, through their eyes. We taste and touch and smell everything as if for the first time, and the world seems so astounding, so magical.

"That's what Christmas is like. Each year when this day comes, we have the chance to feel new, to start new, like the infant Jesus. To be reborn in God's love and his promise. That's the miracle of Christmas. To believe again in miracles. To lose our skepticism and negativity and malaise. To see the world with new eyes, a fresh, energized perspective. To trust in God's love with the innocent, absolute trust of a child. To feel sheltered and protected in His hands . . ."

Emily sat in rapt wonder, the words hitting a perfect bull's-eye somewhere in her heart. That was the gift Jane had given her, both her and Dan. Jane had made them new again. She had refreshed and renewed their spirits. That was the magic of having a little baby. If there was some purpose in God's having sent Jane into their lives, maybe that was at the heart of it.

It would be hard to remain in this state without her, Emily reflected. But she would try.

At the end of the service, they drifted out toward the sanctuary. "Any news yet?" Reverend Ben asked them as they met him in the doorway.

"No, not yet." Emily tried to smile and shook her head.

"Still waiting," Dan added.

"Please call me when you hear something. I'd like to know." Reverend Ben hugged Emily briefly. "Have a peaceful, blessed Christmas," he said to them.

"Thank you, Reverend. We will call you," Dan promised.

Emily swallowed hard. She didn't know what to say. She met Reverend Ben's gaze and somehow knew he understood her feelings perfectly.

Out in the sanctuary, they were immediately surrounded by family and friends. Jessica came up and hugged her tightly.

"Merry Christmas, Emily. Oh . . . I know it isn't a happy one for you, though. How are you holding up?"

"I'm doing all right, as well as can be expected."

"Here, let me have Jane a minute." Jessica reached over and took the baby. She lifted her up in her arms and snuggled her, cheek to cheek. "Look at that pretty little dress. You look like a princess," Jessica cooed to her.

It was a beautiful dress, burgundy velvet with lace on the hem, sleeves, and collar. A matching lace headband with a velvet rose completed the ensemble, along with tiny patent leather shoes. Emily had bought it at a boutique in Newburyport. Price seemed no object when it came to Jane.

"I'm sorry we couldn't come last night," Emily apologized.

"That's all right." Jessica shook her head. "We understand. I made a big tray of leftovers for you. You won't have to cook for a week."

"Thanks, Jess. That was sweet of you."

Emily knew she would be in such a state next week, she probably wouldn't be able to cook or even eat.

Emerging from the crowd, she noticed Sam leading her mother toward them. Emily was glad now that they had spoken yesterday, even though it had been by accident. Afterward, she had wondered if her mother's calling her number had really been an accident at all. Maybe it was her subconscious taking control, or even a ploy. Though, of course, Lillian would never admit to either.

"So here we all are." Her mother sniffed and looked around, obviously trying to be on her best behavior. "I'd wish you a happy Christmas, Emily, but I know that's hardly the case."

"Thank you, Mother . . . for your consideration."

Lillian glanced at her but didn't answer. She looked over at Jane, who sat comfortably in Jessica's arms. "Nice dress. That must have cost a pretty penny, especially these days. Reminds me of one I had for you, Emily, smocking on top, lace collar, all handmade. You were just that age. What a coincidence."

"I suppose," Emily said. Leave it to her mother to make more fuss over the dress than the child wearing it.

Dan soon joined them and they talked for a while. Jessica invited them to come over later for a quiet dinner with just the close family, but once again, Emily and Dan begged off.

"If you change your mind and want some company, just give us a call." Jessica's expression was full of warmth and concern as she leaned over and hugged Emily good-bye. "Let us know if you hear anything?"

"I will," Emily said, hugging her sister back. "You'll be the very first."

Back at home, Jane went down for a nap and Emily

cleared up the piles of wrapping paper and boxes littering the living room. She had a nap herself, though she had gone to bed early the night before and knew she shouldn't feel so tired. It was the stress of all this waiting, she thought.

That evening, she set the table with their best china and crystal, even though it was only for herself and Dan. She didn't want to ignore the holiday altogether, and trying to make things nice provided some distraction. She made a filet mignon roast, with string beans, mushrooms, and a special potato recipe she had gotten from Jessica. The meal was one of Dan's favorites, and despite his teasing, it came out just right.

They had just sat down to dinner and were saying grace when the phone rang. Emily felt her heart skip a beat, but Dan kept tight hold of her hand. "Don't get up. Let the machine get it. We just started dinner."

She looked up at him for a moment, about to agree, then jumped up out of her seat. "Sorry, I have to go see who it is," she called over her shoulder as she ran into the kitchen.

She heard a woman's voice murmuring on the answering machine, but she didn't recognize it. She grabbed at the phone and greeted the caller breathlessly.

"Emily, I didn't think you were there," Nadine Preston said.

"I'm here." Emily tried to catch her breath but now her heartbeat raced. "We were just starting dinner."

"Oh, sorry to interrupt."

"No, that's okay. I guess this must be important if you're calling on Christmas."

"Yes . . . it is."

Emily felt so light-headed all of a sudden, she thought she might pass out. She sat down quickly in a chair, her hands shaking. She hadn't realized, but Dan had followed her. He stood behind her with his hands pressed solidly to her shoulders.

"We did not find anyone related to Jane," Nadine said.

"I can't tell you much more than that, only that the information we had didn't lead to an appropriate guardian. The investigation isn't officially closed yet, but it will be shortly and Jane will be available for adoption."

Emily gripped the phone so hard, her hand shook. "She will? Do you really think so?"

"Yes, Emily. I wouldn't tell you if I thought it was in doubt. It will just take a few days more for the paperwork to go through. How do you and Dan feel about that?"

"Thrilled . . . overjoyed . . ." She suddenly remembered Dan standing behind her and realized she shouldn't speak for both of them. "I need to tell Dan about this," she said hurriedly. "Can we talk tomorrow?"

"Yes, of course. Call me at the home number or on my cell phone. I'm taking a few days off to be with my family."

"Good for you. Have a good holiday, Nadine. Thanks for calling. Merry Christmas!" Emily said in an ecstatic rush.

"Same to you, Emily. Same to you."

Emily hung up the phone and turned to Dan, who watched her with a questioning expression.

"I can guess from your reaction, Nadine didn't say social services was taking the baby any time soon."

"She said a relative wasn't found and that they're closing the investigation. Jane will be free to be adopted in a few days, after all the paperwork goes through."

She felt breathless again, waiting and watching for his reaction. "Isn't that great news?" she prodded him.

Dan swallowed hard. He looked stunned, she thought, like he was processing the news slowly. But that wasn't necessarily a bad sign, was it?

"I don't know what to say, Emily. It seems like a mixed blessing to me."

"What do you mean?" she asked incredulously. "It's just what I've been hoping for, praying for. I don't see anything mixed about it. Don't you want to adopt her?"

She hadn't intended to ask him so bluntly. The question

had just popped out. But she needed to know. They needed to get this out on the table right now.

"Emily, this all puts me in a very difficult spot. Sending the child to a relative would have been hard, no question. But it would have been a solution to the problem that I think we both would have been able to live with in time." Dan paused, pacing across the kitchen. "I don't think that you could have objected that strongly, when all was said and done, to sending the child to live with her own family. But now . . ." He shook his head, looking confused and upset. "Now we're forced to sort this out, between us. And I'm sorry, but I know we are not of one mind about this, Emily, though we may be of one heart."

Emily sighed. Why did she have to go and marry such an eloquent, intellectual man? It made it all the harder to win an argument.

"Dan, just think about it," Emily started off reasonably. "Jane isn't going to a family member. She'll be placed with perfect strangers, some couple like us or even not as caring. Why not us, Dan? I know what I promised. I know I said I wouldn't do this . . . but honestly . . . why not us?"

He rested his hands on her shoulders. "I know that deal you made, promising we would only keep her as temporary guardians, was a ploy from the start, Emily. Just a scheme to get this baby into the house. And I forgive you for it," he said tenderly. "How could I not? But I have a more objective perspective on this situation, dear. I'm looking at the bigger picture."

"Which is?" she asked quietly.

"Is it really fair to the baby to be stuck with such older parents? When Jane is eighteen, I'll be . . . almost seventy." She winced and pulled away. "Well, I will be. That's a plain fact."

"It's still not a good enough reason, Dan. Lots of older couples have children these days, and you'll probably live into your nineties."

"Emily, don't you think it will be painful for me to give her up when the time comes? But we have to be realistic. The baby has changed our lives, turned this place upside down. This isn't the way I planned to live when I gave up the paper. Is this fair to me?"

She sighed and let out a long frustrated breath. No, it wasn't fair to him. It wasn't what he planned at all.

"It would be a great sacrifice for you," she agreed. "I mean, unless you had a change of heart and it didn't feel like it really was a sacrifice. I mean, if you loved her and really wanted to do it . . ." Her voice trailed off. She could see that he was getting irritated.

"Don't make me out to be the villain here, please. You know that's not what's going on."

"Yes, I know. I'm sorry," she said quickly.

"I've already had the experience of raising children, Emily. I don't feel unfulfilled in that area. Some men my age do, but I don't," he told her. "I'm sorry if it sounds selfish to you, but we need to be honest. I've worked hard all my life and didn't envision my retirement years filled with homework and soccer games and band concerts. I want to travel, write. I want you to give up your office so we can have adventures together, maybe live in another country for a year or two—"

"We can do all those things, Dan. Just because we have a child doesn't mean we'll be stuck in the house for the rest of our lives, that you can't write or we can't travel."

"Emily, you don't understand. It's not that easy—"

"It doesn't have to be the way it was with you and Claire, raising your kids. It can be different. It can be anything we want it to be, Dan. Don't you see that?"

When he didn't answer, she pushed on. "We both love her. What's more important than that? Yes, it's been confusing and scary and hard work. And yes, it's totally turned our lives upside down. But for the good, Dan. All for the good, I feel."

He started to say something, but she wouldn't let him interrupt her. He had had his turn; now it was hers. She felt as if she was fighting for her life—not just for Jane's fate, but the fate of her very marriage.

"What is a more worthy 'retirement' project than raising a child? Basically, saving this child's life? Writing a book? Taking a vacation?" she asked, meeting his gaze squarely. "There are many benefits to being an older parent. I've already seen it with me and Sara. You're calmer; you have more life experience and more to give the child. You're not chasing after your career goals anymore. Wasn't that the real problem when you were raising Lindsay and Wyatt? Isn't that really why you feel so overwhelmed by this idea?"

Dan faced her a moment, then stalked across the kitchen. He poured himself a glass of orange juice and drank it out of their best crystal. "I wasn't a very good father when the kids were young. You know that. I've told you," he said curtly.

"Perhaps, but you're good with Jane. Maybe it's different for you now."

"I've been a little better with her," he admitted. "But let's be realistic. It's only been a month. I was a washout as a father, Emily, plain and simple. It's not something I really want to relive."

Emily walked closer to him and looked him in the eye. "You grieve over those years, Dan. I don't see why you wouldn't want to try again and do a better job this time. I know you could."

He stared at her, shocked by her frankness she realized.

"Do you love me?" She spoke in a clear, even voice.

He blinked and shook his head. "You know I do. For pity's sake, don't do this."

"I'm sorry, Dan. That's what it comes down to for me. If you really love me, you'll find a way to make this happen. I know you love the baby," she said simply.

"Yes, I do," he finally admitted. "Though, unlike you, I don't see how that changes the hard realities."

"The hard realities." She nearly laughed at him. "My hard reality was giving up Sara. You know that. Finding her again should have been the cure, but it hasn't been. The experience of raising her, which you take for granted, was stolen from me, Dan. It can never be replaced, I know that. But maybe this is a chance for both of us to do it over right. Did you ever think of that?"

"Emily—"

"I believe in my heart that finding this baby was meant to be, Dan. I believe she's meant to be with us. You and me."

Dan shut his eyes momentarily, rejecting the idea, she thought. But maybe—hopefully—just having a tough time letting it in?

"They say that when God closes a door, He always opens a window," Emily went on. "I closed the door on God, and now He's had to send Jane through a window. Don't you see that?"

"No, I don't." Dan's voice was even, not angry or emotional in any way. "I think it's easy for you to cling to some . . . some fantasy and say, 'This was meant to be. We just have to go through with this because I have this feeling,' instead of looking at it realistically, unemotionally. Then you'd see that there are plenty of couples out there, younger couples with lots of love and care to give, who would be good parents to Jane—just as good as we might be, if not better."

His words seemed harsh, almost cruel, and Emily reeled back, as if she had been struck. There didn't seem to be any hope left here. He would never budge an inch on this.

She suddenly wished that she was single again and had her own life and could just do as she pleased. Then she felt shock at even thinking such a thing, it seemed such a betrayal of Dan. She had been so happy with him, so thrilled to have fallen in love with him. She had never once yearned for her old life, except for now. Wanting Jane so much, she couldn't help but think that when she was single, she never had to ask anyone's permission to do what she wanted. She never had to work for a consensus and compromise.

Now when it felt as if a gift from God had been placed at her doorstep, she couldn't embrace it without Dan's permission. She felt so frustrated at that moment, she wanted to scream.

"I'll tell you what your fantasy is, Dan," she said finally, unable to let it go. "You're always talking about adventure and the new experiences that are out there. The real adventure is right here, Dan, right under this roof. It is for me, anyway."

"That isn't fair, Emily."

"Why not?" she challenged him. "I think it's fair and true."

"What if the shoe were on the other foot? Can you try for just a minute to imagine that? How would you feel if I were trying to talk you into something so momentous by pulling every trick in the book?"

"If I saw how much it meant to you, I would do it," she told him. "That's what I think marriage is about. We can't split things right down the middle all the time; sometimes it's one person getting 100 percent of what they need, and the other getting zero."

He stared at her, his head tilted back. She knew that look. He had had enough.

"Are we done now?" he asked angrily.

Emily didn't answer. The phone rang. Maybe it was Nadine Preston again with more news. Emily didn't feel able to talk to anyone right now.

Dan didn't either. They both stood and listened as the machine picked up the call.

"Emily, it's Dick Sanborne." She recognized the town

fire chief's voice. "There's a fire down at Wood's Hollow. We've sent two trucks and both ambulances, the equipment from the midstation, too."

Emily ran to the phone and picked it up. "I'm here, Dick. I heard what you said. Where are you calling from?"

"I'm down here at the site. We're working on it. It's bad. We have a call into Essex for more trucks and men. We came up short on crew, with the holiday and all."

"I'll be right down."

Emily hung up the phone and turned to Dan. He'd heard the message, too, and his anger had vanished, replaced by deep concern.

"I'm going down to the fire," she said.

"Yes, of course. It sounds bad."

"I think it must be. Dick hardly ever calls me, and he sounds worried."

She sat in a kitchen chair and yanked off her heels, replacing them with a pair of heavy boots. She didn't have time to change out of her suit but pulled a heavy sweater she found in the mudroom over her silk blouse, and then put on her down jacket and woolen gloves.

Suddenly she remembered Jane, who was still napping. She would be up soon, though, and somebody had to take care of her. They couldn't call Blanche Hatcher, not on Christmas night.

She glanced at Dan as she pulled on her woolen gloves. "Can you take care of Jane? She'll need a bottle when she wakes up."

"Of course I can." Dan seemed almost insulted by the question, or maybe ashamed now of arguing so forcefully against adopting her.

She started out and then, on second thought, turned back and quickly kissed him on the cheek. She was still angry, but you never knew what was going to happen. The truth was, she still loved Dan, no matter what.

"Just be careful," he called after her. "And call me."

"I will," she promised.

EMILY'S RIDE TO WOOD'S HOLLOW WAS IN PITCH-BLACK darkness on a seemingly endlessly curving road. But when she finally reached the lake and the scene of the fire, it seemed as if someone had stuck a hundred-watt lightbulb in her face.

The scene was chaotic, the tall, burning wood building billowing with smoke and bright yellow flames licking out the windows. Burned beams were crashing through floors, walls were collapsing, and windows were exploding from the heat. Balconies that lined the old building were consumed by flames; they gradually crumbled and crashed as the fire roared. Men were running and shouting as the burning pieces flew down to the ground. Geysers of water from giant pumps converged on the flames, the spray and puddles turning quickly to ice in the frigid air.

The burning hotel reminded Emily of a monster in an old science fiction movie, wounded but reeling and roaring, refusing to yield to the tiny men who ran frantically, trying to subdue its might.

It was an awesome, terrifying sight to behold. The two buildings nearby were also in danger, she knew, but it appeared that all the residents had been evacuated. Several ambulances stood at the scene, with people on stretchers or just sitting on the ground taking in oxygen, their faces and clothing soot covered. Some sat in groups, wearing overcoats over nightgowns and slippers. Others huddled in blankets, clutching black plastic bags that held the few possessions they grabbed as they were forced from their homes.

Emily walked around, trying to get her bearings. She spotted Tucker Tulley and several other officers from the police department. Everyone was so busy, no one noticed her.

She slowed as she saw a group of terrified residents being hustled away from the buildings. Most were in their pajamas, and many were barefoot. Young and old and middle aged, mothers with children, there had to be a hundred of them who had completely lost their homes, and as many more who couldn't return to their residences that night and would need shelter. Emily felt overwhelmed, wondering how to help them all.

Someone touched her arm and she turned around to see Luke McCallister. "Emily, are you all right?"

"I'm fine," she said distractedly. "But this fire—look at all these people out in the cold, Luke. What can we do? We have to take them somewhere, get them places to stay."

Tucker Tulley waved and started walking toward them. Harry Reilly, who owned the boatyard in town, was there too. He stood with Grace Hegman and Sophie Potter. The red lights of the police cars swirled around, illuminating their faces. Emily couldn't tell what they were saying, but Sophie was talking in an animated fashion, looking as if she were directing traffic.

"Tucker," Emily said, "what are all these people from church doing here?"

"I called Harry and Luke, and the word just spread. We've decided to bring most of the people here back to the church and put them up in Fellowship Hall. Some can even sleep in the sanctuary on the pews. Sophie is going take a group back to the orchard, and Luke is going to take a bunch over to the center. We're calling around, too, to see if we can find some families in the congregation to take the others in."

"Do you think that will work?" she asked skeptically.

There were so many homeless, and it was Christmas night. Were people really going to interrupt their family get-togethers to take in a bunch of dirty, dazed strangers?

Tucker shrugged. "We already tried the hospital and the armory. Nobody will take them. It has to work."

"Does Reverend Ben know?"

"I tried to call him, but I guess he's not home. I left a

message on his cell phone. I'm hoping he'll call back soon, but I think we just have to go ahead and do what we have to do. I *am* the senior deacon," Tucker reminded her. "I have some say in these things. Besides, do you think he would really object?"

"No, of course not." A siren screamed, adding to the noise and confusion. Emily realized she was wasting precious time. "I'll help, too. Let's get this organized . . ."

Emily was used to being the one in control, especially in a situation that involved a crisis and public safety. But when she met up with the folks from her church, she soon found herself taking directions from Sophie Potter. Sophie, along with her granddaughter Miranda, Grace Hegman and her father Digger, Harry Reilly, and a host of others were working on their cell phones, packing the fire victims into their cars and SUVs, figuring out places for everyone to spend the night.

As she was working, helping a group into her Jeep, she spotted her brother-in-law, Sam, riding up in his truck.

He pulled up beside her and called from the window, "Emily, are you okay?"

"I'm all right. It's awfully cold out here, though. We're trying to get these people into some shelter."

"I know. Luke called me. I brought some blankets."

Of course, Sam would be here. If he heard of someone in trouble, he was there, no questions asked. She wasn't surprised that Luke called him. They were good friends.

"Park your truck and check in with Sophie. There are plenty of people who will be awfully glad to see those blankets."

IT WAS JUST PAST MIDNIGHT WHEN BEN REACHED THE church. He had been spending Christmas Day with

Rachel's in-laws, Jack's parents, who lived over an hour away. His cell phone service was spotty out of the area, and it wasn't until they were nearly home that he noticed the call from Tucker Tulley. He and Carolyn bypassed the turn to the parsonage and headed straight to the church.

The church was ablaze with light. Even from a distance, Ben and Carolyn could see the activity. As they walked from the parking lot, cars were driving up as if it were the middle of the day. Members of the congregation hurried about, carrying bags of clothing and groceries and boxes filled with blankets, pillows, and towels.

"Ben, look at all this," Carolyn said, awestruck.

Ben was speechless with astonishment, gazing around as if he had landed in some parallel universe. Everything and everyone looked familiar. Yet it wasn't at all.

Inside the church, he found Emily Warwick and Sophie Potter in charge. His church had somehow been transformed into an emergency shelter.

Sophie was in the Fellowship Hall, helping all the fire victims get settled down with bedding. There were long tables set up with cooked food and hot drinks—tea, coffee, hot cocoa. Carolyn went over to speak to Sophie and Emily, but Ben wandered around, wanting to take in the entire situation.

There were other tables with piles of clothes, almost enough for a mini rummage sale, he thought. It was sorted, he noticed, for women, children, and men. Members of his congregation were helping the people from Wood's Hollow pick out what they needed. A long rack of coats and jackets stood just past the tables. And if all that wasn't enough, there was a small table at the end of the hall where Grace Hegman sat, collecting donations.

Where in heaven's name had all this come from? How had they organized and managed to produce such an abundance? It was like the story of the loaves and fishes, he thought. Only it was even more poignant to him. He'd never seen anything like this—this outpouring of kindness and neighborly love in action. He had never imagined it. The place that he'd so recently found stagnant and complacent was now brimming with God's love.

He was standing right in the midst of a miracle.

The fire victims gazed up at him as he walked through the big room. Some were already sleeping, curled on their makeshift beds, feeling lucky to be alive, perhaps, but facing total devastation. Everything they owned was gone.

A mother with a little girl who seemed about four years old sat on the floor nearby, settled on a nest of blankets.

The little girl stared up at him, her face streaked with tears. He crouched down and tried to smile at her. "Don't be scared," he said. "It's going to be all right."

He glanced at the mother. She didn't smile or even try to. She was plainly in shock, and Ben knew that it wasn't going to be all right for her, not for a very long time.

"Can I bring you anything? Some food or something to drink?"

She shook her head.

He didn't know what else to say to her. "I'm so sorry . . ."

She nodded. Ben wasn't sure she spoke English, but she seemed to understand him. She turned to her daughter and stroked her hair.

"I'll keep you both in my prayers," he promised.

She nodded again, as if to thank him. Ben stayed for a moment more and moved on.

EMILY RETURNED HOME AT DAYBREAK. SHE STAGGERED into the house through the back door, sooty and exhausted. Her good suit and blouse were ruined, but she didn't care.

She walked into the bedroom and found Dan sleeping in a rocking chair, dressed in his bathrobe. It looked as if he'd been up with the baby . . . or perhaps waiting for her.

She tried to be quiet as she got undressed, but he slowly opened his eyes and looked at her. "You're back, thank goodness. What time is it?"

"Almost five. It's going to be light out soon. I just want to grab an hour or two of sleep. I have to get in to the office and start working on this fire situation. Oh, Dan, you wouldn't have believed it. It was terrible."

He walked over to Emily and put his arms around her. "Were many people hurt?"

She nodded. "Lots in the hospital, smoke inhalation mainly. A few firefighters were injured, though nothing was serious. No deaths so far. That part's a miracle."

She gazed up at him. "The most amazing thing happened. All these people in town heard what happened and came out to help. They just up and left whatever they were doing—their Christmas dinners, family, whatever—and came down to the church with clothes and food. It was incredible."

She crawled into bed and he followed her. "Sounds so," he said. He put his arm around her and she rested her head on his chest.

"The old hotel building burned to the ground," she explained. "And the others had to be evacuated. Some people will be able to go back eventually, but the buildings that are still standing will have lots of damage from the smoke and water. All the tenants in the burned building are homeless. All of their possessions are lost." She turned her head to look at him. "They're not the type of people who carry insurance, you know? I don't think the building owner will come up with much help either. This is a real tragedy."

"Yes, it is. Get some sleep now. You're exhausted." He put his hand on her head and she rested it again on his shoulder.

"How is Jane?"

"She's fine. She hardly made a peep."

"I have to get in to the office early and start cutting through all the red tape to get these people some public assistance. There's so much to do. Mrs. Hatcher is off for the week, though, Dan. I had planned on staying home." Emily paused for a moment. "Can you take care of Jane while I'm at work?" she asked carefully.

The question of adopting the baby had been tabled for now, but Emily still didn't know how Dan would react to this request.

"Of course I'll take care of her. You don't have to worry. It sounds as if you have a big job on your hands this week, Emily. I'll help you any way I can."

Emily smiled at him and kissed his cheek. She put her head down again and closed her eyes, her mind racing with the sights and sounds of the fire scene, as well as with lists of all she had to do—all the bureaucrats and agencies she had to call.

Still, within a few seconds, she fell into a deep, dreamless sleep.

CHAPTER TWELVE

BEN CAUGHT A FEW HOURS OF SLEEP AT HOME AND returned to church just before seven the next day. As he walked across the village green from his car, he wondered if last night had been a dream.

But no, it hadn't been a dream at all. He entered the church to find that the miracle continued.

There were dozens of people working in the kitchen, preparing breakfast—pancakes, eggs, bacon, piles of buttered rolls, and donuts. Coffee and tea, hot cocoa, and cereal for the kids were all being served on long tables in the Fellowship Hall. Other tables held piles of clean socks and underwear, toothpaste, toothbrushes, little bars of soap, and various hygiene items. The room was filled with the fire victims and helpers. Most were still asleep of course, but a few were awake and even smiling. Maybe, he thought, they were just happy to be alive after their terrifying ordeal.

Curious as to what else was going on in the church, Ben left the hall. Later, when everyone was up, he would return, welcome everyone, and say a blessing.

Tucker Tulley met him in the hallway. "I've called a meeting of the deaconate, Reverend. Everyone is here. We're in one of the classrooms downstairs," he said, leading the way.

Reverend Ben followed Tucker downstairs to a church school classroom, where he found just about all the deacons assembled.

"Reverend, would you lead us in the invocation?" Tucker asked after calling the meeting to order.

Reverend Ben bowed his head. "Heavenly Father, please guide us, continue to give us the energy, resources, and wisdom to help the victims of this devastating fire. We thank You for the grace that has touched this church and all the people in it. We thank You for the amazing miracle we witnessed last night, the outpouring of love, kindness, and generosity. Please guide us with Your light, keep our hearts open, and let this miracle of love and faith continue."

"Amen." Tucker lifted his head and surveyed the group seated before him. "We need to help these people upstairs," he began simply. "They're burned out of their homes and don't have clothes to put on their backs or shoes for their feet. They need clothing, money, and a place to stay until the town or whoever figures out what to do with them, which from my experience could take awhile."

He looked around, but no one interrupted him. "We did a good job last night. We can be proud of that effort. But we have to keep it up. This is going to take time. We can't get bored with it or lose momentum." He picked up a pad from one of the front-row desks. "Does anyone know how much money was collected?"

Harry Reilly raised his hand. "A little over three thousand dollars."

"That's a start," Tucker said, jotting down the figure. He

went through some other categories of need, clothing and food donations. Someone else produced a list of church families who were inviting the displaced fire victims into their homes.

Ben was cheered by that response. It didn't seem to matter that this group was the poorest in the community, with many who did not even speak English. His congregation was willing to take them in just because they were neighbors in need. They were willing to do it just because it was the right thing to do.

The meeting soon concluded, with everyone assigned their tasks to keep the miracle rolling. Ben went upstairs again, where he found the outpouring of love and generosity continuing in countless ways.

They had done all this without him at the pulpit spouting Scripture and reminding them of their Christian duty. Maybe he was right. He wasn't needed here, but not because his congregation didn't have spirit. He felt so ashamed for having misjudged them, thinking they had no spiritual vigor. Yes, they were a social community, but different from the Elks Club or the Rotary or the group at the country club.

They were very different. How had he been so blind and not seen that? He felt ashamed for finding them lacking and asked for God's forgiveness.

Lord, forgive me for misjudging these good people. Forgive me for losing faith in them . . . and myself. Thank You for all You've done here—and continue to do—through us.

WHEN HE FINALLY GOT HOME LATER THAT EVENING, Carolyn was waiting for him. She had also come to the church to help during the day, working mainly in the kitchen, but they had barely seen each other.

"You must be exhausted, Ben, up all night and working all day."

"I'm not tired at all." He smiled at her, following her into their own kitchen. "I feel like I've been charged up like an old battery by all this wonderful energy at church. It's still hard to take it all in, Carolyn, their acts of compassion and generosity."

"You're proud of them," she noted. She lifted a cover on a pot and stirred. "You should be."

"I am. But I hardly deserve any credit. I was wrong to sell them short. I was projecting my own malaise. The lack of spirit was in me, not them."

"Maybe this event woke everyone up."

Ben nodded. "I think it gave them a way to put their spiritual side into action. There's more to be done, though, than just providing food and shelter for a few days."

"Yes, you have to think of the long-term problems, too."

"Most of those people are at risk of ending up homeless," Ben said. "Emily Warwick is doing what she can, working with the county. But you know how that goes. The best the county might do is stick them all in some dumpy motel somewhere, where they'll be out of sight and soon forgotten. The community can't let that happen," he insisted. "The church can't let that happen."

"Agreed." Carolyn touched his wrist lightly, her expression thoughtful. "But what exactly can the church do?"

"I'm not sure, but that's a failure of imagination and knowledge on my part right now. Yesterday morning I never could have dreamed of what they've already accomplished."

"Well . . . at least you're honest."

"I'm not sure how to figure this all out. There are so many factors to consider. All I know is that the church must play a big role now in keeping these people on track. That much I'm very sure of." He sighed and leaned toward her. "Did you know that several of the men have already lost their jobs for missing one day's work? One day, because of a fire."

Carolyn's look of loving support turned to one of outrage. "How could their employers do that?"

"That's the situation we're dealing with. It's not enough that these poor people have lost their homes and everything they own." He stood up, feeling suddenly restless again. "Maybe the church can help build new housing, some affordable apartments. Maybe we can get the county to cooperate . . ."

"That sounds like a big job, a real mission project. Too bad the church will have to do it without you."

Ben turned and looked at her, wondering at her comment. Then he remembered. The sabbatical . . .

"Didn't you want to leave at the end of January?"

"I've been reconsidering that plan, Carolyn. It might have been a bit impulsive. You know, I never actually filed the papers. Maybe I was depressed, self-indulgent, too." He shook his head regretfully.

"I think the feelings were very real to you, Ben. Don't be so hard on yourself. The thing is, suddenly, there's a lot of work for you here. A real opportunity, don't you think?"

She was so kind to him, always giving him the benefit of the doubt. Even in his folly.

"Absolutely. I can't leave now. The congregation needs me. The fire victims need me."

"The sabbatical idea will have to be postponed, then," she said, a smile hovering on her lips.

"Yes . . . indefinitely," he added.

"Whatever you say, dear." Carolyn's tone was only slightly sarcastic. He knew he deserved far worse for what he had put her through.

"I think that's a wise choice," she continued, turning to the stove again to serve dinner. "There's a lot of work ahead if you plan to have the church help these people."

"Yes, there is. A mountain of work, and an abundance of energy to draw upon. The congregation has inspired me. They've renewed me, just as I was trying to say in my sermon. This is my Christmas miracle," he said quietly.

*　*　*

IT WASN'T UNTIL WEDNESDAY NIGHT, THREE DAYS AF-
ter the fire, that Emily and Dan were able to sit down to a
meal together. Emily had been up and out early every
morning, not returning until late at night. The county and
local Red Cross had taken some action to help the fire
victims, but the church congregation had done the lion's
share so far, offering the kind of support and caring that
government agencies could never provide. She was encouraged by the progress so far, but downright exhausted.

She sat at the table and took a sip of the soup Dan had
prepared for them. There were toasted sandwiches on thick
crusty bread and a big green salad.

"This looks like the best meal I've seen all week." She
took a big bite of her sandwich as Dan looked on.

"The roast is from Christmas night. It didn't go to
waste."

The mention of that debacle of a dinner reminded her of
their awful argument. They hadn't talked about it all week.
But the truth was, they hadn't had the chance. Dan had
been very considerate of her these past few days, caring for
Jane and doing nearly everything around the house.

But although they hadn't talked, she had had a chance to
think things over. She could see now that she had been trying to impose her own feelings on him. It just wasn't fair,
or right.

They talked about the fire victims awhile. Dan, too, had
been at the church helping out when he was able to leave
Jane with Jessica for a few hours each day.

"So they don't think it was arson?"

Emily shook her head. "Reasonable to suspect, all
things considered. But the fire department investigators all
agree it was started by bad wiring. By the time anyone
smelled the smoke inside the wall, it was too late."

"I suppose that proves the other buildings need to be renovated and upgraded." A familiar look of affection came into his eyes. "Maybe the mayor can do something about it. I hear she's good with things like that."

"I'm already on it," she assured him with a weary smile. "I had the county inspectors out there today."

Finally, Emily decided it was time to bring up the question that still hovered over them. "I had a call from Nadine today," she began carefully. "She wanted to know what we were thinking now about Jane. I told her that it's doubtful we'll apply to adopt." She stopped there and looked at Dan. His expression was blank, unreadable.

"I didn't blame it on you," she added in a conciliatory tone. "I didn't say much at all. I've been thinking it over the past few days, what you said when we argued. And maybe it is unrealistic to think we're young enough to keep up with the demands of a child. Maybe it would be better for Jane to have younger parents," she said, though she felt her heart breaking as she said the words aloud. "If I can force myself to look at this objectively, like you asked me to, I know Nadine will find a loving couple who will be happy to give Jane a good home."

She paused, trying hard not to get overly emotional about this. There would be enough time for that later.

"We're not the only people in the world who could be good parents to her," Emily continued. "And I've thought about you—your needs and hopes. I know it's probably seemed as if those things don't matter to me at all, but they do," she assured him. "We agreed when we got married that we wouldn't start a family. It isn't fair to you for me to go back on my word. I don't want to force you into adopting this baby and then find out you regret it. That wouldn't be good for you or me or Jane."

She stared at him, waiting for some response. He had been listening to her with his head bowed, staring down at his plate.

Now he looked up again. "Wow . . . that was some speech. No notes, either. I'm impressed."

She managed a small smile. "I told you, I've been thinking a lot about this."

Despite his small joke, she couldn't tell how he felt about what she'd said.

"Poor Nadine Preston," he said finally. "She must be extremely confused."

Emily frowned. "What do you mean?"

"I spoke to her today, too, and said we wanted to start the process to adopt Jane."

Emily felt her jaw drop. She just couldn't believe it. But she knew very well he would never joke about this.

"You don't have to do this, Dan," she said quickly. "I don't want to force you into it. I can see that now. It's not the kind of thing you can talk someone into. I was wrong to try—"

"Hush up now. You had the floor, my dear. Just let me finish," he said, giving her a mock stern look. "I've been thinking, too. I've had a lot of time here the past few days, alone with Jane. I've even talked it over with her from time to time," he confided. Emily had to smile, pleased to hear he talked aloud to the baby, too.

"You know me, I don't much believe in fate, but even I have to admit it was a conveniently strange turn of events that had me stuck here, all alone, caring for her lately."

Emily had been thinking the same, but hadn't dared to say it.

"And I've had to conclude, I love her madly. I've tried to imagine giving her up. I even tried talking myself into believing it's the best thing for her. But my heart can't buy it, Emily. And I know for sure it's not the best thing for you."

He gazed at her fondly and paused for a moment. "I've come to really understand what this means to you. At least, I think I do. You're a wonderful mother to this child and to

Sara. I can't deny you the chance to try to adopt this baby. We might not be chosen, you know," he added quickly, "That's still not certain."

"Yes, I know." Her heart was beating so hard it felt like a drum inside her chest. She felt so happy, she wanted to jump out of her skin.

"You were right when you told me I was grieving the past," he admitted. "I had a lot of shame about not being a good father. But it would be different now. I wouldn't be distracted by work, and you're nothing like Claire. I think I could be a good father now, Emily. I want to give it another go."

Emily blinked back tears of joy. "Dan, I'm so happy, I don't know what to say. I don't know where to start . . ."

He got up, walked over to her, and pulled her up from her chair. "You can start by telling me you love me."

"You know I do." She jumped into his arms and held him close. "You just can't imagine how much."

"Thank you for seeing my side of it," he whispered in her ear. "Even though I was mostly wrong. I get that tunnel vision thing going sometimes. I nearly lost you once because of it. You would think I had learned my lesson."

Emily laughed softly. "Thank you for this . . . this amazing gift, Dan. I can never thank you enough."

He didn't answer, just gazed down into her eyes. He pulled her close and kissed her deeply, his strong embrace enfolding her completely.

Emily kissed him back. She loved him so much. Not just because he was willing to adopt Jane. But because of all that he was, right and wrong.

That's what marriage was all about. That's what love was all about.

Finally, he stood back, looking down at her, his arms looped around her waist. "You were right about something else, too, Emily. The real adventure is being married to you, and whatever comes along with that, even if it's a baby. What I realized this week is that caring for Jane has deepened my love for you and made our marriage even stronger. Why would I ever want to give all that up?"

Emily hugged him close again and squeezed him so tight he practically cried out for mercy. "I have an idea," she said. "Let's go tell Jane."

He smiled and kissed her again. "I already did."

"SARA! WHEN DID YOU GET BACK?"

Emily had just walked out of the church on Friday morning and could hardly believe it when she saw Sara walking in. She quickly hugged her daughter and leaned back to look at her.

"I just got here five minutes ago. Lindsay called and said they needed me back at the newspaper right away. There's so much going on because of the fire."

"It was terrible. But it's amazing the way the town has pulled together to help these people. That's the real story." Emily paused, feeling full of news and not knowing where to begin. She was also dying to know what happened with Sara's job interview but was trying not to pounce on her about it. "How is everyone in Maryland?" she asked. "Did you have a good time?"

"It was great to see them. They want to come up here soon again for a visit. Maybe in February."

"Oh . . . will you still be here?" Emily was happily surprised. "What about Philadelphia?"

"That didn't turn out to be much. I would be back at square one, taking phone calls and bringing *real* reporters coffee. I don't need to work on a big paper that much."

Emily tried not to look as thrilled as she felt. "You'll know when the right opportunity comes along."

"This certainly wasn't it, believe me."

Emily took her hand. "I have some great news. Dan and I have applied to adopt Jane."

Sara's face lit up with happiness. "That's wonderful! When did you decide? I thought Dan was against the idea."

"He was," Emily said slowly, smiling. "But we talked it out—argued, really—and we both took some time to think things through. And then he decided he couldn't live without Jane, either. It's still not certain, of course, but at least we're trying."

"Oh, I know you'll be the ones," Sara said, hugging her. "I have a feeling this will all work out for you, Emily."

"Thanks, honey, I hope so." Emily had a feeling, too, but she was too scared to say. So far her feelings in this matter hadn't been all that foolproof.

Prayer had helped, though, she was certain of it. And now her prayers were mostly full of gratitude.

"Listen, we're having a get-together on New Year's Eve. Will you come?"

"Sure. I don't have any plans," Sara said honestly. She hesitated a moment and then asked, "Is Luke around? I heard he's been helping." Sara's voice was tentative, shaky. Emily felt for her.

"He's been a tremendous help, as always. He's not at the church right now, though. A few families are staying at the center. He's been out there with them mostly."

"That makes sense." Sara nodded. "I guess Christina has been helping, too. Just to show what a good sport she is," she added. "Did she bang out some big feature about the fire for the *Globe*?"

Emily had to smile. "I haven't seen Christina around, Sara. As for that *Globe* article, maybe you're the one who ought to get working on that." *In addition to getting back together with Luke*, Emily wanted to add. She didn't say that, though, just gazed at her daughter a minute. Then she hugged her quickly once more. "See you tomorrow night. Come around eight."

"I'll be there." Sara waved, ran up the steps to the big wooden doors of the church, and slipped inside.

Emily was so glad Sara was back, and even happier that she would be staying. She had a lot to celebrate this New Year's. *What in the world did I do to deserve all this happiness?* she wondered.

EMILY AND DAN WORKED ALL DAY, CLEANING THE HOUSE and rearranging the furniture to get everything set for their New Year's Eve party. Everyone was bringing a dish, so Emily didn't worry too much about the menu. It would all blend together somehow, she decided.

Dressed for the party in a gold satin top and black velvet pants, she hustled about, putting a few finishing touches on her decorating. She filled the living room and dining room with votive lights and sprinkled golden confetti and festive streamers on the white linen tablecloths. She set out piles of silly Happy New Year hats and noisemakers, hoping everyone would be inspired to make a racket at the stroke of midnight. And for the crowning touch, she let loose a huge bunch of helium balloons that had Happy New Year stamped all over them and let them float up to the ceiling.

When Dan came downstairs, dressed and ready to receive their guests, he gazed around in wonder. "What in the . . . balloons, too? What is this, Times Square?"

"Not quite, but not bad for Cape Light," Emily remarked, admiring her handiwork.

Dan walked over to her and took hold of her shoulders. "You're so happy, you're on cloud nine. That's a good start to the New Year."

Emily smiled up at him. "I haven't been this happy since . . . the day I married you."

"Me either," he agreed, pulling her close. "Hard to believe it's just been a year."

"It went by so quickly. So much has happened—"

"And keeps happening," he finished, drawing her to him for a kiss.

The doorbell rang and they slowly drew apart. "Meet me right here at midnight," Dan said softly.

"I will," Emily promised him.

Molly Willoughby and Matt Harding were the first to arrive. Molly was so impressed by the decorations, she jokingly offered to hire Emily to join her catering business. Jessica and Sam came in next, then Betty Bowman with her latest boyfriend, a lawyer named Scott Craft who lived in Hamilton. Scott seemed funny and smart and kind, and Betty looked radiant. Maybe, Emily thought hopefully, Betty had finally met the "one." Ever since her painful divorce, Betty had been very wary of commitment.

Emily sometimes wondered if that was Sara's problem, too—a fear of settling down. But Sara was so young, she certainly had time. Still, Emily hoped her daughter and Luke could resolve their differences and at least get on speaking terms again. She knew it wasn't right to interfere and had purposely not invited Luke so that Sara would be comfortable coming to the party. But Luke had a way of showing up at these events, invited or not. Emily was holding out hope for one of his infamous "party crashings," as her mother called them.

Dr. Elliot had driven Lillian over, and they entered bickering, as usual. "Watch out, you two. You're standing right under the mistletoe," Dan teased them, hoping to break up the argument, Emily was sure. At Dan's words, her mother leaped so quickly out of the threshold, Emily half feared she'd fall and break her hip again.

Emily was trying not to laugh at her mother's sudden display of athleticism when Sam came up and drew Emily aside. "Listen, I ran into Luke today. He wasn't doing anything tonight, so I mentioned the party, told him to take a ride over later. I hope that's all right. I didn't think you and Dan would mind."

"Of course I don't mind. I like Luke." Emily's gaze strayed across the room to Sara, who stood chatting with Betty and Scott. "Does Sara know?" she asked quietly.

Sam shrugged. "No, should I tell her?"

Emily sighed, unsure of what to do. "Well . . . he might not even come. Why get her all concerned? Let's just wait and see what happens. I'll handle it." She patted her brother-in-law on the arm, acting far more confident than she really felt.

The hours passed quickly with lively music, good food, and good company. Even her mother seemed to be relaxed and having a good time, telling stories about the days when she was a young girl growing up in Boston society—the coming-out parties and winter white balls and *peau de soie* silk gowns imported from Paris. Emily gazed at her wistfully. No wonder her mother sometimes seemed so out of step with everyone around her. Lillian had come from another world altogether, and now nearly all traces of that world had vanished.

Sara seemed subdued, Emily noticed, and the reason was no mystery. All alone on New Year's Eve. Emily had been there more than once; it wasn't a good feeling. Her heart went out to her daughter, but she promised herself she wouldn't meddle.

At eleven o'clock, Jane woke up for her late-night bottle, and Emily brought her out to the party. The guests flocked around the baby, happy to see her and happy for Dan and Emily's decision to go ahead with the adoption.

Jessica sat the nearest to Emily on the sofa and leaned

over for an impulsive hug. "I'm so happy for you, Emily. This is really a miracle."

Emily nodded. "It is, isn't it?"

"She is an attractive child," Lillian said quietly, "and appears to have a reasonable disposition."

Emily and Jessica turned to their mother, both looking shocked. Lillian shrugged. "Of course, you never know. They do go through so many stages," she added, quick to withdraw some of the good feeling generated by her prior comment. "You can never be sure what you're going to get."

Emily glanced at her sister, trying hard not to laugh. "I'll just have to roll with it, I guess, Mother," she said.

"Believe me, you will," Lillian promised her with a curt nod.

The doorbell rang and Dan quickly walked over to answer it. Emily was not surprised to see Luke standing there, though everyone else seemed to be. Her gaze flew to Sara, who was talking with Sam and didn't notice Luke at the door.

Sam did, though. He leaned over and said a few private words to Sara. She turned and stared at Luke and seemed to swallow hard. Then, with Sam at her side, she walked over to greet him.

Despite Dan's encouragement, Luke didn't come in. He looked a bit sheepish, Emily thought, standing around in the cold, his hands dug into the pockets of his blue jeans.

Lillian spied him and gave a loud sniff. "That gate-crasher again. Of course. I could set my watch by his arrival."

Jessica laughed. "Sam told Luke about the party, Mother. It's okay."

"That's what I call hearsay, not an invitation. I thought I taught you better manners." Lillian sat back in her chair, looking disgusted.

Meanwhile, Sara had slipped outside with Luke, and Sam had closed the door. Emily glanced heavenward.

Dear God, I know it's not my place to meddle in Sara's relationships . . . but surely You can? Please help her sort things out with Luke. He's such a good guy and I know they really love each other. Please let them at least hear each other out?

Okay, I'll stop now, Emily said silently, ending her prayer.

SARA WORE A WOOL SWEATER AND A SUEDE BLAZER BUT still felt cold outside. She crossed her arms over her chest, hugging herself for warmth. She felt shocked when she saw Luke in the doorway and then afraid to talk to him. Sam had more or less pushed her out the door.

"So . . . how was your holiday?" she started off, not knowing what to say.

Luke shrugged. "All in all, pretty lousy. Though it was good to hang out with the kids at the center. Some of them didn't have anyplace to go, so we cheered each other up a little."

Sara nodded, staring down at her boots. "What about Christina? Didn't she cheer you up?"

"Not exactly. Christina left town. She wasn't around for Christmas."

"Oh?" Sara looked up at him, surprised. "I thought she rented a cottage, planned to write her book here."

He shrugged. "I guess Cape Light turned out to be too quiet for her."

Sara considered his words carefully. Christina had been disappointed, she gathered. But maybe not just by the town being too quiet.

"I thought she had her sights set on you," Sara said frankly. "She seemed pretty determined."

"I think she had some big fantasy about how great it

would be if we got back together. I think the real me disappointed her," he said with a little laugh.

"Really? Now I know she's a complete idiot," Sara said.

Luke laughed. "That's the first nice thing you've said to me in weeks. Does that mean there's some hope?"

"Some," she admitted. She met his gaze and looked away again. He stood apart from her but stared at her so intently, his steady focus seemed to draw her closer.

"So what about your holidays? How are your folks?"

"They're fine." *Asked a lot about you*, she almost added, but couldn't quite get the words out.

"And that job interview in Philadelphia? How did that go?"

"It was a complete dud," she admitted. "Sounds like I'd be a glorified secretary for years before they would even let me proof copy, much less write a story."

"Oh . . . that's too bad." He crossed his arms over his chest, finally smiling.

"Or not, depending on how you look at it." She met his gaze again, then smiled back at him. "I'm sorry I acted out about Christina, Luke. That night we went out to dinner . . . I acted like a child, the way I ran out and left you two there. That wasn't right. I shouldn't have been mad at you, either." She sighed. "I was just pretty jealous, I guess."

"So I gathered," he said quietly. "I didn't mind that part that much. Two gorgeous women, fighting over me. That wasn't what I'd call a bad evening out."

She glared at him and he laughed. "Just kidding," he added. His expression grew serious. "Okay, so Christina's out of the picture. She never really was in it to begin with. That was all in your imagination, Sara."

She nodded, finally knowing what he said was true.

"So where does that leave us? Are you still scared of making a commitment? Do you still want to work at a bigger newspaper, no matter where that turns out to be?"

Sara swallowed. "I need to be honest with you, Luke. I am scared of making a commitment. You talk about getting married and having a family so easily. It's not that easy for me to see myself doing those things right now. Especially having a baby."

He nodded. "We don't have to start a family right away. I understand if you're not ready yet. Hey, look at Emily and Dan. If they're just starting off, we have loads of time left."

The comparison made Sara laugh in spite of herself. She felt relieved to see he really did understand. She took a step closer and took his hand. "I'm scared of this engagement and marriage thing," she said quietly, "but I realized something down in Maryland. I don't want to be away from you, Luke. I don't want to make new plans, or take a new job, or do anything anymore without you. I want us to start a life together. I think I'm finally ready for that. Will you still have me?"

"Hmm . . . can I think about it a little?" he asked. His voice was serious but his expression was teasing. When he saw the crushed look on Sara's face, he laughed and drew her close in a tight embrace. "Of course I'll have you, you silly goose. Don't you get it yet? I don't want anyone but you. That's just the way it is for me."

Sara buried her face in his shoulder, crying with relief and love. She felt him suddenly pull away and didn't understand what was happening, until she saw him drop down on one knee.

He took her hand and looked up at her. "Sara, you are the most wonderful woman I've ever met in my life. The most remarkable person, really. I love you with all my heart and soul, and I'll do all I can to make you happy. Will you marry me? I'd be the happiest man on Earth."

Sara felt breathless, overcome with his words and his tender loving look. She took his face in both of her hands. "Yes, I'll marry you, Luke. I love you more than anything."

He jumped up, put his arms around her, and kissed her deeply. Then he pulled back and dug his hand into his pocket. He pulled out a small blue velvet box and handed it to her. Sara was speechless.

"Go on, open it," he whispered.

Sara opened it slowly, knowing what she would find: the ring from the jewelry store, the round solitaire in the gold and platinum setting. But even knowing, she wasn't prepared for its beauty, its fire beneath the light of the winter moon. "Oh, Luke, you didn't have to get this ring. It was so expensive."

"That was the one you liked, wasn't it? We can change it if it's not right," he added quickly.

"Oh no . . . it's perfect. I love it." She took the ring out and he put it on her finger. He held her hand a moment, admiring it, then smiled into her eyes. "It is a nice ring."

"I adore it," she said, hugging him again. "Wait a minute. You came here with this ring, knowing you would propose to me?"

Luke shrugged. "I didn't know what was going to happen. I figured if not tonight, I would just hang on to it and try again some other time."

Sara didn't know what to say. She couldn't believe that anyone could love her that much, could want her that much. She felt like the luckiest woman in the world to have a man like Luke so in love with her.

They held each other close for a long time, until Emily appeared at the door. "I'm sorry," she said, sounding embarrassed. "But I thought you'd want to know, it's almost midnight."

Luke and Sara quickly went inside and joined the rest of the party, who were now gathered around the TV in the small sitting room. They watched coverage from Times Square in New York, counting down the seconds along with the television as the end of the year drew nearer.

"Ten . . . nine . . . eight . . . seven . . . six . . . five . . . four . . . three . . . two . . . ONE!"

They blew their noisemakers, whooped and laughed, cried and hugged and kissed each other, stumbling around the small sitting room in a frenzy of good wishes.

Emily hugged Sara close. "Happy New Year, sweetheart," she said. Sara said the same, then pulled back, and silently showed Emily the engagement ring.

Emily screamed, causing everyone to turn in alarm. "Sara! Oh my goodness!" She turned to her guests. "Sara and Luke . . . they're engaged!" she announced, half laughing and half crying.

Luke stepped up beside Sara and slipped his arm around her shoulder. Emily hugged him, too. Then everyone else quickly gathered around, offering their heartfelt congratulations.

Everyone except Lillian, who stalked off, shaking her head. But no one seemed to notice.

EMILY FELT A SPECIAL EXCITEMENT IN CHURCH ON NEW Year's Day. She had expected to be too tired to get up for the service, but somehow it hadn't been much trouble at all to make it there on time. The weather was cold and dry, the sky clear and cloudless. *A clean slate for the year ahead*, she thought, glancing up as they walked toward the church's front doors.

The sanctuary was full, which was unusual for a service right on New Year's Day. She glanced around. It looked as if many of the displaced families from Wood's Hollow were there, filling the pews to capacity. She wondered if the congregation would attract new members now, after the work they'd done helping the fire victims. It was a good feeling to see new faces and feel the church growing, like a living thing.

Reverend Ben had a certain bounce in his step as he

walked up front to address the congregation. "First, I want to wish everyone a happy and blessed New Year. Our congregation enters the New Year as witnesses—and participants—in a miracle. There are simply too many of you to mention by name who came here on Christmas night and have continued to come here this past week, to help our neighbors who were forced from their homes by the fire in Wood's Hollow.

"The crisis was devastating and there is so much work still to be done, so much aid we can continue to give. But I, for one, stand in awe of the effort I've seen from all of you. Surely, our church has been touched by God's grace, and out of the rubble and ashes of that fallen building, we have risen here with new purpose and new life."

He paused, gazing around the congregation. Emily heard his voice go thick and strained with emotion, and for a moment, she thought Reverend Ben was about to cry.

"I have a confession to make to all of you. For the past few weeks, I've been feeling discouraged, even disappointed in the level of spiritual energy in our church. I blamed myself mostly, for not being able to lead and inspire all of you.

"The irony is that when the real moment to act came, you had no need of me. I was miles away, oblivious. You saw the problem and sprang into action. You shared whatever you could—more than you could, in some cases—food, clothing, money, even the roofs over your heads. This is the Christian spirit in action. This is what it means to live out the lessons of the Scriptures. This is God's spirit and love working through us."

He paused, taking a deep breath.

"I am humbled by what you have all accomplished, and I'm grateful. I was in a place of darkness and confusion, and your acts of compassion led me back to the light, or rather, to see the light that is always around us and part of our eternal spirit. I stand in awe of your miracle. I am proud to be your minister, to continue to learn from you, to serve you, and to serve with you.

"Let us come together now to worship and to ask God's help and blessing so that we may continue this New Year to do the good work we have only just begun."

The sanctuary was absolutely silent.

Emily didn't dare take a breath. Reverend Ben stood a moment before them, his head bowed. Then he slipped a white hanky from his pocket, quickly dabbed his eyes under his glasses, and slipped them in place again.

Suddenly the organ sounded and the chorus began the choral introit. Everyone slowly came to their feet and began to sing. Emily stood up with Jane balanced on her hip while Dan held up the hymnal for them. She felt her own eyes growing misty for a moment and blinked the tears away. She agreed with Reverend Ben. The congregation's work for the people of Wood's Hollow had been a miracle, a strange and wonderful coming together of so many hands and hearts united by one purpose. There was no question in her mind that the work itself had been its own reward. Still, she couldn't help but feel that God was smiling down on them.

She was suddenly reminded of a quote from the New Testament: "Be not forgetful to entertain strangers; for thereby some have entertained angels unawares."

Angels, indeed. She looked down at Jane, who gazed back at her with the kind of wise and knowing expression that babies seemed to have at times. Perhaps there were more angels around than she had ever realized.

The rest of the service seemed to pass quickly, with a light, joyful feeling. A feeling of unity, Emily thought.

At the end of the service, they walked to the back of the sanctuary where Reverend Ben stood greeting the congregants.

"Happy New Year," he said to them.

Emily smiled and wished him the same. "We have some good news. We've decided to apply to adopt Jane."

Ben's eyes widened with surprise and he beamed at her. "That is good news! Well, well . . . I'm very happy for you, Emily . . . for all of you," he added, his gaze taking in Dan and Jane as well. "How long will the process take?"

"Several months," Dan answered. "We're just starting to file the necessary papers this week. Then we'll be going before a judge to finalize everything and make it legal."

"It's a little nerve wracking," Emily admitted. "I wish it could be settled more quickly, but Jane's social worker said she thinks everything will go smoothly."

Ben nodded. "I think it will, too. I just have a feeling." He glanced down at Jane. "I'll keep you in my thoughts . . . and in my prayers."

"Thank you, Reverend." Emily squeezed his hand as they said good-bye. After all these years, Reverend Ben was perhaps the only one who knew just how much adopting Jane meant to her.

Lillian was not having her usual family gathering this Sunday. She had announced last night that she was too tired to have them all over, and also that the conversation would be too boring, since they had all been together for New Year's Eve.

Emily and Dan were both relieved. They had enjoyed entertaining but were now looking forward to a quiet afternoon—just the two of them and Jane—to celebrate their good news privately.

"So where to?" Dan said as he started up the car.

Emily clipped Jane into her car seat and then got in the car next to Dan. "Oh, I don't know. I thought we'd just go home and relax."

"We can relax later. I think we ought to do something special. We have a lot to celebrate—adopting Jane, Sara and Luke's engagement, our first anniversary. You know I'm not much of a praying guy, but we do have a lot to be thankful for, Emily. We really do." He glanced at her.

She reached over and took his hand. "Yes, we do," she said quietly.

"You know, when I was listening to Reverend Ben today, I had to say to myself, 'Hey, I've had a few miracles in my life lately, too.' There's you, Emily. You made me feel happy again just to be alive." He gazed at her with a loving look that touched her heart. "And now there's our little girl." He glanced back at Jane, cozy in her car seat. "Definitely a miracle. She's made me feel young again, the way only a baby can."

"Me, too," Emily agreed happily.

"I can't believe we've only been married one year. It seems as if so much has happened." He shook his head. "I'm almost afraid to wonder what the next twelve months will bring."

Emily laughed, then leaned over and kissed him. "Me, too," she agreed again. "But that's the adventure."